D0049603

The Dangerous
Edge of Things

The Dangerous Edge of Things

A Tai Randolph Mystery

Tina Whittle

Poisoned Pen Press

Copyright © 2011 by Tina Whittle

First Edition

10 9 8 7 6 5 4 3 2 1

Library of Congress Catalog Card Number: 2010932102

ISBN: 9781590588178   Hardcover
        9781590588192   Trade Paperback

Poisoned Pen Press
6962 E. First Ave., Ste. 103
Scottsdale, AZ 85251
www.poisonedpenpress.com
info@poisonedpenpress.com

Printed in the United States of America

To James, who always has, and always will be.

Acknowledgments

It takes a village to write a novel. Here's a brief roster of those whose generosity and smarts made this work possible. Thank you to my fellow writers whose insights shaped this manuscript— Jon Bryant, Laura Cooper, Susan Newman, and David Starnes (we miss you, David). Professor Mary Hadley deserves special kudos—the idea for this book was born during my semester in her Mystery Writing class. She and her husband Charles Martin have been staunch supporters from the beginning. Many specialists contributed their expertise and put up with my endless questions about cars and guns and burn marks: Steven Brown, Guy Antonozzi, R. Steven Eckhoff, Mike Kerce, Carl Stover, and Tanya Terry. Fran Johnson rendered me photogenic, and Joel Caplan put up with my camera shyness—without them, there would be no author photo at the back of this book. And my best friend Antonia Deal went above and beyond the call of duty in ways that my legal team says it's best not to describe—thanks, Toni! I'll see ya in Vegas!

My deepest gratitude to the loved ones who have believed in me through the years—my parents, Dinah and Archie Floyd; my out-law parents Yvonne and Gene Whittle; my brother Tim and siblings-in-law Lisa, Patty and Rich; and of course my husband, James, and daughter Kaley Grace. I am blessed to count them in my circle.

Our interest's on the dangerous edge of things.
The honest thief, the tender murderer,
The superstitious atheist...
        —Robert Browning

Chapter One

Don't look left, I reminded myself. Look left and you throw up again. So I made myself look right, where I stared at an azalea bush until it blurred into a pink and green blob. Luckily for me, the police officer returned at that moment with a cardboard cup of water. I accepted it with shaking hands as he appraised me.

"Are you sure you're okay?"

I faked a smile. "Still shook up, but okay."

His nametag read Norris, and he was dark and squat and as official as a fire hydrant. He'd discovered me retching behind my brother's new forsythia and bustled off to fetch some water. Then he'd offered to track down some breath mints. I'd declined. What I wanted was a cigarette, and I wanted it fiercely.

It was the only thing I could think of that might get the dead girl out of my head.

I remembered strange details, like the rhinestone barrette just above her left ear, a clean metallic gleam in the dark clotted mass of her hair. A silver cuff bracelet encircling a slender white wrist. And the smell when I'd opened the car door—copper sour and stale, like the bottom of a meat drawer, with a tang of something dank and sewer-ish at the edges.

I took a sip of water and willed my hands steady. And I didn't look left, where the body still slumped over the steering wheel of the white Lexus, which was still parked across the street at the curb. Up and down the cul-de-sac, Atlanta police officers clustered with EMTs from both Grady and Crawford Long. I was a part of this scene too, secluded in the back of a patrol car, protected by a ring of yellow tape and nice Officer Norris, who was just beginning to get down to business.

He took out a pen and a small notebook. "It says here your name is…Tai?"

I knew what he was thinking. Curly caramel blond hair, hazel eyes, pale freckled skin. Not a drop of Asian blood.

"It's a nickname. My real name is Teresa Ann Randolph. I can show you my driver's license if you want."

He wanted. I could tell he was getting suspicious, his tight appraisal cataloging my frowzy hair and unmade face, my tee-shirt and thrift store jeans. I didn't belong in this neighborhood of ivy-laced cottages and tidy window boxes, and he knew it.

"My Aunt Dotty started calling me Tai when I was a baby," I said, digging in my tote bag for my wallet. "She said it meant 'little drop of heaven,' which is totally made up, of course, but—"

"This is your brother's place, correct?" He consulted his notes. "Eric Randolph?"

"That's him."

"Do you live here too?"

I started to explain that I'd only been in Atlanta for a week, that I'd just moved up from Savannah, that I used to have a part-time job leading ghost tours, so I usually didn't get freaked out around dead people, or cops, except that the dead people in Savannah were crumbly and six feet under, and the cops were all related to me, but I liked Atlanta cops, so far anyway.

Luckily, I caught all that before it escaped my mouth. "I'm staying here until I find an apartment."

I handed over my license. Norris scrutinized it and handed it back. "Where's your brother?"

"He left this morning for a cruise to the Bahamas."

He narrowed his eyes and underlined the word "Bahamas." Twice. I scrambled to explain.

"It's for work, some pop therapy seminar-at-sea thing. Like Dr. Phil, only on a boat. I took him to the airport this morning for his flight to Miami."

"Was he behaving out of the ordinary?"

"You mean homicidal?"

The response came out peevish, not what I'd intended. Officer Norris kept his pen poised while I scraped wax off the cup with my fingernail. Why had I decided that this was the week to quit smoking?

"What I mean is, he seemed perfectly normal. A little tense, maybe, but nothing that would have anything to do with something like...that."

I gestured toward the Lexus. Eric's Virginia Highland cul-de-sac was usually quiet, the only noise the distant murmur of North Highland traffic. It was a place of Arts and Crafts bungalows and kitschy specialty shops, a place where you strolled to the corner café for a petite serving of organic peach gelato. Not the kind of place where you stumbled into corpses on the curb.

"So your brother was tense?" Norris said.

Oh great, I thought. Now I'd done it.

"Not tense like guilty," I corrected, "tense from worrying about passports and stuff. A perfectly innocent tense."

This was not the whole truth, but I didn't feel like explaining the rest, the part where we'd argued, the part where he'd told me to grow up and I'd told him to shove it. The part that would make any cop's nose twitch with interest. I knew it wasn't relevant and would only distract the police from what they *should* be doing, namely, finding out why there was a corpse across the street.

"You picked him up here, at the house?"

"No, at work, some place by Perimeter Mall. He's a PhD, you know, an industrial psychologist."

I had no idea why I added that last part. Perhaps I was trying to make Eric seem stable and ethical, not the kind of man who'd murder some woman and then flee the country. Officer Norris didn't seem concerned about his character, however. He remained focused on the timeline.

"So you picked him up at work, dropped him off at the airport, and came back here?"

"No, not immediately anyway. I went to the shop first."

"What shop?"

I hesitated. It was looking like I didn't have a non-suspicious answer in me.

"Dexter's Guns and More," I finally said. "Up in Kennesaw. I'm the new owner."

Norris' eyes dipped to my chest, to the tee-shirt with Dexter's logo and the slogan "From My Cold Dead Hands" on it. I'd found a bag of them in my uncle's desk and pulled one on while I cleaned the storeroom, so not only was it politically incorrect, it was filthy with dust and cobwebs.

"Look, I know it sounds bad, me with a gun shop just forty-five minutes away and a murdered person on the curb, but it's entirely innocent."

I held up my cell phone and showed him a photo from that morning. There I was, standing in front of a display case chock full of dangerous things, a Confederate flag hanging brazenly behind me.

"Interesting," Norris said. His ebony features betrayed no emotion.

I tried again. The next shot didn't have any rebel paraphernalia in it, just the prominently displayed city ordinance requiring all Kennesaw citizens to own a gun. And me, beaming brightly. But it *did* have the time and date, proving that I was telling the truth about my whereabouts.

"Uncle Dexter left the place to me in his will. Well, he left it to my mother actually—she's his sister—but she's been dead for over a year now—my dad and Aunt Dotty too, a long time ago—and we were next in line, me *and* Eric, but Eric will have nothing to do with it, loathes the whole concept, so technically—"

"Can anyone verify your story?"

I took a deep breath. "Sorry. I run on when I'm nervous. My friend Rico was there, I'll give you his number."

Norris wrote down the information, which I knew was going to piss Rico off royally. Rico didn't like being asked to go on the record for anything; he never had, not even in high school. But he'd forgive me, just like I'd forgive him for not returning my four messages and three texts.

Norris turned the page. "Tell me how you found the body."

"I left the shop a little after four, got here sometime around five-thirty. I noticed the car right off, but I didn't think much of it, not until I went to the mailbox. That's when I saw the woman slumped over the steering wheel. So I went over and knocked on the window, and when she didn't look up, I opened the door. And that's when I saw the blood."

A camera flash popped as the crime scene photographer circled the car, stepping on the neighbor's pansies. Another cop placed squarish yellow markers on the concrete. Someone's radio squawked, staccato and abrupt.

Behind Norris, I saw two new arrivals duck under the tape, one male, one female. The woman was average height and athletic, with the kind of bleached straw hair and nut brown skin that come from too many hours in the sun. The man was only a little taller, with deep-cocoa skin and hair clipped close to his head. Both wore the same thing—charcoal pants and jackets, gold shields clipped at the belt.

APD detectives. They knew better than to step on the pansies.

"And you have no idea who she is?" Norris said.

"No. Do you?"

He seemed surprised at the question. "Would I be asking you if I did?"

"Of course you would, you're a cop. You ask all kinds of questions you already know the answer to."

I said it with a smile, and he smiled too, just a little, which was a relief. Not as big a relief as a Winston Light, mind you, but something.

Just then, I noticed a dark gray sedan pull up close to the crime scene tape. A sandy-haired business type pushed himself out—a stocky guy, with broad shoulders and a purposeful stride.

One of the uniforms shook hands with him and pointed him toward the detectives.

Not a cop, I decided. Probably a GBI agent, maybe even a Fed. Which could only mean one thing—this dead girl I didn't know was somebody important.

The patrol officer led the detectives and the sandy-haired man under the yellow tape to the crime scene itself. The sandy-haired man peered inside, then shook his head. The female detective held up a plastic bag with something small and white inside. I squinted to get a look. And then, as if on cue, all three turned and looked at me. With interest.

Not a good thing.

My belly sloshed. And then the two detectives headed toward my patrol car, leaving the sandy-haired man at the crime scene to do things I didn't want to think about. I peeked at my cell phone. Nothing from Eric, nothing from Rico, nothing from anyone at all. Abandoned.

And then they were upon me.

"Ms. Randolph?" The male partner leaned down and extended his hand. His grip was dry and warm, but his eyes were skewers. "I'm Detective Ryan. This is my partner, Detective Vance."

The woman unfastened her gaze from the dead girl's car and swiveled her head my way. She reminded me of a hawk, right down to her small hook of a nose and round unblinking eyes. I fought the urge to get still and small.

Ryan smiled. "Is it all right if we talk inside?"

The way he phrased it wasn't a question.

My mind raced. I watched *CSI*, I knew what it meant to let a cop in your house with their little vials and black lights and rubber gloves. Should I demand a search warrant? Tell them to wait until I heard from Eric? Call a lawyer?

I thought all of these things, but what I said was, "Sure. Okay."

Chapter Two

Eric's office was decorated with the military zeal that only a civilian could muster—navy carpet, gold brocade drapes, coat-of-arms wallpaper. Dueling pistols crossed above the loveseat and mock samurai swords above his desk, this bombastic creation as pitched and massive as a merchant schooner.

In the middle of the excess was one spot of hominess—an old family portrait on the wall, taken when I was barely eight, Eric on the edge of twenty. We were both dark blondes, but while he was tall and slim, I was short and compact, with Dad's broad shoulders. All I remembered from that day two decades ago was how excited I'd been to have us all together for once.

The detectives didn't care about Memory Lane, however. I waited in the doorway while Vance walked a slow circle around the office, as if she were printing it with her mind. Ryan stood by Eric's desk, looking pointedly at the stacks of papers and manila folders, including Eric's desk calendar.

"Did your brother have any appointments scheduled for this afternoon?"

"Why would he? He was leaving for the Bahamas."

Ryan eyed the calendar. I stepped forward and moved a notebook on top of it, but not before I'd caught a glimpse of the day's agenda—two items, both in the morning: Tai pick-up: 7:30, flight to Miami: 11:05. I wondered how much Ryan had scavenged from his brief perusal.

He smiled. "Maybe he forgot, made a mistake."

"My brother doesn't make that kind of mistake."

"Thorough guy, huh? Organized, a good planner?"

I folded my arms. "Yes, Eric's all those things. Why do you make it sound like that's a crime?"

"Not my intention. I'm just wondering why a young woman would come to his home office unless she had an appointment."

"What makes you think she was coming to see him? The car was parked across the street."

Vance flanked me from the left. "Because we found your brother's business card under the front seat."

The white square I'd seen in the plastic baggie. So Eric had known the dead girl. And she'd heard of him.

Through the picture window, I saw movement across the street as the EMTs loaded the body into the ambulance, threading past a crowd that had swelled to include a news crew. Bars of waning sunshine cut through the branches of the oak tree, slanting across the hood of the Lexus. The sandy-haired man watched from the sidelines, cell phone pressed to his ear.

I noticed Ryan looking at me then, his expression alert. Vance seemed to be cataloging everything in her periphery—leather reading chair, framed Kandinsky print, cut crystal whisky decanter—and using it to decide who my brother was, who I was, what had really happened. Like Norris, she'd decided I didn't fit. And she was right—I didn't. But that didn't make me, or my brother, a criminal, and I was determined to prove it.

"Is there anything else?"

Vance snapped her notebook shut. "We appreciate your cooperation, ma'am, but that probably does it for here."

Ryan nodded in agreement. "For here."

I felt a surge of relief. It was almost over. And then it hit me. "For here?"

Ryan nodded again.

"I know what that means. That means you're taking me downtown, doesn't it?"

Vance laughed. Ryan crooked a half-smile at me. "Oh yes, ma'am. You are definitely going downtown."

I sighed and dug in my pockets for a piece of nicotine gum. God, I wanted a cigarette.

Waiting in the interrogation room felt very much like being kept after school. Boxy and square, off-white and badly lit, it had the same smell as a principal's office—Pine Sol and plastic and industrial air conditioning—and the same sense of imminent unpleasantness.

Detective Ryan brought me coffee. Detective Vance turned on a video camera. And then I repeated a lot of the same information I'd told them before. But before I could explain once again how very little I knew, I actually learned something.

"Eliza Compton," Vance said, slapping a file folder on the desk. "That name sound familiar?"

So they had an ID. "I'm sorry, no."

"Did your brother ever mention knowing her?"

"No."

"Not even in some offhand casual way?"

"No."

I didn't tell them that Eric and I had spent the majority of our lives being offhand and casual. But now, thanks to the gun shop, our every conversation was tinged with exasperation of the most personal sort. Still, we were trying to get along, and I was ready to follow our relationship wherever it led.

Of course, if I'd had any idea it would lead to the APD interrogation room, I'd have been a little more hesitant.

Ryan shifted forward and put his elbows on the table. "Any idea why she might be leaving him a voicemail message?"

"What message?"

Ryan motioned to Vance, who pulled out a small digital recorder and hit play. The voice that came from the machine was female and young, with a deep Southern accent. Her words were clipped and nervous at the edges: "Dr. Randolph? It's Eliza.

I'm sorry I couldn't make it last night. I tried, but there was a problem, a big problem. I'm headed over right now, though." Then a robotic voice announced the time: three-fifteen p.m.

Ryan looked at me. "You don't recognize her?"

"I don't know Eric's friends."

"She called him Dr. Randolph. Sounds like she's a client."

"I don't think he works with individuals any more, just businesses."

"If that's true, then why would she be meeting him at his home, and not at work?"

I started to say she wasn't really *at* his home, she was on the curb, but I dropped that idea. I'd heard rumors about Atlanta's finest from Rico—taser-gun waving, bad cop/bad cop scenarios—and decided pretty quick the last thing I wanted to be was an uncooperative witness.

"I honestly don't know. I take my brother to the airport, go to check his mail, and suddenly, there's a dead girl across the street and everybody's asking me what I know, which is nothing. Have you talked to Eric yet?"

"We're still processing that information."

Uh huh, I thought. That meant they were using me to verify whatever it was he'd told them. I wondered—again—why he hadn't called me yet and took a sip of my coffee. It was surprisingly good, creamed and sugared with a heavy hand.

"How did you find out who she was?"

"We got an official ID on the scene."

The sandy-haired business type, I decided. Mr. G-Man.

"Then I'm not sure what more I can tell you. If she is the woman on the answering machine, then it's obvious my brother didn't kill her—he was on the plane by eleven, on a cruise ship by two. I'm assuming you've verified that by now, along with my alibi."

"I wouldn't call it an alibi, Ms. Randolph. You said yourself that your friend Rico can only account for your whereabouts until about four o'clock, when you left Kennesaw. After that…" He spread his hands.

I put down my coffee. "Wait a minute, you don't really think I had anything to do with this, do you?"

"Now why would we think that?"

Which wasn't a no.

"Well, do you?"

"No, Ms. Randolph, we don't. But the fact is, you found the body. And that makes you very important, whether or not you had anything to do with how that body got there."

"What about my brother? Is he important too?"

"Of course. He was the person Eliza Compton was trying to see when somebody blew her brains out a hundred feet from his front door."

He leaned forward, and I caught the smell of secondhand smoke on his jacket, probably from some other innocent bystander he'd been interrogating. The tips of my fingers itched. I rubbed them on my jeans.

"Do I get to go soon?"

"Yes, very soon. A few things to sign and you're on your way."

I sighed. "Good."

"Just don't leave town."

"What?"

He smiled. "I'm kidding. We can't make you stay in town—that only happens in the movies." He got up and his chair scraped backwards. "But seriously…don't leave town."

Detective Vance escorted me to the lobby, where I sat in an anti-ergonomic chair and waited for a patrol car to take me back to Eric's. She perched on the check-in counter, reading rap sheets and ignoring me. When my phone rang, however, she gave me her full attention. I got up and moved to the far corner of the waiting area.

It was Eric. "Tai! Thank God! I've been worried sick!"

Vance cocked her head. I turned my back on her.

"You've got some explaining to do!" I hissed.

"I've already talked to the cops."

"So have I. Down at the station. Still here as a matter of fact, wondering what the hell—"

"Don't worry, I've got this under control."

"That's easy for you to say. You didn't just get interrogated."

Vance rustled her paperwork. I ignored her.

"I'll explain soon, I promise, but right now the important thing is getting you someplace safe."

"Why isn't your place safe?"

"Tai—"

"I mean it, Eric. Who was that girl? Why was she—"

"Look, I had nothing to do with what happened, but I'd still feel better if you stayed someplace else. And I don't mean that room over the gun shop."

"Don't start. This has nothing to do with the shop."

"You'd better hope not. That's the last thing I need right now."

My temper flared. "When did this become about what you need? I'm the one stuck at the police station with you being all bossy and mysterious and suggesting I might be in danger—"

"Which is why I'm trying to help!"

I glanced at Vance. She raised an eyebrow. I lowered my voice. "So what do you want me to do?"

"I'm setting you up at the Buckhead Ritz-Carlton. I've got a corporate account there, and the security is top notch."

"But—"

"Just for tonight. Call it a favor."

He made it sound simple, which made me suspicious. I decided to take him up on the offer, however. Rico still hadn't called me back, so his place was out. And I didn't really want to stay at Eric's, not until I could close my eyes and not see blood.

"Okay," I said, "but—"

"There's a car on its way to pick you up."

"I don't have my things."

"Get some things on the way, I'll pay you back."

"But my car—"

"You can get it tomorrow."

"I just—"

"Look, I know this is hard. I'll explain everything tomorrow, I promise, but until then, stay put at the hotel. And relax."

He hung up, and I stared at the phone. Something was happening, of that I was certain. I felt like a minnow in a trawl net, flopping about with sharks.

Just then Ryan joined Vance in the lobby. She frowned and looked a question at him. He nodded, then looked at me. A taut smile stretched his mouth, but his eyes were sharp enough to slice brick as he said, "Rumor has it the Mercedes out front is for you."

Chapter Three

The Buckhead area of Atlanta is the ninth most expensive zip code in the United States. Often called Beverly Hills East, it houses two five-star restaurants, one governor's mansion, and the Ritz-Carlton Buckhead. When I crossed that opulent threshold, carrying a plastic Rite Aid bag filled with deodorant and a three-pack of underwear, I entered virgin territory, as daunting a frontier as confronted any pioneer.

It was almost eleven, so except for a few businessmen returning from late dinners, the lobby was deserted. My first impression was the smell—lemon verbena mingled with leather and the ghosts of expensive perfumes. Velvety light gilded the dark wood and golden fabrics, making everything seem deeply textured. Even the fire in the stone fireplace was well-mannered, a tidy blaze in coordinating flickers of auburn and yellow.

The doorman directed me to the marbled swath of the check-in counter, where a crisp young woman took my information. She eyed the plastic bag with no reaction and summoned a bellboy to cart it to my room. He pressed his lips together tight, fighting a grin, then bore it away.

That was when I noticed the man standing at the other end of the counter, watching me. He was very good looking, broad-shouldered and lean, with coal-colored hair brushed back neatly from his forehead. His attire marked him as one of the corporate crowd—black suit, white shirt, black tie, all of it perfectly tailored, probably designer.

The clerk noticed the man too and smiled his way. He didn't smile back. I noticed the earpiece then—tiny, black, discreet.

"Security guy?"

She smiled. "That's Mr. Seaver, yes. He usually works upstairs, but he's watching the lobby tonight."

"Is he always this…intense?"

"He's very thorough." She laughed a little. "You must have done something to make him suspicious."

"Discovered a dead body earlier. You think that could be it?"

Her eyes widened. "The woman they found in Virginia Highland?"

I nodded. The man was still watching me. Pointedly.

The clerk looked concerned. "If you require any special safety measures, I'm sure—"

"No, I'm good, thanks."

I signed my name just as my phone went off. I tossed the key card in my tote bag and moved behind a luggage cart. Security Guy stayed focused.

It was Rico. I tried to keep my voice low. "Where have you been? I called you six hours ago!"

"Don't even start, baby girl. Boss Lady's got me working the Kanye concert—I told you this, like, a million times—and I didn't get a break until fifteen minutes ago. Are you okay?"

Across the lobby, Security Guy moved down the counter, where he exchanged a few words with the clerk. She smiled at him, chatting while she worked the computer. He nodded at whatever she was saying, but kept his eyes slanted in my direction.

"I'm fine. Under surveillance, but fine."

"Uh oh. That sounds bad."

"We'll see. Damn, it's good to hear from you."

"Same here. Well, except for the part where you gave my name to the cops. Who just showed up, by the way, and asked me a bunch of questions about where you were this afternoon."

I apologized and filled him in on my situation. At his end, I heard muted crowd noise and the flurry of keystrokes on his laptop. He had steelworker hands with long thick fingers, dark as chocolate, but he could type like a house on fire. He worked tech support at a local PR firm, which meant that he logged some crazy hours, but it also meant he was on top of virtually every piece of breaking news in the Greater Metro area.

"Glad to hear your side of things," he said. "All I knew was I came over to Mick's to grab a burger, and there you were on the big screen, looking all Courtney Love and shit. And then I saw your seventeen messages, and then the cops—"

"I'm on TV? What channel?"

"All of them, all saying the same thing—that you found a body, somebody named Eliza Compton." More tap-tapping. "The Fox website has footage up."

"What else are they saying?"

"Shot to death in quiet cul-de-sac. Neighbors shocked. No leads. Anyone with information blah blah blah. They're calling it a homicide. That true?"

An Asian man got off the elevator and stood within three feet of me. He wore an Atlanta Braves baseball hat and carried a big foam hand on a stick. It was yellow. He was grinning.

"Oh yeah," I replied. "Definitely a homicide. No gun in the car, though, not that I could see anyway."

The guy with the baseball hat stared and his grin faded. I smiled his way, did the tomahawk chop. He smiled back and returned the gesture, then headed out, humming a war chant under his breath.

"So yeah," I finished. "Murdered."

Down the counter, Security Guy remained vigilant. Another clerk chatted with him now, this one a dazzling brunette. She ran a hand through her hair, tucked it behind her ear. He kept his gaze fastened on me.

Rico's voice was serious. "This is deep shit you're talking. You called a lawyer, right? Doesn't your brother work for some fancy people who would know a fancy lawyer?"

I made a noise. "Don't worry about Eric, he's good at covering his ass."

"We're not talking about his ass, sweetie. That's your ass up there on 11 Alive News at Ten."

"I didn't even know this girl!"

Rico snorted. "Like the APD cares. They got prostitutes to push, drug cartels to run—"

"This is ridiculous."

"So say all suspects."

"Rico!"

"I'm for real! And don't think for a second they're not looking at that assload of weapons you inherited and—" He muttered a curse. "Crap, I gotta go. You gonna be okay tonight?"

"It's the Ritz. Safe as Disneyworld. I'm just gonna get one drink—"

Rico made a noise.

"C'mon, Rico, it's on my wayward brother's tab. One drink. And then it's lights out for me, I promise."

"In that case, comb the hair," he said. "And some lipstick wouldn't hurt, you know what I'm sayin'?"

The Ritz-Carlton bar was low-lit and walnut-paneled, plush in a very masculine sort of way. Mostly empty too, which was not unwelcome. I sat down and ordered a top shelf mojito. The bartender slid a napkin in front of me and pulled down the rum. That was when I noticed Security Guy standing at the entrance of the bar, arms folded. Staring at me. Again.

I crooked a finger his way. He cocked his head and frowned, but to my surprise, he came right over. Up close, he was not as tall as I'd first thought, maybe six one tops. Narrow of hip, long of leg, the kind of build made for running.

I smiled up at him. "You're Mr. Seaver," I said. "And you're kind of relentless, anybody ever tell you that?"

He didn't reply. His eyes were blue, startlingly so, and he directed them like x-rays. The bartender pretended to be engrossed in mashing up mint leaves, but his ears pricked our way. I lowered my voice.

"Look, I know you're watching me, so just do me the courtesy of admitting it, all right?"

After the slightest hesitation, he nodded once, crisply.

I smiled wider. "See how easy that was? Now we can be friends." I patted the stool beside me. "Would you like to sit down, maybe have a drink? I'm putting everything on somebody else's tab tonight."

He shook his head. "I don't drink. Except for water. And hot tea."

"Water like in ice water?"

"Water like in Pellegrino."

"Ah." I signaled the bartender. Then I stuck out my hand. "I'm Tai Randolph, by the way. Hi."

He took my hand. He had a good handshake, firm enough for me to know what was behind it, but not so powerful that I thought my knuckles might pop.

"Yes, you are," he replied. "Hi."

The bartender delivered my mojito, which I charged to the room, along with one Pelligrino. My first sip was heaven, like sunshine and honey on the tongue, almost better than a cigarette. I took two more sips before continuing.

"So what was it about me that tipped you off? Oh God, please say it wasn't Fox News. Apparently I looked terrible."

"Not the news."

"Courtesy call from the cops?"

"No."

The bartender popped a bottle of Pellegrino and a glass on the counter. Mr. Seaver poured the fizzy water into the glass, then positioned the bottle exactly in the center of a napkin, which he then positioned exactly in the middle of the bar. He adjusted it a millimeter to make sure this was so. I studied him through this procedure.

"You're wasting your time with me, Mr. Seaver. I had nothing to do with that girl's death."

He cocked his head. "Say it again."

"Say what?"

"The last part."

"You mean the part where I assure you I'm not a murderer?"

His gaze moved deliberately across my face, focusing on my mouth, then returning to my eyes. There was appraisal in it, but no emotion.

"Well?" I prodded.

He nodded. "I believe you."

"You do? Now why is that?"

"Because you're telling the truth."

One hand rested on his thigh, but the other toyed with the green Pellegrino bottle, a restless gesture completely at odds with the smooth blandness of his expression. Why did I feel strangely opened before him, as if I didn't have a single secret anymore?

Something wasn't right. Why was this man shadowing me like I'd just debuted on *America's Most Wanted?* Eric had said the hotel had good security, but this was ridiculous.

I took another sip of mojito. "Must be a relief to know I'm not a killer."

"It is."

"I mean, it must be annoying to have some random woman show up at your hotel, RiteAid bag under her arm, her picture all over the news. Stuff like that probably makes your job really stressful."

"Not stressful. Just complicated."

I chewed on a spring of mint. "So as long as I stay here, you have to stay here, right?"

"Right."

"Even if I'm just sucking down rum and hitting on the bartender?"

"Even then."

This man was giving me nothing to work with. In some other bar, on some other evening, I might have tried flirting him into submission. He was a fine-looking creature, even if he never smiled, and I was pretty sure the suit disguised a first-class physique. But I had other plans, and tempting though he might be, Mr. Seaver wasn't in them.

I finished off the mojito. "So I should just go to my room then? Get out of your hair so you can get on with your other important duties?"

"That would be helpful, yes."

"You're going to follow me up there, aren't you?"

I expected him to smile at that, but he didn't. Instead, his mouth curved just the slightest, a quirky pull to the left.

"Of course," he replied.

I lost my key on the way up. I was legendary with keys, leaving them in restaurants, in taxis, finding them weeks later in my sock drawer or the glove compartment. He watched patiently as I searched my wallet, patted down my pockets. I finally found it in my tote bag and slid it through the slot. To my relief, the light flashed green, and he held the door open for me.

I saw my Rite Aid bag waiting for me at the foot of the king size bed along with a white cotton bathrobe and a tea tray. Through the window beyond, the Midtown skyline skipped and jutted across the dark horizon like an incandescent EKG.

"I'm sorry if I've been obnoxious," I told him. "But first, there's this dead girl, and then my brother vanishes, and nobody will tell me crap, especially not the police."

As I talked, I heard the soft purr of his cell phone. His gaze dipped to examine the readout, and a tiny wrinkle appeared right between his eyes.

"And I'm tired, and stressed out of my mind, and I want a cigarette so bad I might steal one, if I could find one. I mean—"

"I have to go now." He slipped the phone in his jacket pocket. "If you have any problems, call the front desk. They'll find me."

He was less than two feet from me, and he smelled good, a hint of crisp aftershave mingled with warm maleness and soap. I noticed a scar on his chin, caught the pattern of other scars, webbed and barely visible, at his right temple. This was a man with history.

"Mr. Seaver?"

"Yes?"

"I never got your first name."

"Oh. It's Trey."

I smiled up at him. "Goodnight, Trey. Thanks for the escort."

"You're welcome, Ms. Randolph. Please enjoy your stay."

Then he was down the hall and in the elevator. I watched the doors close after him. Enjoy your stay, he'd said. As in stay put. As in Eric's last remark. As in be a good girl and let the menfolk take care of this.

Phooey. I grabbed a bag of M&Ms from the mini-bar, plus some peanuts for later. I stuck my head into the hall—empty. Then, after making sure my key card was in my jeans pocket, I headed back to the lobby.

Taking the stairs, of course. Also keeping to the less-traveled hallways and finally slipping sideways into the bar, where I asked the bartender to call me a cab.

"And a coffee to go," I added. "Heavy on the cream and sugar."

Outside, Atlanta churned in all its chaos. Inside the Ritz, however, it was all potpourri and feather duvets and squares of dark chocolate on my pillow, none of which provided a single clue to what was going on.

I checked my tote bag one more time. Car keys, house keys, office keys—every tool of access I needed to get back into Eric's and see what was in that desk of his, especially his calendar.

Returning to the scene of the crime. Excellent girl detective behavior.

Chapter Four

Eric's cul-de-sac reeked of spooky. Police tape still ringed the neighbor's driveway even though the Lexus had been towed, and with the exception of the crime scene clean-up crew, the street was deserted. I saw a white panel van parked nearby, probably a plumber or exterminator, and I prickled. All of a sudden, even the ordinary felt dangerous.

His office had a similar vibe, especially in the half-light of his desk lamp. I took several swallows of coffee, hoping the caffeine would clear my jumbled head. I allowed one pang of guilt, then I sat down and got to work spying on my brother.

His password was easy to guess—BFSKINNER. He used it for everything, despite my telling him what a dumb idea that was. Now I was glad he hadn't listened, because with that one word, I suddenly had access to his entire life—files, programs, photographs, everything.

But the first thing I did was pull up the Internet and type in the name Eliza Compton.

Her murder flashed front and center, the top story. I saw myself in several background shots, looking unfocused and vaguely guilty. And awful, Rico had been right about that. I looked like I'd seen a ghost, and then I realized with a start that I had. From the second I'd peered into that car, my vision had been clouded with a stranger's ghost.

Eliza Compton was haunting me, only not in some super-natural way, like in the stories I spun for the tourists down in

Savannah. She haunted me with the smell of her blood, the sound of her voice, the gleam of the silver bracelet, strangely untouched with gore.

Her Facebook profile intensified the feeling. She'd been very pretty, with liquid brown eyes and bobbed chestnut hair layered with wispy bangs. In her profile shot, she wore a silver halter top, low rise jeans, and a coquette's smile. She'd ignored the concept of privacy settings, which meant that even though I wasn't her "friend" I had complete access to her life. Within two minutes I knew that her favorite band was Slipknot and her favorite club was Vortex, the grinning goggle-eyed skull unmistakable even if the photo seemed to have been shot out of the window of a moving car. No mention of where she lived, but she worked at a place called Beau Elan, a mixed-use development Rico had briefly considered before finding a more appropriately artsy loft over in Sweet Auburn.

Beau Elan. Cookie-cutter and predictable, I was betting. Not words I would have associated with the girl on the page.

I sifted through her friends, her photos. Lots of beautiful people, but no photos of Eric, which was a relief. Just this parade of sharp young faces, generic in their prettiness. It occurred to me that one of these attractive darlings might be her killer. I knew the statistics—more often than not, people were murdered by some-one they knew. Someone who snowboarded, who liked macaroni and cheese, who posted videos of sleepy kittens to YouTube.

It was too much, this life spread out before me like a dumped-out drawer. How was my brother connected to this, my respect-able brother with the gold-rimmed glasses and the hair just beginning to gray at the temples? What could he possibly have in common with this beautiful, tasteless girl?

I glanced at our family portrait. I'd never noticed the way his upper lip curled, the way his eyes narrowed. Like I was betraying not only him but our entire genetic line.

"Stop looking at me like that," I said. "If you'd just get your ass back to Atlanta, I wouldn't have to be digging through your drawers."

I turned my chair so I was facing the ridiculous crossed swords, not the portrait, and got back to work.

I found his cache of business cards in the top drawer. Most were unfamiliar and uninteresting, but one caught my eye—Marisa Edenfield, Executive Partner, Phoenix Corporate Services. The name sounded familiar, as did the address on Ashford Dunwoody Road.

The office building where Eric worked—I'd picked him up there that morning.

I stuck the card in the back pocket of my jeans along with the only other card that seemed useful—Dan Garrity, Senior Investigator, Atlanta Police Department. That card had a private phone number scrawled on the back. I could see that coming in handy.

Then I scanned Eric's calendar. I noticed my arrival time marked in blue ink, an unexpectedly touching flourish which only ratcheted up the guilt even more. I ran down the rest of his appointments and saw nothing out of the ordinary, for even though the word Phoenix appeared a lot, and the name Marisa, Eliza Compton was nowhere to be found.

I peered at the computer screen. One of his folders was entitled Phoenix Confidential. I clicked on it. But before I could get a good look, I heard a noise in the kitchen—the swift open and shut of the back door, then footsteps coming toward the office.

I jumped up, and hot coffee tumbled all over my shoes. Panicked now and lacking any better idea, I snatched down one of the Japanese swords hanging above Eric's desk. The footsteps came closer, coupled with a masculine voice, low and indecipherable.

I hefted the sword. I knew the thing wouldn't cut warm butter, but it was shiny and intimidating. I tightened my grip. The blade shook violently.

And then he stepped through the doorway right in front of me. Trey.

I pointed the sword right at his throat. "Stop right there, you son of a bitch!"

He froze. "You're not supposed to be here."

"It's my house, I get to be here if I want!"

"No, it's your brother's house, which means—"

"Shut up!"

I wrapped both hands around the sword, trying to hold it steady. He was dressed differently than at the Ritz—black nylon pants and a long-sleeved black shirt—and he looked stiffer, less graceful. Exactly like a burglar caught in the act.

I pointed the sword. "You followed me!"

"I did not. I was here first." He cocked his head. "Did you follow me?"

"No!"

"I didn't think so."

He still hadn't moved, was just standing there examining me, just like he had at the hotel.

I waggled the sword. "You make one move and I *will* run you through."

"I know."

"Do you? You don't seem to be taking me very seriously."

He held out his right hand. It shook with the slightest of tremors, even though his expression remained blank and neutral.

"Adrenaline," he said.

"Hands behind your head," I shot back.

He complied just as his cell phone started ringing. I pointed at it with the sword. "Who's that?"

"Probably Simpson. He's tech support." The phone stopped ringing. "Since I didn't answer, he should be calling my supervisor, who should be calling back in approximately thirty seconds. Assuming he's following protocol."

The phone remained silent. Trey shook his head slowly. I reached for Eric's phone and started to dial 911.

"Wait," Trey said.

"Why? So you can steal something else?"

"I haven't stolen anything."

"Right. What else would you be doing here?"

He just looked at me some more.

"Fine," I said, and reached for the phone.

"Wait."

I sighed. "Look, here's the situation. You lied to me at the Ritz."

"I did not."

"You told me you worked there, but you don't, and now here you are, breaking and entering at my brother's place."

"I'm not breaking and entering, and what I told you was—"

"Your name probably isn't even Trey, is it?"

"Yes, it is, but—"

"And now you're stalking me, aren't you?"

"No, I—"

"Stop interrupting! And keep your hands where I can see them!"

He closed his mouth and put his hands back up.

"Give me one reason I shouldn't call the police," I said.

He thought about that for a second. "It would be the next logical step, of course. But if you'll call Detective Dan Garrity—"

"Who?"

"Dan Garrity, with the APD. He's a friend of your brother's. He'll vouch for us."

"Us?"

"My team." He frowned. "If I still have a team. He'll vouch for me, though, regardless. And Phoenix."

"Phoenix? As is Phoenix Corporate Services?"

"Yes. I'm one of their agents. Your brother is one of our consultants."

Eric. Trey. Phoenix. Things weren't making sense yet, but I could feel some sense forming beneath the chaos and weirdness. I checked the clock. Almost two a.m. Detective Dan Garrity was most likely asleep. But then, he was a cop, and cops were used to being startled awake and confronted with strangeness.

I fished the business card out of my pocket and dialed the handwritten number. A man answered on the second ring. "Yeah?"

"Detective Garrity?"

"Yeah?"

"This is Tai Randolph, Eric Randolph's sister? Anyway, sorry to be calling you at home, but I'm in my brother's office holding this guy at sword point—"

"Sweet Jesus, what in the hell!"

"He says he's a friend of yours. Name of Trey. Works for some place called Phoenix. Any of this familiar to you?"

An unnerving pause. "Listen to me, Tai, you put that thing down right now!"

"I don't think so. Not until—"

"He's on the level. Really. But first, I want you to put the sword down. And get the hell away from Trey, I mean, right now. Back up slowly."

"I'm not an imbecile—"

"You're not hearing me—put down that sword. Now!"

There was a panicked edge in his voice. Trey watched, hands raised, eyes flat. Curious, perhaps, but not the least bit distraught.

Just then, I heard the squeal of brakes outside, followed by a slamming door and footsteps sprinting up the front walk. Silence, then a polite knock. A business card slid under the door.

"You're supposed to pick that up and read it," Trey said.

"I am, dammit, just give me a second!"

The doorbell rang, and I cursed. Keeping Trey in sight, I backed into the hallway. I could still hear Garrity on the end of the line, calling my name. I knelt to pick up the card, eyes on Trey.

Kent Landon, the card said. Managing Partner, Phoenix Corporate Services.

I tucked it in my back pocket under Trey's watchful eye. Then I lowered the sword a fraction of an inch. "Is your name really Trey Seaver?"

"It really is."

There was another knock at the door, more insistent this time. I backed up and opened it. A stocky, sandy-haired man waited on the mat. He had his hands shoulder high, palms out, an expression of weary frustration on his face. He looked familiar, but I couldn't place how.

"Ms. Randolph?" he said.

I nodded.

"May I come in?"

I nodded again. He stepped inside and shut the door behind him. Trey watched from the office, hands still in the air.

The man shook his head in his direction. "Get back to the van."

Trey lowered his hands and stepped forward, his face unnaturally composed. He walked past me toward the door, then paused at the threshold and looked back over his shoulder.

"Simpson?"

"Fired," Landon replied.

"Thank you."

And then he was gone. I put his phone to my ear. "Hey, Detective? It looks like the show's over. Trey's booked it, and there's a Mr. Landon here now, so—"

"Where's the sword?"

I tossed it in the umbrella stand with a clatter. "Gone."

"Good. I'll be there in thirty minutes. Keep your hands empty, you hear me?"

He hung up before I could reply. Kent Landon waited in the entrance, and I suddenly remembered where I'd seen him before—he was the sandy-haired guy talking to the detectives at the crime scene earlier that afternoon, Mr. Big Dog G-Man in the gray suit.

"Detective Garrity's on his way," I said. "I think he's pissed."

"I assumed as much." Landon folded his arms, looked weary. "Is it my imagination, or do I smell coffee?"

"Coffee?" I shot a quick glance at my sneakers—they were soaked brown. "Maybe."

"Mind if I have a cup?"

I threw my hands in the air. "What the hell, I guess I'll go make some."

Chapter Five

I rummaged in the back of the freezer until I found Eric's stash of Blue Mountain blend. Then I piled paper towels on the Ritz-Carlton coffee, which was now a fragrant puddle on the carpet. I didn't even try to clean my shoes.

Landon settled himself at the kitchen table and pulled out a cell phone. His manner was open and casual, but despite the nonchalance, there was obviously an agenda somewhere. He reminded me of my high school guidance counselor, and I shuddered a bit. Same pink complexion, broad face, let's-get-down-to-business air.

I dumped coffee into the filter basket. "Okay, let's start with what you people are doing in my house."

"This is your brother's house."

"Same difference."

"Actually, no." He kept his eyes on the keypad, his fingers moving efficiently. "It's his house, so what we're doing here is his business, not yours."

"You got a piece of paper to prove you belong here?"

"Of course." He paused. "You're going to make me go get it, aren't you?"

I waved the pot at him. "Damn straight."

"I figured as much." He put the cell phone in his pocket. "Look, can't this wait until morning, after everybody's calmed down a bit?"

"Right. And the minute I leave the house, you people are all over it again."

"Well, that *is* our job."

I turned on the coffee maker and leaned against the counter. "All the same, I think I'll wait for Detective Garrity."

As if on cue, the doorbell ding-donged, followed a split-second later by a half-dozen assertive poundings.

Landon chuckled. He had a nice laugh, rich and deep. It caught me off guard. "Better let him in before he starts threatening to kick things down. In the meantime, I'll call my partner, see if there's anything we can do to salvage this situation."

"What about Trey?"

The banging at the door grew louder, more insistent. Landon gestured toward the porch with his chin.

"Why don't you let the nice policeman in first? Then we'll all have a long talk."

I did as he suggested. The guy on the front stoop was all cop, right down to the sturdy khakis and navy jacket, rumpled from a day's wear. He looked about five-ten, slim and wiry, with thick auburn hair cut short and a face like a fox—deep-set brown eyes, a neat sharp nose, and a mouth with crinkles at the corners, a mouth made for smiling.

It wasn't.

"A sword?" he said.

"Hey, there, Detective." I held up my hands. "No more armed and dangerous, see?"

"Garrity, please." He took the steps, pausing warily at the entrance, a cop stance.

"I'm Tai, Eric's sister. Hi."

"Hi, yourself. And it's nice to finally meet you, Tai, but good Lord." He shook his head, raked his hand through his hair. "This is a mess, you know that?"

"Sorry. It's not like I planned it, you know?"

"Yeah, yeah." Then he smiled, just a little. "So how are things?"

"Fine. Well, they were until I found a corpse at the end of the driveway, but I suppose you heard about that."

"Yeah, I just didn't know Eric was involved. Or you. Or Phoenix."

I stepped back. "You wanna come in? Apparently I'm making coffee for everyone."

He raised his eyebrows. "Coffee? Oh sure, I got nothing better to do at three in the morning."

◇◇◇

The three of us sat in the ladder-back chairs circling Eric's kitchen table, artisan-crafted mugs in hand. Garrity didn't bother hiding his annoyance at Landon. "Look, this is Eric's sister. Can't you just tell her what's going on?"

"C'mon, Garrity, you're a cop. You have rules just like we do, so you know the minute you start breaking them, it's—wait a sec, that's me." Landon checked his phone and stood up abruptly, scraping the chair back. "I've got to take this."

He took his coffee with him. Garrity waited until he was gone, then cut me a look. "Where's the sword?"

"It's not like it was real or anything."

"Where is it?"

"In the umbrella stand."

"And where's Trey?"

"Hightailing it back to the van, last I heard." I took a slug of coffee and burned my mouth. "He's lucky I didn't stick that thing right through his—"

"Drop that thought, my friend." Garrity put his mug down hard. "Trey used to be my partner, and I'm telling you, he's not somebody you mess with."

"Trey was on the force?"

"Yeah, a long time ago, back in my patrol days. We did Red Dog together."

The phrase was familiar. "Red Dog? The gangs and drugs unit thing?"

"Yeah, that thing. I moved on to Criminal Investigations—Major Crimes, the fraud division—but Trey started working in Special Ops."

"Ops? Like in SWAT?"

"Exactly like in SWAT."

I suddenly remembered Trey's unnatural composure, his placid blandness. So cool under pressure, even in the face of a crazy woman with a sword at his throat.

"That explains some things," I said.

"Some things, maybe. But that's too much to get into right now."

I started to ask him what he meant, but Landon returned to the table, rubbing his hands together. The expression on his face was that of a smart man told to execute a real stupid order.

"That was Marisa," he explained. "She said that since we have everything we need here, we can close up and go home. And you. Ms. Randolph, you can get your things and go straight back to the Ritz. If you'll do that—no fuss, no 911—then we bring you in for a full briefing in the morning."

Marisa. The name on the business card in my back pocket. Phoenix's Executive Partner.

I looked at Landon. "We leave together, all of us?"

"Yes."

"And you don't come back?"

"No. And neither do you."

I considered his words. "Why should I trust you?"

"You don't have a choice. This isn't your house, you don't get to call the shots. But frankly, the situation being what it is, we don't have much choice either."

"So it's mutual distrust? That's what you're offering?"

"Looking like."

I thought about it. As trade-offs went, it wasn't so bad. I lowered my mug. "Okay, Mr. Landon. You've got yourself a deal."

Chapter Six

Nothing about Phoenix Corporate Services LLC screamed elite security firm. Its location was in the unsexy industrial area north of the Perimeter, and the building matched its surroundings—three bland stories and a smattering of overlygroomed shrubs. Somewhere I heard the burbling of a fountain against the mono-drone of I-285 traffic.

I shouldered my tote bag and stepped inside, the automatic doors opening and closing with a pneumatic hiss. The receptionist swiveled toward me.

"Hi," I said. "I'm here to see Kent Landon."

She made a check in her book, then looked up. She had a sweetheart face framed with tumbling coffee curls, soft round eyes, and the straightest, tightest mouth I'd even seen on a human being. She handed me a clipboard and an ugly badge the size of an index card that proclaimed VISITOR in bright blue letters.

"Do I really have to wear this?"

"That's the rule."

I fastened it at the hem of my sweater. "I am so sick of rules. Everywhere I've turned the last twenty-four godforsaken hours, there's been someone there spouting off about rules."

"Take the elevator to the second floor, third office on the right. Mr. Seaver will be waiting."

I looked up. "I thought I was seeing Mr. Landon?"

She shook her head.

◇◇◇

Trey's office was, without a doubt, the most freakishly neat piece of square footage I'd ever seen. More like a MOMA exhibit than a workspace, it featured matte white walls and a slick black floor. Late morning sunlight cut the room into acute angles.

Trey himself was seated at his desk, dressed once again in a black suit and tie. He glanced up as I knocked.

"I thought I was seeing Mr. Landon," I said. "Then the woman out front told me to find you instead."

"That's Yvonne. She's the administrative assistant." He returned his eyes to his computer. "Landon assigned me to answer your questions, since your brother's case was filed under premises liability."

"What about Mr. Landon?"

"All field work comes under him. But I'm your contact for this matter." He gestured toward the client chair in front of his desk. "Have a seat."

I sat. His desktop was a study in geometric precision: mechanical pencils in a row, meticulous stacks of papers with the edges exact. He wheeled his chair backward, pulled something from the printer and handed it to me. It was a formal release of information request with an X where I needed to sign.

"I've got an appointment with the firearms certification team in…" He checked his watch. "…twenty-seven minutes. What can I tell you about the case before then?"

I borrowed one of his pens. "You could tell me what's going on for starters."

"Starting when?"

"Starting at the beginning."

"That would be the day before yesterday. Wednesday." Trey laid a manila folder exactly in the center of his desk. "I met your brother as he was returning from lunch, and he mentioned that he would be working late that night."

I waited for the rest of the story. There was none. "Okay, so…"

"So he was lying."

"What makes you say that?"

Trey's shifted his gaze to the wall behind me. "When he was speaking, his eyes slanted to the left and up, with too much blinking. The rest of the time, his eye contact was too direct and—"

"What does any of this have to do with why he hired you people?"

"Once Eric learned that you'd discovered the body, he requested that I be assigned a level-one personal protection order." He slid the folder across the desk to me. "Read the case notes so far."

I did. Mostly it was a repetition of what he'd just told me, all of it time-stamped and cross-indexed—the suspicious conversation, Eric's request, Landon's clearance to proceed, official yada-yada, yeah, yeah, yeah—at which point I noticed my name.

"Why am I on the—what is this, the personal protection order?"

"Because you're the protected party."

"My brother hired you to be my bodyguard?"

"That's not the official term, but yes, he did."

I examined the fine print at the bottom. It looked very official and bloodless, completely at odds with the churning in my gut. "I needed guarding? I was in danger and nobody told me?"

"The danger was hypothetical. My job was to get you from your brother's house to your hotel room, safely, with no complications."

"You could have told me!"

"Not without violating client confidentiality."

"But I was your client!"

"No, your brother was. Is. And I'm certain that he'll eventually explain—"

"But he's not explaining anything, not to me, not to you! He's on a boat somewhere in the Caribbean sipping daiquiris while I'm dodging cops and robbers and—oh yeah—a murderer!"

Trey almost frowned at that, but caught himself. "As I said—"

"I heard what you said. I just don't like it" I slapped the folder shut and slid it back to him. "So what the hell were you and Landon doing at the house last night?"

"Your brother requested that Phoenix collect his files and computer records for safekeeping. Simpson is the technical expert, but since I'm premises liability, Landon thought I should assist even though hardware is not my field of expertise."

"Let me guess. Your 'field of expertise' is the James Bond stuff while Simpson gets to rewire things." And then I remembered. "Until you got him fired."

Trey narrowed his eyes. "He was negligent enough to desert his post, which allowed you to infiltrate the premises—"

"I didn't infiltrate anything!"

"—which then created an unpredictable situation that could have ended badly."

He had a point there. Nothing like an edged weapon through the gullet to end things badly.

Trey continued. "Simpson was entirely unsuited for surveillance work, and I have no idea why Landon assigned him to my cases. However, it's immaterial now. He's been terminated."

I scanned his features. Was he hiding something behind that professional blandness? Or was I just getting paranoid? I rubbed my temples against an encroaching headache.

Trey stood. "I'm fielding a conference call with your brother and Landon tomorrow morning. You're welcome to join us. In the meantime, wait here. Yvonne is on her way with the last of your paperwork."

He walked around the desk and stopped right in front of me, uncomfortably close. I stood too, toe to toe, refusing to be muscled.

"Look," I said, "I want to work with you on this. A woman is dead, and my brother is involved, which makes me involved, like it or not. Anyway, what I'm trying to say is this: I'm sorry I threatened you with a sword, and I'm willing to forget the whole thing if you are."

He shook his head. "I don't forget."

And then he walked out of the office, not even looking over his shoulder, leaving me standing there furious, but unsurprised.

Chapter Seven

I had a perverse desire to trash his office, maybe dump his pencils on the floor, toss some paper around. Instead I sat at his fancy desk and put my feet up, then took off the stupid badge and threw it in his in-box.

Trey Seaver. Who the hell did he think he was?

Who the hell was he?

The hallway was quiet, the door half-closed. The opportunity was irresistible. Keeping my eye out for Yvonne, I tried the file drawers on Trey's desk. As expected, they were locked up tight. But then I tried his top drawer, and to my utter astonishment, it slid right open.

Too damn easy, I thought. Probably a trap, probably being recorded on some hidden camera. I didn't care. If anyone asked, I would say I was looking for a pen.

There wasn't much to inventory, however. One bottle of prescription medicine—Topomax, half-empty—and two bottles of over-the-counter pain reliever. A black silk tie, neatly laid out. Four fountain pens. A box of pencil lead. And two manila folders, one labeled LEGAL and the other labeled MEDICAL.

I checked the hallway. Still deserted.

The first folder contained a stack of official papers, including a last will and testament, a power of attorney, and a living will, all of them in Trey's name and recently updated. In every case, the name Dan Garrity featured prominently, as beneficiary, as executor, as carrier of Trey's final wishes concerning his departure from this world.

The medical file was even heavier. I paged through an ominous alphabet soup of words: Glasgow coma scale, Serum S 100 B readings, ICP monitor. There were copies of x-rays and MRI scans too, head shots, all of them listing the patient as Trey Seaver, and all of them featuring gray squiggles and gray fuzzy spots and gray blotches.

What was it Garrity had said the night before, about Trey? *This explains some things, but not all.* I hadn't had a chance to ask him what he meant then, not with Landon stomping around like Alexander the Great. But I knew one thing—I was gonna make that chance as soon as I got out of Phoenix. Most people didn't have a desk drawer full of cranial scans, and I wanted to know why this one did.

"Miss?"

I jerked. A man slouched in the doorway, silver hair swept across his forehead, white teeth brilliant under a matching slash of a mustache. I casually slipped the folder back into the drawer, but one of the papers slipped to the floor. I covered it with my tote bag.

Then I stood. "May I help you?"

"I was looking for Trey."

"He just stepped out, Mr....?"

If this gentleman knew I was snooping, he wasn't showing it. He had an odd face, like Cupid gone bad, but the rest of him was tastefully dressed in stone-colored trousers, white shirt open at the neck. His entire manner said that even though it was obvious I knew who he was, if I wanted to play like I didn't, he could be a regular joe about it.

He came into the office and stuck out his hand. "Mark Beaumont."

He was right—I should have recognized him. Mark Beaumont was Atlanta's version of Donald Trump, and he walked, as they say, in tall cotton. If I remembered correctly, he was the owner of Beau Elan, the apartment complex where Eliza Compton had worked.

An interesting development, this.

I took his hand. "Tai Randolph. Pleased to meet you."

"Same here." He gave me the up and down. "You must be new."

"You could say that."

"So I can leave these with you then?"

He pulled a stack of photographs from an envelope and handed them to me. The top one gave me goosebumps. It was Eliza, a black and white headshot. She looked serious and pleasant; only the tilt of her head revealed the playfulness I'd glimpsed on Facebook.

"That one's for the press release," Mark said. "The rest are for Trey, that one especially."

He pointed to the second photograph in the stack, a glossy 5X7, the kind of party shot popular with society magazines. I recognized Mark Beaumont, looking tan and fit, in a handshake with Trey, looking pale and stiff. An auburn-haired beauty I didn't recognize stood at Trey's side, her hand resting on his shoulder, and there was a woman next to Mark too, a dark-haired exotic creature.

Mark tapped it approvingly. "Not bad, huh? This new guy took them. Trey doesn't usually do photos, but look, he's almost smiling in this one."

Mark was wrong—Trey was nowhere near smiling. There was something subtly alert in his expression, however, and I suspected it had to do with the redhead at his side. She was barely five feet tall, as delicate and exquisite as a music-box ballerina, and unlike the others in the photo, she had no interest in the camera. She had eyes only for Trey.

I nodded like I knew what Mark was talking about. "And this was taken at the…"

"Blue Knights Mardi Gras Ball."

Mardi Gras. Tuesday night. Three nights ago.

"It was Charley's first time chairing the event, but she did great. The police chief himself said so."

Charley Beaumont, the black-haired woman in the photo. Mark's wife. I paged through the rest of the shots. The framing was always askew and the subjects looked startled, as if the photographer had bounded at them from behind a bush. There were more of the Beaumonts, including a shot of them with the mayor, Mardi Gras masks in hand. And then, sudden and startling—

My brother.

He looked every inch the society guy—black tux, champagne glass, an open smile on his face. Utterly at ease, even with strands of purple and gold beads around his neck. When had he gotten this life, these friends? When had I stopped knowing anything about him?

As I studied the photograph, Charley Beaumont herself came through the door. I recognized her even before she slinked her arm through Mark's elbow. Sharp-featured with high maintenance hair, she looked older in person, pushing forty easily. A red sheath dress skimmed her size-two frame.

Mark waved in my direction. "Meet Trey's new assistant."

I didn't correct him, just stuck out my hand. "Tai Randolph."

Charley took it silently, still holding onto Mark. She had no grip whatsoever, and I felt self-conscious, like someone had handed me a Ming vase. Her eyes dipped to the photos in my hand. "What's that?"

Mark explained. "It's the shots that new photographer sent over, from Mardi Gras."

"When did you get these?"

"Wednesday morning."

"Let me see."

I handed the photos over. She took them to Trey's desk and fanned them across the surface, like a magician performing a card trick. "I didn't like that photographer. He kept lunging at people."

"So don't hire him again."

"I didn't hire him this time." She restacked the photographs into a sloppy pile. "I just spoke with Landon. He's not going to make the meeting."

So I wasn't the only one Landon had stood up. I wondered what he was up to, and didn't like any of the answers that sprung to mind.

Mark's expression sobered. "I'm sure you've heard about the young girl who was murdered. She was one of our employees at Beau Elan, our newest development. She was a tenant too, a fine person. Charley and I are offering a reward."

I waited for him to recognize that I was the woman who'd found his murdered employee. It didn't happen. He was too busy waiting for my reaction.

"Wow," I said, "that's very generous."

"The least we can do."

Charley removed Eliza's black and white from the assorted other shots and placed it in Trey's inbox. The rest she shoved in her purse. I tried to sound curious and not confrontational.

"You decided not to leave them?"

Charley froze. "What?"

"The Mardi Gras photos."

Her eyes snapped with annoyance. "I prefer more traditional shots, not this paparazzi crap." She took Mark's elbow again. "We'll find a better one for Trey, sweetheart. In the meantime—"

"I know. The interview at Channel 11." He exhaled loudly. "It's such a tragedy, a young woman's senseless death."

"Eliza Compton."

"Yes. So young." He shook his head somberly, then held out his hand for a final shake. "Very nice to meet you, Tai. I assume we'll be seeing you next weekend? At the reception?"

I had no idea what he was talking about.

"Of course," I said. "Wouldn't miss it for the world."

Yvonne came to walk me out before I could return the fallen MRI to its proper place, so I left Phoenix with the contraband tucked in my tote bag. I hadn't planned it that way, and was convinced alarm bells would go off and burly men would take me by the elbow as soon as I went through the doors.

To my astonishment, nothing happened. It was ridiculously easy.

I cranked the car and breathed a fervent wish that returning the thing would be just as easy. But first, I needed some answers. And that meant a call to Detective Garrity.

Chapter Eight

I remembered Piedmont Park from the previous summer, when Rico and I had watched *Casablanca* one midsummer night, blanket to blanket with the soccer mom/buff gay guy demographic, drinking moscato straight from the bottle. At that time, barely a month had passed since Mom's death, and I remembered feeling like I was in an overturned fishbowl, separate from the rest of the city. Every sensual detail had been as rich and distinct as an oil painting—the hazy islands of candlelight around us, the smell of crushed grass, the latent heat.

Now it was bright spring, dogwood time, and instead of Rico, Dan Garrity waited for me at the edge of the meadow, the spires of midtown jutting up behind the spreading green. He was dressed in his cop khakis and when he saw me, he tapped his watch. "You insist on seeing me during my lunch hour and then you make me wait?"

"I know, I know. I got lost." I threw my tote bag under the tree. "Every other street in this town is freaking Peachtree—North Peachtree, West Peachtree, Peachtree Avenue Boulevard. Not a single actual peach tree anywhere."

"They chopped it down last year. Miserable little thing. Had one peach on it, like a shrunken head."

Garrity held a rolled pita sandwich in one hand, binoculars in the other. Every now and then he'd peer through them at the crowd on the meadow, scanning the green space. A uniformed policeman stood in the center with a microphone and a German shepherd at heel, but I couldn't hear what he was saying.

"What's going on over there?"

Garrity lowered the binoculars. "K-9 demonstration. That's my buddy Lawrence, he works that unit. This is the dog's first time out, and I'm making sure no PETA nuts show up and start making noise about turning man's best friend into an assassin."

Another person lumbered into the cleared center, dressed in gray sweats and a baseball cap, like a slovenly Michelin Man. I guessed he was the bad guy. Too bad real bad guys weren't that easy to spot.

Garrity took a bite of his sandwich, which smelled like garlic and roasted meat. "You told me you wanted to talk, so start talking. I got thirty minutes."

I decided to start with something safe. "You know the Beaumonts?"

"Those two, huh? What are they doing at Phoenix, filming some commercial?"

I explained what Mark had told me about Eliza and the reward he was offering. Garrity didn't seem impressed.

"I'm not saying Mark doesn't have good intentions, I'm just saying he never passes up a good PR opportunity when he sees one."

"So how does the redhead factor into this scenario?"

"What redhead?"

"The one who went to the Mardi Gras ball with Trey."

Garrity put the binoculars up again. "Oh, that's Gabriella. She runs some spa boutique place over in Buckhead. She was at Phoenix?"

"No. But she *was* in this picture Mark brought over which Charley promptly confiscated. The woman did not like that picture, not one bit, and I suspect it had something to do with what's-her-name."

"Gabriella," Garrity supplied. "And I don't see why. They're friends, those two. They're even working on the reception together." He held out the sandwich. "Wanna bite?"

"No, thanks. What reception?"

"The one for Senator Adams. It's being held next weekend out at the Beaumonts' new resort property, up at Lake Oconee. Private affair." He waggled the sandwich in my face. "You sure you don't want some? Beef shawarma, best in the city."

I had no idea what shawarma was, but I took a bite anyway and got a mouthful of beef chunks and hot sauce. I wiped my mouth with the back of my hand. "Adams is a state senator, right? Running for governor?"

"If he wins the primary, yes, which is why this reception is so important. It's for the heavy-hitters donation-wise, the twenty thousand and over camp. You interested in going?"

I made a noise. "Yeah, sure, I'll just put a donation on my Amex."

Garrity laughed and returned to watching the demonstration. I knew very little about Senator Adams, except that he was a popular guy, especially in the rural parts of the state. Not so many friends in the urban areas, but that was changing, I suspected, especially with friends like the Beaumonts. And it sounded like everybody else was big fans too—Phoenix, the redhead, my brother, Trey. All in it together.

Suspects. The word bubbled up from my subconscious. I was looking at these people as suspects.

Garrity watched the dog strain at its leash. When the trainer released it, the creature flew across the grass, lunging at the villain's upper arm as he lumbered away. The dog leapt, clearing the ground, a furred missile. The force of its blow took the man to the ground, and the dog proceed to shake the padded biceps between its teeth.

"Got a little fast off the mark there, but he's new. He'll learn." Garrity took another bite of sandwich. "Look, I know you didn't come out here to talk about the Beaumonts. What's up?"

So I took a deep breath and told him what I'd learned that morning from Trey. I started with the conversation he'd had with Eric, detailed the whole personal protection gig, then finished up with the upcoming conference call. Garrity listened seriously, not smiling. Not a good sign.

"But here's the topper," I said. "Trey swears that Eric's lying."

"About what?"

"Some conversation they had." I frowned. "Is that for real, that stuff he was spouting about blinking and eye contact?"

Garrity kept his eyes on the demo. "Trey can do that. He can tell if people are lying."

"You're kidding."

"No joke. A heightened sensitivity to micro-emotive readings, the doctors say. Trey lasers in on things that most people ignore—subtle eye movements, tics at the corner of the mouth."

"Does this have anything to do with the brain scans in his desk?"

Garrity switched his cop eyes my way. Across the grass, on some signal I didn't see or hear, the dog suddenly released the bad guy and loped back to its trainer for a pat and a treat.

"Well?" I said.

"You were snooping."

"I was looking for a pen."

Garrity raised the binoculars once again.

"Okay, fine, I was snooping—so what? Trey's a secret agent. If he didn't want people snooping in his desk, he should lock the drawers."

"He can't. If anything goes wrong, the EMTs need access to those files."

"Why?"

Garrity sighed. "This is where it gets complicated. You might want to sit down."

I sank down cross-legged on the grass. Garrity did too, propping his back on the tree and stretching out his legs. Across the meadow, the dog's tail swept back and forth like a metronome, while at the other end of the field, the padded bad guy staggered to his feet for a second attack. I envied that dog—it had somebody to tell it what to do.

Garrity kept his eyes on the demo. "What did you see in those folders?"

"Bunch of legal papers. Your name everywhere. Some head x-rays." I signed and reached into my tote bag. "Like this one."

"Where did you—"

"It was an accident. I'll put it back, I promise."

Garrity took it with a frown. "This is an MRI scan, one slice of it anyway. You're not a doctor, or you would have noticed the subdural hematoma, right in the frontal lobe." He handed it back to me. "The diagnosis was coup contrecoup. Closed skull injury. Which means that compared to a normal brain—"

"Normal?"

"Uh huh. Because Trey's isn't. Not anymore."

I hung out with this knowledge for a little while. Damn, why'd I picked this scent to follow, the one that was suddenly uncomfortable and complicated and very personal.

"So what happened?"

"Car accident. Killed his mom at the scene, put him in a coma for five days. He came out of it, of course, but it left permanent cognitive impairment."

"Are you telling me he's brain-damaged?"

"Actually, I prefer screwed-up." He said this without a hint of a smile. "The technical term is TBI—traumatic brain injury. But Trey doesn't care what you call it, that's part of how he's screwed-up."

I felt light-headed. This wasn't making any sense, but then again, it made perfect sense. I remembered the faint silvery scars at his temple, in the middle of his chin, the prescription medicine in the drawer.

"But he seems so—"

"Well, he's not." Garrity's tone was sharp. "Don't get me wrong, he's still smart as a whip. You saw his office, right? He can find anything in it in two seconds. His brain's the same way—one giant flowchart filled with rules and subsets of rules and addendums to rules. Memory like a bank vault."

"He doesn't forget," I repeated, feeling dazed. "He told me that. I thought he was just trying to piss me off."

"No, just being blunt-ass honest. He has no sense about what to say, what not to say. He lets things slip if he's not careful, which is why he stays so damn quiet most of the time."

I swore under my breath. I'd noticed that too, the nonsequiturs, the pauses, the cautious bare-bones responses.

"He has trouble finding words sometimes. There's some amnesia, mostly the two years before the accident, and some damage in comparative analysis. He thinks in a straight line now, lots of focus, but no periphery. No shades of gray. Right or wrong, yes or no, stop or go."

"Is this why he's not a cop anymore?"

"Yes."

It was a clipped response. I waited for him to continue, but he changed the subject suspiciously fast.

"Look, I've known him for ten years. He was my best man when I got married, he was there when my kid was born, there when I got divorced. We played poker and drank beer and went to Braves games and then one night—bam!"

He bit his words back. I didn't pry further. There are minefields in everyone's psyche, and the best thing you can do when you realize you've stepped into one is to stop moving. So I did. We sat in the quiet shade, cocooned in bird song and traffic murmur and distant applause as the dog readied for attack once more. Garrity crumpled up his shawarma wrapper and stuffed it in his pocket.

"I was on duty that night," he said, "so I got there right after the ambulance. Semi crossed the median on 400, just past the Perimeter. Trey managed to avoid it, but ended up head-on with the overpass embankment. Anyway, he got a huge out-of-court settlement from the trucking company, almost three million. And what's the first thing he does with some of the two million or so left after bills? He pops for a freaking Ferrari. Trey was not a Ferrari guy; he had a Volvo. Secondhand. A condo in Buckhead was next, one of the high rises. And I'm sure you've noticed the wardrobe."

"Rather limited in color."

"Yeah, black and white all the way. Armani, most of it, or some other Italian crap I can't pronounce. I mean, he was my best friend and then suddenly—"

"Was?"

"Yeah, was. But then he was gone and then he was back, but it wasn't him anymore, so we just…" He shrugged, too casually, then stood. "Look, I have a nasty feeling this thing with your brother is about to snowball, so you'd better have your ducks in a row, you and your brother both, and figuring out how to work with Trey is a good start."

"Does Eric know about Trey's…?" I waved my hands around my forehead.

"Of course he does. It's part of what he does at Phoenix—compiling mental health profiles. Didn't you know that?"

The folder on Eric's computer labeled Phoenix Confidential. I had been five seconds from getting into it. Now it had been collected and stored at Phoenix, out of my reach, thanks to the efforts of Trey and Landon and the recently unemployed tech support dude.

Across the green, the padded bad guy was spinning in a circle, the dog fastened tight on his arm, its tawny body pinwheeling like a ride at the fair. The applause ratcheted up in volume, punctuated with hoots and whistles. I stood up too.

"No," I said, "I didn't know that."

I was discovering there was a lot about my brother I didn't know. But I did know one thing—there was more to this story than I was getting over shawarma and K9 demos.

The new key to Dexter's shop was silver and efficiently shiny. The lock was not. I jiggled the handle and bumped hard with my knee, but the door remained stuck. It took two more bumps before I got inside.

Dexter's Guns and More was more like Guns and Less now, the firearms and knives having been stowed in the safe, leaving the display cases and wall hooks empty. Only the Confederate flag and its associated paraphernalia remained—an infantryman's jacket, a box of buttons, a single boot.

I put the keys on the counter. The fluorescent lights washed the beige walls into blandness. The smell of linoleum and floor wax tangled with the vanilla potpourri I'd put in the ashtrays. It looked empty and blank, but not fresh-blank like a new canvas. Empty-blank like a hole.

I had no idea how to fill it. I pictured the racks single file with rifles, the cases lined row after row with matte black metal—Walther PPKs and Glock 19s, weapons both utilitarian and exotic. Magazines and clips and the ammo that came in cardboard boxes with the texture of playing cards. Shot cartridges and shells. Camo and holsters.

A gun in your hand isn't just a gun, Uncle Dexter told me once. *It's part of you. Don't ever pick one up unless you know exactly what you're capable of doing with it.*

He should have warned me the same was true of gun shops. Stripped and bare, it was even more daunting than when stuffed wall to wall with weapons. Part of me wanted to bolt right back to Savannah. Right after I smoked seven cigarettes in a row.

Instead, I stuffed another piece of nicotine gum in my mouth and went to the safe. Then I pulled out one of the revolvers, a Ruger .357 double action. Petite, with a cushioned grip and shiny stainless steel frame, it nonetheless packed a wallop. This one was unloaded, but I could feel its potential. Unfortunately, until Cobb County coughed up my carry permit, it remained in the shop, untested.

I put it back in the safe and prepared to return to the Ritz, hoping I wouldn't run into Trey there. As long as my tote bag contained his MRI, I knew guilt blazed across my forehead. But until I could come up with a plan, its plush bubble of security was best, at least for the night.

A plan, yes, one that was smart and flexible and included strategies for dealing with a human lie detector. An action plan. Because I knew the first part of my strategy had to include a face-to-face with Mr. Seaver.

Chapter Nine

As it turned out, Trey wasn't at the Ritz. I didn't find him until the next morning, when I showed up at Phoenix. Yvonne escorted me to a different room this time.

"In there?" I said. "Are you sure?"

She nodded, then handed me a new VISITOR pass. Her eyes glittered sharply. "Don't lose this one. And leave that here."

I gave her the Krispy Kreme bag—it only had a tiny greasy scrap of donut left inside anyway—and stepped into the room. Yvonne closed the door behind me. It was dark and narrow, with a bright projection screen at one end. There I saw Trey silhouetted against the clear white light, standing with his back to me. He had a gun, but I knew from his lack of protective gear that it wasn't a real one. His attention was concentrated on a body target projected on the screen.

I felt a little thrill from knowing what this was—a training simulation room, and a fine one at that. All Bluetooth technology, no wire or tethers to destroy the illusion that you were pumping hot lead into someone. Such set-ups were all the rage, my gun aficionado magazines reported, and very very expensive.

Trey pulled the trigger three times fast, and the gun kicked in his hands. He lowered it and examined the results—a definite kill shot, with nice tight grouping.

I moved beside him and clapped softly. Trey kept his eyes on the target. He wasn't going to make this easy.

"I accidentally took this with me yesterday," I said, pulling the MRI from my bag and handing it to him. I'd spiffed it up with a new manila folder, to show that even though I might be a thief, I was a conscientious one.

Trey gave it a quick glance, then looked at me, hard. "How did you get this?"

"I could tell you I was looking for a pen, but you'd know that was a lie, wouldn't you?"

He placed the folder on the table and picked up the gun again. His eyes never left the target.

"I saw Garrity yesterday," I said. "He explained some things."

Still no reply. No reaction.

"Like that you really can tell if people are lying. Micro-emotive readings, he said. Is that true?"

He sighted along the barrel. "Yes."

"Show me."

He fired off one more shot, then turned to face me. His eyes met mine, moving to my mouth and lingering there before meeting my gaze again. It reminded me of how he'd looked at me the night we'd met, at the Ritz, and I realized he'd been sizing me up even then.

Say it again, he'd said.

Say what?

That you're not a murderer.

I made my expression as blank as possible. "I have mace in my tote bag. I had pancakes for breakfast. Which is the lie?"

He didn't even hesitate. "The second one."

"Okay, that was too easy. Do it again. I was elected prom queen in high school. I'm allergic to shellfish."

"Both of those are lies."

"How about this one, true or false?" I took one step closer, just enough to breach his personal space. "I don't usually let strange men escort me to my hotel room."

He tilted his head, then shook it slowly. "Technically true, but deliberately evasive."

I decided it was as accurate a judgment as any. Which meant I was going to have to be real careful with this man. I gestured toward the gun in his hand. "Can I have a try? Or is that against some rule?"

"There no rule about that."

He handed over the gun and stepped back. It was a Glock, a 9 mm. I was surprised at how realistic it felt, with the heft and balance of the real thing.

Trey moved to a computer station and tapped out a key sequence while I took some deep breaths. Thanks to my recent marksmanship lessons, I'd learned that I enjoyed shooting. It was like yoga, only with weapons. Breathe in, breathe out, focus on the still point between.

The target appeared again, and I pumped it full of holes, amazed at the realism of the mock pistol, right down to the simulated recoil.

"You're good," Trey said.

"You sound surprised."

"I am. You've only been taking lessons for a month."

"The guy teaching it says I have natural talent." And then it hit me. "Wait a minute, how did you know that?"

"It was in your dossier."

"I have a dossier?"

"Just basic background—residence, employment history. Several university transcripts, no degrees. Two speeding tickets, no other criminal record. Concealed carry permit still in process. Identifying marks include a recent tattoo on your left bicep and an appendectomy scar. No birthmarks."

He'd missed a tattoo, an old one, in a very private place. This information pleased me.

"Why do I have a dossier? Because you're my bodyguard?"

"No. Phoenix always runs background on job applicants. It's standard operating procedure."

"I didn't apply for a job here. Who told you I did?"

Trey took the gun over to the pneumatic refill and pumped it full of air again. "Your brother."

I fumed. Eric. Once again meddling in my life, trying to make it into something more along the lines of his life.

"I don't want to talk about my dossier, I want to talk about Eric. The cops think my brother is involved with this murder, or maybe they think I'm involved with this murder. Either way this is *not* good news for my burgeoning career as liberal feminist gun shop owner. And then there's you."

"Me?"

"Yes, you. Garrity says if I'm gonna make any headway here, I've got learn how to work with you, and that means I have to trust you."

"You don't trust me?"

"Why should I?"

"There are several reasons." He slipped into his jacket. "I've got an excellent record, with good references. I'm proficient with firearms and most small weapons. I'm Krav Maga trained, other self-defense too, including judo. Special certification in security risk assessment and management."

I studied him. "So you'd take a bullet for me?"

He straightened his tie. "Of course."

"That was a joke."

"Oh."

"But that's not the kind of trust I'm talking about. I'm talking about the kind where you don't lie to me, deceive me, withhold information from me. I found a corpse yesterday, and it's been downhill ever since. I need to know you're on my side."

"Is this why you looked in my desk without asking me?"

I suppressed the burn of shame. "I'm sorry about that. It's an old habit. Won't happen again."

"Okay." He cocked his head. "I'm sorry if I've seemed untrustworthy. Garrity explained that part, didn't he? Because I don't want you to think that I'm…I'm looking for a word."

"Devious," I offered. "Shifty. Underhanded."

His eyes did this funny little crinkle. "Yes, any of those. I'm not any of those. I'm not good at them anymore."

Behind him the screen was blank, but I remembered the target. Shot after shot clustered around the heart, kill shot after kill shot, expertly and coolly delivered. I looked up at him. His eyes weren't empty, just impassive, like the ocean.

"Were you serious about taking a bullet for me?"

"Are you still joking?"

"No."

A pause. "Yes, I would. It's part of my job." Another pause. "Does that make you trust me?"

"Not yet. But we're getting closer."

He nodded, then headed for the door. "The conference call begins in eight minutes. Landon's office is this way."

Chapter Ten

Kent Landon's office was the epitome of masculinity, like a plush cave. Bigger than Trey's, it was stuffed with heavy dark furniture, including a library table scattered with official-looking detritus—maps, files, memos.

Landon was already on the phone when we arrived. He waved us in, and I seated myself in front of his half-acre desk. Trey, however, remained standing at my side, arms folded. He checked his watch.

Unlike Trey's blank walls, Landon's featured a hodgepodge of portraits and diplomas and certificates, mostly from the Air Force. The photographs were telling: Landon and Ron Reagan, Landon and Colin Powell, Landon and Dubya, all candid shots, not staged grip-and-grins.

Trey took a seat, checked his watch one more time. I leaned his way. "What's the AFOSI?"

"Air Force Office of Special Investigation. Landon worked there before starting his own agency."

"Phoenix?"

"No, a smaller one. He sold it when Marisa offered him a partnership here."

"Oh."

"Hold on a second," Landon said into the phone. "I'm putting you on speaker phone."

And then I heard my brother's voice. "Are you there, Tai?"

I took a deep breath. "Yeah, Eric, right here."

"God, it's good to hear you." He cleared his throat. "Look, I know you guys have lots of questions. So go ahead, fire them off. I gave Kent here the short version—"

"How did Eliza Compton end up dead in front of your house?" I cut in.

Eric sighed. "I figured you'd start with that."

According to Eric, Eliza met him at the Mardi Gras ball. She told him she was a receptionist at Beau Elan, talked about her psychology class at Georgia State. It was a polite conversation— party chit chat—and he thought nothing more of it until she dropped by his home office Wednesday morning.

Which was very different story. She was nervous, upset, asking if there was a place they could talk. She said it was urgent, but she didn't want to do it in his office. She insisted they go someplace in public, maybe that evening. She kept repeating the word "urgent."

"She said it had to be someplace where no one from work would see us," Eric explained. "She was very specific about that."

Eliza then quizzed him about the ins and outs of therapist-client confidentiality, especially—and this was the interesting part—whether it applied to criminal wrong-doing. Eric told her privilege was a complicated matter and suggested that if she knew of something illegal, she should talk to the police. She told him she couldn't go to the police, and that if he would just listen to her story, he would understand why. In the end, he agreed to meet with her that evening at a restaurant several miles out of town in Duluth.

Trey leaned toward the phone. "Did you meet her?"

"No. She never showed, so I went back home. I never saw her again. But here's something strange. When she pulled out of my driveway on Wednesday morning, this dark blue pick-up truck that had been waiting at the curb pulled right after her."

I stared at the phone. Why had nobody mentioned this before now?

"Did you see the driver?" Trey said.

"There was a guy behind the wheel, but I didn't pay attention to him until the truck peeled out and took off down the street right behind her."

"So he was following her?" I said.

Landon frowned. "Let's not jump to conclusions."

"I didn't actually *see* anybody, just a guy in a truck," Eric insisted.

But I wasn't letting this one go. "Do you think this person knows you saw him?"

"It doesn't matter."

"It matters if he figures out you can ID him."

"But I can't ID him!"

"This isn't getting us anywhere," Landon interrupted. "Eric, listen to me. Have you mentioned any of this to the cops?"

"I told them exactly what I'm telling you."

"You didn't tell anyone when Eliza first came to you?"

There was a long pause. "No."

"Why not?"

"She asked me not to. I saw no reason to get the police involved because there wasn't a crime. Not then anyway."

Trey again. "Then why did you lie to me Wednesday afternoon, about where you were going that night?"

"Look, Trey, no offense, but I couldn't exactly tell the truth without having to explain everything, and I knew where *that* would lead."

Landon had a look of perplexed frustration on his face. "Didn't Eliza's moves strike you as strange? Or alarming?"

"No, just odd. Then Marisa called me about the murder. She told me that it could be some kind of set-up, so she sent you to take care of the house and Trey to take care of Tai."

Marisa. The CEO of Phoenix. Her name sure was coming up a lot for someone I hadn't seen yet.

Landon's voice was all business. "Listen to me, Eric. The media are going to be crawling all over this thing, which is a royal pain in the ass, especially with Senator Adams' reception coming up. The cops want you back here ASAP."

"But my workshop isn't done until Sunday afternoon. Can't you talk to the detectives?"

Landon didn't reply. Eric kept talking.

"If I have to cancel, it's going to cost Phoenix big time. And it's not like I had anything to do with her death; that should be obvious. You know the strings to pull."

Landon neither argued nor agreed. "We'll see. In the meantime, I'm alerting legal that you'll be talking to them as soon as you get back to Atlanta. Until then, you talk to no one. No reporters, no strangers at the bar, no one. Got it?"

"I've got it, don't worry."

"Good," Landon said. "Keep every scrap of paperwork— receipts, tickets, billing statements. You'll need all the alibi you can get. As for Tai, I think we'll all feel better if she's safely back in Savannah."

I shook my head. "No, I don't think so."

Landon's voice was flat. "Excuse me?"

"I'm not going."

Eric made a noise of frustration. "Then we need to extend the personal protection order."

Trey shook his head. "My job is premises liability. I don't usually do—"

"No, you don't," Landon agreed, his eyes lasered on mine. "Which is a moot point, because the better idea is for her to go back home."

"Atlanta *is* my home," I countered. "I own a business here, which I'd like to get back to."

Landon's cheeks pinkened, but his gray eyes went hard. "There's been a murder, do you understand that?"

"I'm the one who found the body; I understand that better than anyone!"

"So understand this. Trey is escorting you back to your hotel, where you are picking up your things and getting in your car and heading back to Savannah. Got it?"

"I got that you don't get to tell me what to do. So I'm staying." I shot a look Trey's way. "With or without a bodyguard."

"Personal protection," he corrected.

◇◇◇

The meeting ended swiftly after that. Landon threw me out, then had a quick confab with Trey. I couldn't make out everything they were saying behind the closed door, but I did catch the word "liability." Suddenly, the door opened, and Trey came out. He didn't look the least bit perturbed, but Landon glared at me and slammed the door. Hard.

"Did you just get in trouble?" I said.

"No. But I think you did. Landon requested your dossier."

"Oh." I folded my arms. "I'm still not leaving town, you know."

"I know. Marisa told him so. She said that until Eric returned, your hotel room is on her dime. Her words."

He held the elevator door for me. I got on.

"So the Executive Partner of Phoenix Corporate Security Services is intervening with Landon on my behalf?"

"Correct. She also okayed the extension of the personal protection order for as long as necessary."

"Why?"

"Because Detective Ryan has requested that you come into the station for a formal interview, and she decided that a security presence is still needed, for our protection as well as yours."

"What interview? Nobody told me about any—"

My phone rang. Trey looked at it, then at me. "You should get that."

Chapter Eleven

Thirty minutes later, I was waiting out front for Trey to pick me up and take me downtown yet again. I had Rico on the cell phone. He was thoroughly intrigued.

"A hot guy who drives a Ferrari? I'm jealous."

"Don't be. It's weird and complicated and the hot guy is more trouble than he's worth."

"So why are you messing with him?"

"I'm not! But my brother's in trouble, which means I am too, and like it or not, that means messing with Hot Guy." In the distance, I heard the roar of an engine, coming fast. "We'll discuss this later. I may be in need of some technical assistance. You feel like helping out?"

"On what?"

"I don't know yet. But these Phoenix people are playing it close to the vest, and I suspect their version of the truth is very different from the truth-truth."

I heard him tapping at his computer. "I gotta ask, you know."

"Ask what?"

"If you think your brother—"

"Of course not! He may be a corporate stooge, but he's no killer."

"You sure? He abandons you with a murder in your lap while he hunkers down in the Bahamas. That sounds suspicious to me."

Rico had a point, but the car was coming closer, so I put one hand over my free ear and raised my voice. "Are you up for cyber-sleuthing or not?"

"What do you think?"

He hung up before I could thank him, just as a black car slammed to a precise stop right in front of me. It was a Ferrari, the real deal, and like all Ferraris, it was sleek and loud and predatory. Trey didn't get out, but he did lean over and open the passenger door for me.

I eased in as best I could. The interior was black on black with brushed aluminum detailing, including a serious dash display with about eight different readouts and a speedometer that arched up to—I did a doubletake—200 mph. I shut the door, and the leather seat molded intimately to my body, like a caress. Trey shifted into first and accelerated with jaw-dropping velocity.

"This is a Ferrari," I said.

"Yes, a 2008 F430."

And we hit the street in a dazzling burst of sunlight.

It's amazing how abruptly Atlanta happens, how mile after mile of strip mall sprawl rolls on by and then suddenly, everything goes enormous and vertical. Not once did we venture above the speed limit, however. Cars zipped by us. Other drivers stared. Trey let them pass with placid indifference.

"This is it?" I said. "You take me out of the parking lot like a bat out of hell and then you go forty-five?"

"Forty-five is the limit here."

"But nobody goes the speed limit in Atlanta!"

"I do."

"Well, obviously." A motor home passed us. "Don't you ever take this baby to the triple digits?"

He slowed for a jaywalker pushing a charcoal grill across the street. "No. But I would under certain circumstances."

"Like?"

"Like emergencies. Life or death situations."

"What about chasing down suspects?"

"What suspects?"

"Hypothetical suspects. Dangerous escaped maniacs who don't obey speed limits. What about them?"

He didn't reply. He just put on the left turn signal, glanced at his mirrors again, then started easing into the left lane

"Hold on," he said.

Suddenly, he wrenched the car right with a sickening lurch, cutting off this VW bug and veering into a tight turn. I shrieked, the Volkswagon honked furiously, and the guy with the grill flashed us a bird. Trey kept his eyes on the road.

I whirled to face him. "What the hell was that?"

"A tail."

"No, the...what do you mean, a tail?"

"I mean someone following us in a black late-model Explorer, tinted windows. Male driver, sunglasses, baseball cap. Vanity plate reading D MAN."

I craned to catch a glimpse of the vehicle but couldn't. "Are you sure?"

"I'm positive. I saw the same car Thursday morning at Phoenix, in the parking garage. That afternoon, Marisa discovered two security cameras destroyed."

"So you've got somebody following you?"

"Following us."

"No, following you. People don't follow me."

He slipped me this sideways look.

"Okay, besides you. But why would anybody be following me besides you?"

"I don't know."

He downshifted and took the car into a tight left. And in that moment, in that completely coincidental convergence of angle and motion, I saw the break of his jacket on his left side. And there it was.

I pointed. "You brought a gun."

He looked puzzled. "I usually carry a gun."

"And it never occurred to you to say, oh, by the way, Tai, I'm armed and dangerous?"

"I don't tell people I'm carrying a weapon unless they ask."

I couldn't argue. It didn't pay to go around advertising that you were armed and dangerous. But then, I doubted few people were in Trey's league of dangerous.

"So you think something's going to happen?"

"Something?"

"Yes, something." I scanned the traffic nervously. "You know, something like finding a dead body, getting surprised by intruders, getting tailed, getting shot at. Those kinds of something."

"You haven't been shot at."

"I'm just saying! Do you think things are getting dangerous? For me, I mean, not you—I'm sure things are dangerous for you all the time. But I'm not used to this, not at all!"

He turned onto Memorial. He looked thoughtful.

"There has been a murder. And now there's someone following us. That means things already are dangerous."

My heart did a sick little shimmy.

"However," he continued. "I've been assigned to protect you. I intend to do so."

The way he said it was serious and matter-of-fact. It was surprising and reassuring and a little touching, all at the same time.

"Thank you," I said.

"You're welcome."

I gestured toward the holster. "So what you got under there?"

"H&K P7M8."

Heckler and Koch, a nine-millimeter. I was familiar with the brand. Very expensive and hard to get now that they'd gone out of production, but very smooth and virtually jam proof once you got the hang of working the squeeze cocker. It was also heavy and hot and required a strong grip, but I imagined Trey had no problem with the latter.

"That's an unusual choice for a service weapon."

"Phoenix issue. Landon's choice." His expression turned mildly curious. "Does it bother you that I'm carrying a weapon?"

I thought about the question. Guns in a display case were one thing. Guns in a holster to protect me from a deranged killer were quite another.

"No, but will you just tell me from now on, as a courtesy?"

"Of course."

And that was that. But I was glad he hadn't been looking straight at me when I'd said no.

He'd have spotted the lie for sure.

Chapter Twelve

Trey escorted me into the station, where Detective Ryan shook hands with him. Apparently they knew each other from Trey's days with the APD, and even though there was no attempt at small talk, some strange off-the-radar communication zipped between them. I decided it was a cop thing.

"I'll wait out front," he said, and left me to it.

Ryan indicated a drawing on the table in front of me. "This person look familiar?"

It was a police sketch, a guy with a military buzz cut and thick flat features. The eyes were blank—not mean, just vacant—and there was something solid about the guy, something close to the ground.

I shook my head. "Nope. Who is he?"

In the fluorescent light, Ryan's cocoa skin looked ashy, but his eyes were sharp as ever. "That's a good question. The manager at the apartment complex where Eliza lived gave us this description. He said he'd seen him around her place, maybe a boyfriend?"

"I wouldn't know."

"Ever seen him hanging around your brother's place?"

I tried to remember everyone I'd seen in Eric's neighborhood. The woman next door walking her pug dog. The race walker with the exotic stride. The mother with the whiny toddler who pulled up people's flowers. But not this guy. This guy made me think of pool halls and construction sites.

"Has the manager ever seen him driving a dark blue pick-up?"

Ryan's eyes went even sharper. "You hear that from your brother?"

"Yes." I tapped the sketch. "Or maybe this guy sometimes wears a baseball cap and drives a black Explorer with the license plate D MAN?"

"Now why do you ask that?"

So I told that story, too, which got Trey dragged into the room to surrender his version. He told the story better than I did, knew things like exactly what time it happened and exactly what intersection we'd been at. Ryan nodded every now and then, like Trey's story was utterly profound and fascinating. Then he thanked us for our time, told us he'd be in touch, and escorted us right out of there.

I'd been expecting something different from the second official interview—the chair under a bare light bulb, maybe some trick questions. The whole episode felt more like a job interview than an interrogation.

"That's because it wasn't an interrogation," Trey explained afterward. "Detectives only interrogate people they think are guilty."

We were headed back to the Phoenix, the heart of the city behind us now. The sun was still out, but a chill remained. I blamed the pavement and concrete, the slick-walled buildings and glass and steel. Sometimes I tried to picture the whole city ablaze, as it had been during Sherman's March. But even imaginary fire didn't take.

"So they think I'm innocent?" I said.

"Probably not innocent. Just not a suspect. Unless they find a motive."

Which I didn't have. Means and opportunity, however, were a different story. I'd found the corpse, after all, right after returning from my shop full of potential murder weapons.

"They told me they were letting Eric finish his cruise," I said. "Unless something else comes up."

"Unless he becomes a suspect."

The same refrain. "He told Landon to pull some strings. Do y'all really have that kind of power at Phoenix?"

"I don't. But Landon does."

Trey stuck to the back streets on our return to Dunwoody, avoiding 285 North, which looked like a clogged artery, surprising for 3:30 on a Saturday afternoon. The feeder roads weren't much better, but at least traffic was moving. The apartment complexes and office buildings alternated in cookie-cutter rhythm, vernal and urban intermingling—Forest Hills, Concourse One, Summergrove, Centre Square.

We'd stopped at the light, and were just about to make the left that would take us to the Phoenix parking garage when I saw it, just ahead, right beside the Phoenix main building.

Beau Elan, Eliza's apartment complex. She'd lived and worked right next door to Phoenix. I'd been looking for the connection between Eliza and my brother, and there it was, in brick and mortar.

"Wait!" I pointed. "Take me there!"

"Beau Elan? Why?"

"Because I'm curious. I know you need a pass to get past the gate, but I figure you have one, right? Being that Phoenix works for the Beaumonts."

He neither confirmed nor denied my hypothesis.

"And there's a cybercafé on premises, right? So I can have a look around, get some coffee, check my e-mail. You can do… whatever it is you do."

The light remained red. Trey angled in the seat so that he was facing me. "Say it again."

I looked straight at him. "One coffee. Fifteen minutes."

The light changed. Trey faced front again, shifted into first.

"You're doing it again," he said. "The technically true but deliberately evasive thing."

I didn't deny it. But he took me there anyway.

"Here," I said. "Vanilla chai. No sugar. You'll like."

He accepted. "Thank you."

The Beau Elan cafe pulsed with the same "uniquely familiar" vibe that permeates most coffeehouses. Hardwood floors, bistro chairs, folkish artwork. There was a fake moose head on the purple wall to show they had a sense of humor.

Whatever. They had tea. Trey was content.

We sat at a bank of computers running alone a picture window. From what I could see, the complex looked predictably comfortable—multiple three- and four-story units catty-cornered along a curving driveway, each one washed in a different pastel, faux-aged and earthy. Like Bourbon Street crossed with Disneyland.

Trey peered over my shoulder. "Why are you researching the Beaumonts?"

I'd pulled up a *Home and Garden* feature about their house on Tuxedo Road, a nine-million-dollar property that looked like what Louis XIV would have built if he'd been a plantation owner. The mansion had eight bedrooms and a kitchen the size of a gymnasium where a beaming Charley Beaumont showed off a platter of cheese straws.

"Why is it always cheese straws?" I muttered.

The article also gave a synopsis of the Beaumont Enterprise backstory, how they brought their millions into Atlanta, making some well-received expansions into the niche apartment complex market. Charley's backstory was of the Cinderella variety—broke waitress at the Fontainbleu Miami (her) charms a visiting millionaire (Mark). Two years and one serious pre-nup later, she's the new missus. A few clicks brought me her wedding picture—the caption identified the dress as a Christos Yiannakou silk taffeta—plus a slew of society shots. Mark and Charley at the Botanical Gardens. Mark and Charley at the High Museum.

Trey looked puzzled. "What exactly are you researching?"

"I don't know."

He looked even more puzzled. But I was telling the truth. I didn't know how any of these parts connected—Phoenix, the Beaumonts, my brother, Eliza. But I did know one thing, and

I'd learned it as a tour guide —the truest stories get made from the weirdest bits and pieces.

I scanned the list of links associated with the Beaumont name. One of them was very familiar. I clicked on it.

"That's you," I said.

It was his Phoenix profile, complete with a bio/resumé and a photograph, a serious straight-on head shot. Apparently, he was in charge of Security Needs Assessment with a focus on Physical Security Analysis and Premise Liability (including independent analysis and coordination of vendors). He also conducted CEO training in Executive Protection Services, including threat assessment and special event security.

It was a catalog of competence, undeniably reassuring. I looked from his photograph to the man himself, all neat hair and smooth hands and small weapons proficiency. But Trey looked confused.

"How is my Phoenix profile linked to the Beaumonts?"

"Through the Blue Knights Mardi Gras Ball. See?"

He peered at the list of supporters and saw his name there. This did not please him. "That should have been Landon. He usually works directly with the Beaumonts. He was unable to attend, however, so Mark asked for me. Marisa says he finds me utterly fascinating. Her words."

I couldn't argue with that. Trey was every inch the elegant bad ass. And with bodyguards being the new cutting edge fashion accessory, having one as spiffy as Trey was a coup indeed. There was no way Landon could match his appeal, no matter what Air Force training he had.

I licked at the foam on the inside of the plastic lid. Coffee made me want a cigarette. My fingers twitched, but there was nothing to hold, nothing to steady the physical urge.

I pushed my chair back. "Let's take a walk."

"Why?"

"I'd like to take a look around."

"I have the schematics back—"

"Trey! Can we just go for a walk? Please?"

He took one final sip of his tea, placed the cup precisely in front of him. "Of course."

We walked. The sunshine had warmed the day up, so I took off my jacket and tied it around my waist. Just past the laundry facilities, we saw Eliza's unit—the yellow police tape gave it away. Trey looked over his shoulder at the parking lot. A patrol car sat there, a cop behind the wheel, paying us very close attention.

"There's probably someone inside too," Trey said. "Crime scene investigators."

I knew he was right. This was turning into a high profile crime, with lots of media attention. But right now, the complex was quiet. The only other people we saw were tenants; they talked amongst themselves, moving quickly from car to building. No one went near Eliza's apartment, which was a ground-floor unit, on the corner near the perimeter wall.

"So you did the security plan for this place?"

"I'm still planning it, yes."

"Nice work."

"Acceptable, but hardly up to standard."

I looked around. Besides the gated entrance, I saw a ten-foot concrete wall around the perimeter of the property, nicely disguised with hedges and such, but a wall nonetheless. And I knew from the ad copy that there were security cameras too. Short of providing a bodyguard-slash-butler for each apartment, I didn't see anything that seemed "hardly up to standard" security-wise.

When I told Trey this, he shook his head. "The wall is easily breached from the exterior, and the plants disguising it on both sides provide a means, and a good cover, for anyone attempting to do so. The camera films around the clock, but in many areas, the lighting isn't adequate for clear images. I also explained that a twenty-four-hour manned presence at the gate was the only way to guarantee the kind of limits they wanted on entrance and exit procedures."

"What you're saying is that the Beaumonts went for what looks secure, not what is secure."

"That's what I'm saying."

I noticed the security camera that he was talking about when we passed the swimming pool. The area was deserted except for a deeply-tanned woman stretched out in a lounge chair, engrossed in a magazine. She directed a suspicious look our way over the top of her *Cosmo*. The pool was empty too, its blue surface so flat it seemed fake.

"Do you miss being a cop?" I said.

Trey kept his eyes straight ahead. "I think so. Mostly I miss the…I'm looking for a word. Multi-syllabic, starts with C."

"Camaraderie?"

"Camaraderie. I miss that, I think. It's hard to tell. Everything's different now."

"You mean after the accident?"

He nodded. We were standing outside the Beau Elan main office, right at the center of the complex. It was closed and dark, which was a disappointment. I put my face to the window, peered inside.

Trey started walking again. He was a good fifteen feet ahead of me, already clearing the corner, when the office door opened and a man stepped out. He looked scruffy and annoyed and carried a toilet brush in one hand.

He frowned. "Can I help you?"

I hesitated, tried to think fast. Failed.

"Umm…hi?" I said.

Chapter Thirteen

He was a big guy, stocky, with dark brown hair and a square jaw. He wore faded blue jogging shorts with roughed-up athletic shoes, and in addition to the toilet brush, he carried a can of Comet.

He scratched his forehead. "Look, this is a very bad time. If you're here about an apartment—"

"Actually, no. But if you've got a minute, I'd like to ask you about Eliza Compton."

He opened the door, and I stepped inside the reception area, which obviously doubled as a community room—matchy-matchy sofa and chairs around a fireplace, a small kitchen area. The lights were off, which gave it a staged and ominous feel, but I could see soda cans on the counter, a wastebasket overflowing with paper cups.

"Sorry about the mess," the man said. "With Eliza gone, I'm pulling double duty around here."

He switched on the overhead and stowed his cleaning materials under the sink, leaving me standing by the information desk. A photograph of the Beaumonts hung above the stacks of pamphlets and brochures. I examined it as I slipped some of the sales materials in my bag.

It wasn't the typical display. In fact, it was decidedly unusual, a photograph of Charley and Mark shaking hands with a General Robert E. Lee look-alike in full dress grays. I recognized the figures flanking them too—Senator Adams, who was smiling in an official manner, and the guy with the toilet brush. Only this time he wasn't wearing faded jogging shorts—he carried a musket and wore the butternut uniform of a Confederate infantryman.

I peered closer. I couldn't read the tombstone, but I did recognize the statuary in the background, as any Southern tour guide worth her salt would—the Lion of Atlanta, guarding the tomb of the Confederate Unknown. Oakland Cemetery.

Trey joined me, hands on hips. He didn't look angry; if anything, he seemed extremely calm. "This is inappropriate."

"Five minutes."

"No. We're leaving now."

I put my hands on my hips too. "You can't make me."

I saw it in his eyes—throw me over his shoulder, toss me in the car, slam the door while I kicked and screamed—and I didn't doubt for a minute he could do it. He'd be sorry, and it wouldn't be as easy as he imagined, but he could do it.

"This is police business," he said.

"So?"

"So we're not police."

"So?"

He stared at me, then reached under his jacket. I froze. He pulled out his cell phone. "I'm calling Marisa."

"You do that."

"And Garrity."

"Fine by me."

He moved just outside the door, scowling. While he tattled on me, I grabbed a Beau Elan memo pad from the information table and scribbled my name and number down. The man walked over, looking puzzled.

I held out the slip of paper. "This is my personal cell phone number. Please call me later, Mister..."

"Whitaker. Jake Whitaker. I'm the manager." He accepted the information with two fingers and looked at it earnestly. "The cops have been here already. I let them into her apartment." He lowered his voice. "They're saying she was murdered."

"That's what it looks like."

"They know who did it yet? Or why?"

"That's why we're here, to try to find out."

"So you're an agent, huh? Like him?"

He was looking at Trey, who was still talking on the cell phone while he paced a six-foot strip, back and forth, tight turns at each end. I angled my body so that only Whitaker could see my face.

"Yes, like him. You know Trey?"

"A little. He works for Phoenix, and they're out here a lot."

"What about Eliza? How well did you know her?"

He shrugged. "She moved here about six months ago, right after she started the job. I live in the building opposite hers, so we were neighbors."

"I've heard she had some creepy guy hanging around her. Buzz cut, goatee?"

"Sure, I was the one told the police about him."

I didn't tell him I already knew that. "Ever see what he drove?"

"No, I never paid attention. I didn't have any trouble until Wednesday, when he parked on the street and walked past the gate. Then he was pounding on her door, and she was threatening to call the police. He left. And then the cops showed up here Thursday night."

Wednesday. The morning Eliza had come to Eric's place, only to be followed by the blue pick-up. The night she missed their dinner. The guy must have followed her from Eric's back to her apartment. And then on Thursday…

At that moment, Trey came over and stood at my elbow. The chill was palpable, as if an iceberg had suddenly materialized on a clear horizon.

Jake kept talking. "She was a great girl, you know. Everybody's going to miss her around here."

"We're leaving now," Trey said. He turned on his heel and headed toward the parking lot.

I indicated the memo in Jake's hand. "Just call me? Please?"

Jake nodded, and I hurried after Trey, who was not strolling anymore. I jogged into place beside him. "Sorry."

He didn't look at me. "You cannot interfere in an on-going investigation. There are procedures to be followed—"

"I wasn't interfering! The cops had already talked to him!" I untied my jacket and slipped it back on. "I didn't get much info anyway. All he said was that yes, he knew her, that she was perfectly nice blah blah blah. You ever notice how it's always perfectly nice people who get killed, never nasty people, like on the soap operas."

Trey unlocked the doors to the Ferrari. "He was lying about that last part, the nice part. Now get in."

I almost grabbed his elbow, caught myself at the last second. "Lying? Are you sure?"

"Eighty-five percent sure. Now get in."

We were barely ten minutes down the road when Garrity called me.

"The manager of Beau Elan asked about you at Phoenix," he said. "Seemed to think you were some kind of investigator. Landon referred him to Ryan and Vance. They are not pleased."

I mentally cursed Manager Guy. "Big deal. Trey said he's just a big fat liar anyway."

Trey shot me a look. "I did not."

Garrity wasn't interested in my explanation. "Do me a favor and leave the police work to the police, okay?"

"Oh, please, that's such a cliché. If this were a movie, you'd be dead in the next scene, and your last thought would have been, I should've listened to that smart blonde."

"Go to Trey's. Stay put until I get there. No argument."

"Fine."

A pause. "Now I'm suspicious."

"Look, I found a dead body yesterday, I get tailed this afternoon, I've been dragged downtown twice in two days. A bodyguard sounds like a fine idea, especially one with a nine-millimeter under his jacket."

"Tailed?"

"Yeah, tailed. Trey didn't tell you?"

"Put him on."

I did. Trey kept his eyes on the road as he spoke. He explained things to Garrity rather succinctly, then said goodbye.

"So is this okay with you?" I ventured. "My staying at your place?"

"Of course."

I felt a pique of curiosity. "You kept saying 'I know.' What is it that you know?"

"That you might try to sneak away, and that I shouldn't let you, but since I probably can't stop you without physically restraining you, it's really a moot point. Trying to stop you, that is."

"Were you supposed to tell me that?"

He considered. "Probably not. I guess that's a moot point too."

We turned left, heading back to the Buckhead area. As we turned off GA 400, I imagined I could smell the whiff of money, all flavors—old money, new money, dirty money. Trey didn't head for the residential section where people like the Beaumonts live, nor to the Lenox Mall area where the Ritz-Carlton holds court, nor to the bar-choked party strip close to Midtown, where Peachtree Road changes to Peachtree Street. Instead, he took us down the Peachtree Road corridor, into the heart of the skyscrapers. They lined the road like steel gray dominoes, and I remembered Garrity's words and wondered which one of these looming rectangles Trey called home.

"So Jake Whitaker lied?" I said.

Trey nodded. "Yes."

"About her being such a great girl?"

"Yes."

"So he's covering up something."

"That's an assumption. All I can tell you is that he wasn't being completely truthful."

"I saw a photograph on the wall of him and the Beaumonts. Are they friends?"

"Not friends. He's involved in many of the same causes as the Beaumonts, so he's more of a…"

"Hanger-on?"

Trey nodded, but offered no further commentary. Obviously Jake Whitaker held little interest for him. Or maybe he was just pretending, pulling another one of his tight-lipped cover-ups. But then, from what Garrity said, he didn't do cover-ups. He just kept his mouth shut until you asked the right question, like one of those magic cave doors in the Arabian nights.

He returned his attention to the road. I settled back in my seat and watched him drive. No matter how hard I tried, I couldn't picture him and Garrity as partners. Garrity with his frank, easy-going diligence, his gruff professionalism. And Trey, he of the blank arctic stare, the flat appraisal, the perfectly-pressed trousers and monotone responses. The Ice Man.

I remembered Garrity's words: "And then he was back, but it wasn't him anymore." Like who we were was little more than a chemical soup of neurons and nerve endings, that the slightest rearrangement of our brain cells turned us into different people.

I kept my eyes on him the whole way into Buckhead, and if Trey noticed, he didn't seem to mind. He took off the sunglasses, and in profile I detected the first hint of crow's feet at the corners of his eyes. It made him seem oddly vulnerable.

Screwed up, Garrity had said. Jeez, I thought, aren't we all?

Chapter Fourteen

He thinks in black and white. I hadn't taken Garrity's words literally until I saw Trey's apartment.

It was an open layout, all one room except for the bedrooms. Ebony hardwood floors gleamed darkly, bounded by matte white walls. No artwork marred the bland expanse, not even a clock, and there was little furniture, just an oversize black leather sofa and a low coffee table.

Trey turned on a floor lamp and opened the French doors leading to a wrap-around terrace, letting in the cool smell of night. Beyond him, the Midtown skyline sparkled, like someone had thrown rhinestones at the horizon. We were on the thirty-fifth floor, the streets below us a snaking dazzle of brake lights.

He loosened his tie. "Can I get you anything?"

"A pizza would be nice."

He got a phone book instead. I ordered a meat lover's special with extra mushrooms while he changed clothes. He didn't shut the door to the bedroom, and from what I could see, it was as dichromatic as the rest of the apartment. I heard the closet door open, followed by the scrape of hangers.

Next to his desk, a bookshelf held rows of hardcovers. I ran my finger along the spines, noting a veritable library of neuroscience, cognitive psychology, and behavior modification therapy. A series of triathlon training manuals completed the collection. Not one sentimental novel, not one trashy beach read.

I checked over my shoulder. Trey was still in the bedroom, out of sight. Keeping my eyes on the doorway, I tried the top desk drawer. It slid open easily, revealing another set of neatly labeled folders, another bottle of medicine. Also a bottle of valerian root capsules and a *GQ* magazine, the Italian style issue. In addition—inexplicably, incongruously—he had a tarot deck. I picked it up, splayed the cards. The Fool grinned at me, his eyes bright as he took the step that would send him tumbling down a cliff.

The phone rang, and I dropped the deck. "Shit!"

I got on hands and knees and snatched at cards. I remembered then my promise—no more snooping—and felt ill. To my relief, Trey picked up the bedroom extension instead of coming back in the living room. His first words were unclear, but then, just as I got the deck back in the drawer, I caught his end of the conversation.

"No," he said. "Not tonight. I have a guest."

My fingers itched, and not from nicotine withdrawal. I moved my hand to the phone. I'd done it a thousand times with my last boyfriend—pick up the receiver, press a hand over the mouth-piece, listen for a discreet interval. But then, my last boyfriend hadn't been some super-elite secret agent likely to kick my ass for snooping on his private calls.

"Yes, that's her," Trey said. "The blonde."

I bit my lip and laid one finger on the receiver.

"No, everything's fine," he said. "Goodnight, Gabriella."

Gabriella. The redhead in the photo. Garrity said she wasn't connected, but I was willing to bet she was. I'd seen the telltale glitter in Charley's eyes, and the expression on Trey's face. And now here she was calling Trey.

But before I could wrap my curiosity around the possibilities, Trey returned. He appeared as silently and suddenly as a ghost, and I froze, hands behind my back, guilty fingers still wrapped around the drawer pull. He'd exchanged the suit for a white t-shirt and black sweatpants and he carried two items—a set of keys in his right hand, his Heckler and Koch in his left. His expression was as blank as a piece of paper.

He walked over, moving closer and closer until he was standing right in front of me. I felt the edge of the desk digging into my back.

"Looking for something?" he said.

I held his gaze. "A pen?"

He cocked his head, and I felt it again, the psychic unzipping, especially when his eyes moved to my mouth.

He reached around me and opened the bottom drawer—it contained a black metal gun case. He placed the handgun inside, the magazine too. Locked that. Then he tucked the ammo into a separate box. Locked that too. Then, and only then, did he reach around my other side, pull open the top drawer, and hand me a fountain pen. The inside of his wrist brushed my hipbone.

The pen was black. And fancy. Trey turned and headed for the kitchen, leaving me backed up against the desk, holding a pen I didn't need but wasn't about to turn down.

"I'm making tea," he said. "Oolong. Would you like some?"

He brought it to me in a delicate ivory cup with a saucer. It smelled of herb and caramel and had not one speck of sugar in it. I drank it anyway, chased it with a piece of nicotine gum. Then I dumped my tote bag on the floor and sat cross-legged in the middle of the mess. Trey sat at his desk, a spreadsheet pulled up on his laptop. He had a ruler and a calculator out, and two mechanical pencils, one in hand, the other stuck behind his ear.

I pulled out one of the Beau Elan trifolds I'd picked up while talking to Jake Whitaker. Despite the economic downturn, even a studio seemed out of a receptionist's price range. It boasted cutting edge security features, however—gated entrance, passcard entry, surveillance cameras—all of which must have been worth the expense to a young woman with a stalker-ish ex-boyfriend. Especially considering that Phoenix Incorporated was right next door.

"Did the Beaumonts put this complex so close to Phoenix for a reason?" I ran down the list of features, remembering the ones that Trey had pointed out. "Jeez, you'd think this was Quantico, not fancy apartments in Dunwoody."

Trey got out a highlighter. "Managers like obvious security features. They make good sales tools."

He had a point. Beau Elan's prospective tenants valued themselves pretty highly, and they appreciated people who did the same. Mark Beaumont effectively translated that attitude into brick and mortar. I'd also picked up a brochure for Beaumont Waterway, their new resort at Lake Oconee and the location for the upcoming reception for Senator Adams. Slick, sleek, saturated with color, luxury practically dripped off the page.

This was starting to sound like a financial *ménage à trois*—the Beaumonts, Senator Adams, Phoenix. Throw my brother in the mix, and you had an orgy. I wondered how Trey fit into all of it. He didn't seem interested in politics or social climbing. And despite his multiple quirks and weird complexities, he inspired a visceral trust that I couldn't explain any more than I could explain why he had a tarot deck in his desk.

A small voice poked at me: *if you trust him so much, why are you always going through his things?*

I batted the small voice away. Trey worked diligently at his spreadsheet. Black and white choices, no emotional demands, everything compartmentalized, both literally and figuratively. But how long could a former SWAT warrior push paper before snapping and going Krav Maga on someone?

I put down my brochures. "Are you still on the clock? Being my bodyguard?"

He kept his eyes on the computer. "Personal protection. Yes, I am."

"So you agree with Marisa, that I'm in danger?"

"I don't know. But I think we should err on the side of caution. Considering."

"Considering what?"

"Your connection to the crime, your current situation." He took a sip of his tea, then lowered his cup. "Your pizza's here."

The doorbell rang.

I looked at the door, back at him. "All right, how did you do that?"

"I'll get it," he said. And he padded off to fetch my dinner, taking his oolong with him.

But it wasn't a delivery boy who held my dinner—it was Garrity, looking tired and rumpled and very cop-like. He handed the pizza box to Trey and pointed right at me.

"You. In the kitchen. Now."

Chapter Fifteen

Garrity dumped a handful of grim photographs on the counter. Crime scene pictures, official ones. Lurid and vibrant, they hit me with the force of a punch in the stomach, and yet there was a detachment to them too. An unnerving composure.

"This is what murderers do," he said. "This is what happens to people who get in their way."

The photos were repulsively magnetic. One showed a woman's hand, her palm sliced with a red line, a finger bent at an unnatural angle. The other showed a spreading pool of blood, black-red, clotting tendrils of blond hair.

I peered closer. Blond?

"That's not Eliza," I said. Then I noticed the date stamp on the photographs. "Garrity, these things are ten years old! What are you doing showing them to me?"

"Getting your attention." He collected the images and shoved them in his pocket. "Getting killed is fast most of the time. You never see it coming. Life's all chuckles and then suddenly someone's brains are making modern art on the wall. Are you getting the point?"

I was getting the point. "Fine. I apologize for my behavior this afternoon at Beau Elan. I should have listened to Trey. Can I have my pizza now?"

◇◇◇

Garrity ate like a starving teenager, in quick two-bite attacks. He looked kinetic, even sitting at the table, like his spring was wound too tight. I sat opposite. Trey took up a position near the window, his arms folded.

"I got somebody checking out that SUV following you all this morning," Garrity said. "Guess what? It's registered to Dylan Flint."

My jaw dropped. "You've got to be kidding. *The* Dylan Flint, the Dylan Flint who boffed what's-her-name, that boy toy actress, and then sold the videotape on the Internet, Dylan Flint the sleaze?"

"Flint claimed it was stolen," Trey said.

"Wouldn't you, if you were a sleaze?"

Trey ignored me. "Did anyone ask him why he was following us?"

Garrity shook his head. "No. The officer dropped by his apartment, but there was nobody home. Same at his work, some photography studio over on Luckie Street. "

"So that's it?" I said.

"For now. We can't put out an APB for acting suspicious."

"But Trey said he saw the same car at Phoenix Thursday morning. And then the parking garage cameras at Phoenix got smashed that afternoon."

"Circumstantial."

"What about Eliza?" Trey said. "Has there been any progress in the investigation?"

Garrity got another piece of pizza. "No weapon, no suspect. No purse either, so they're thinking maybe a car jacking gone bad."

"What about the guy who was following her," I said, "the one Eric saw in the pick-up?"

"At this moment, he's a phantom. Just like this Dylan Flint character."

Trey kept his gaze on the horizon, his eyes focused on the ink and brilliance of the city sky. He seemed to be inhabiting his own world, and I guessed in many ways, he did.

"Do they have time of death?" he said.

"Sometime between three and six p.m." Garrity wiped his mouth. "Eliza called in sick around nine o'clock Thursday morning, called your brother around three. It's looking like Eric was the last person to see her alive, on record anyway."

"So you heard his story?"

"I got the basics. Something else, though. She'd been roughed up a bit—bruises on the arms and wrists, chest, back of the neck. ME said probably forty-eight hours or so before she died."

Forty-eight hours. Tuesday night. When Eric was still in town and they'd been at the Mardi Gras ball together.

I picked at what remained of the mushrooms. "So how bad is Eric looking?"

Garrity chewed vigorously. "Hard to say. I'm sure he knew he shouldn't have been meeting some young, single girl under such strange circumstances."

"I can't believe that makes him 'a person of suspicion.'"

"You are, too, you know."

"That's beginning to dawn on me."

"Don't take it personally. Everybody's guilty of something, it's a cop's job to find out what. Your job is to be prepared."

Trey spoke up. "Landon has approved counsel for Eric. I could talk to him about what might be available for Tai, but—"

"But," I interjected, "since Landon has a bug up his ass about my hanging around, I don't think I'm going to be getting any favors from him."

Trey nodded. "Marisa is more amenable, however."

He'd brewed another cup of hot tea for himself and was sipping it at his station at the window. His eyes didn't have that blue flash to them, and every now and then, he tilted his head back against the wall and stared at the ceiling, taking long slow blinks.

I leaned closer to Garrity. "Is Trey okay? He looks kind of…"

Garrity waved off my concern. "He's fine, just tired. A good night's rest and he'll be back to normal. Or whatever."

"So what do we do now?"

"We finish this pizza. Then I'm taking you back to the Ritz."

"But I left my car at Phoenix."

Chapter Sixteen

Garrity proved to be a swift instinctive driver. The nighttime sky loomed gunmetal and dense, like the inside of a helmet, and the view through the windshield of his sedan was dotted with the streaky blur of oncoming headlights. Only a few blocks over, the raucous Buckhead party crowd was grinding into high gear, roaming like drunken gypsies from Pharr Road to East Paces Ferry.

But not me. No, I was cruising with the APD. And the APD was not in a good mood. In fact, the APD was shooting me serious cop looks, and I was starting to regret ever getting in the car with him.

"You're mad," I said.

"I'm not mad."

"Then you're not telling me something, I can tell. You're all squinchy around the mouth. That's either holding back or mad."

Garrity kept his eyes on the road.

"What is it, something about Eliza? Something about my brother? Just tell me, I can take it."

"This isn't my case. I don't know enough about it to hold anything back."

The streetlights flared the car from bright to dark, intermittent slices of illumination followed by darkness. Atlanta had such a gorgeous skyline, even if it was always dotted with cranes and holes and veering half-finished angles. The Ritz-Carlton lay just around the final turn. I could see the brightness of the entrance,

"You can get it tomorrow." He turned his cop eyes on me. "Looks like bodyguard duty falls to me this evening."

Garrity had granite in his gaze. Could I see him killing somebody? Oh yes. Up close and efficient. But he'd have to have a good reason to do it.

"Personal protection," I corrected.

Garrity went to bring his car around front, leaving Trey to make the arrangements. He talked to several people on the phone, then handed me a piece of paper with names and numbers on it.

"If you have trouble, any of these people can help you. I'd prefer if you called me first, however."

I tucked the list into my bag. Up close, he looked exhausted, but he was still being polite, attentive even. He kept his arms crossed, though, and stayed farther away from me than personal space dictated.

"I appreciate everything you did today," I said. "The ride, the pizza, letting me hang out here."

He nodded.

"You've been very considerate," I said.

He nodded again.

I wanted him to say something. But he just stood there, arms folded, his body slanted away from mine.

"This has been the damn strangest forty-eight hours of my life," I said.

"There's always tomorrow."

"What does that mean?"

He shrugged. "I have no idea. It's what people say."

I searched his eyes for the joke. There wasn't one.

dazzling, rich with spotlights. Garrity pulled under the awning and flashed his badge at the valet, who backed away.

"Go to your room," he said. "And stay there. I'll call you in the morning."

I wanted to ask Garrity so many questions—what had Trey been like before, was he going to get better?—but the doorman was holding the door. So I got out of the car.

I crossed my heart and held up three fingers. "On my honor, Detective."

I was true to my word. Sort of. I didn't exactly go to my room, so technically I didn't leave it either. Instead, I took my tote bag full of research to the business center. The beige room was deserted, so I dumped my collection onto the counter. I hadn't realized I'd gathered so much information—the Beaumonts, Phoenix, Senator Adams, and now the disreputable Dylan Flint made a messy mix. Rico always warned that this was the danger of research. He said that it was less about finding stuff and more about knowing what you're looking at, what matters and what doesn't.

I understood. Putting together tours was the same way—too much history would avalanche on you and bore your customers. I always approached the gig like telling a story. You find out the arc, the plot line that's driving all the facts in front of you. The who and why and how come naturally after that.

I typed "Dylan Flint" into the search engine. Just as I expected, twelve thousand hits, most of them referencing the infamous videotape along with other, umm, interesting words. I added the word "Atlanta" and tried again. This time the first entry was for a business, a local one, on Luckie Street next to Centennial Park.

I clicked the link. It was a photography studio—Snoopshots. The images on the home page looked startlingly familiar, with their eccentric composition and off-kilter focus. It was the same nervous energy that I'd seen in the photos Mark Beaumont brought to Phoenix, the ones Charley had taken such an instant dislike to and confiscated.

"Oh yes," I said. "Now we're getting somewhere!"

Dylan had a blog linked to his site—also called Snoopshots—which featured a running commentary of Atlanta nightlife. Lots of seen-about-town photos sprinkled with random fashion don'ts. His most recent post was a photo of Charley Beaumont from the Mardi Gras Ball, her eyes wide, her mouth half open. It was entirely unflattering, and I suspected the entire Beaumont PR machine would roll out first thing in the morning to eliminate it from the blogosphere.

So the same guy who was following us in the Explorer was also the erratic photographer at the Mardi Gras party? But why was he taking pictures of me and Trey in the Ferrari? And even though he was seen on Phoenix property when the security cameras were destroyed, what possible reason could he have for doing such a thing? It made no sense.

I was scrolling though his blog when my cell phone rang—a local number, one I didn't recognize. When I answered, I heard the muted echo of traffic in the background.

"Rico?"

"Look," said a female voice, "I don't know who you are, but I am telling you, do not trust those people, especially not that asshole manager. Or that bitch Janie, do not believe a word that comes out of that crazy redneck's mouth."

Who was Janie? And which cop guy, which manager? Garrity? Jake?

"Who is this? How did you get this number?"

"Listen, I'm not playin' here. This is for real, you hear what I'm saying?"

"I can't help you unless—"

"Shit, baby, I'm trying to help *you*, so you'd best listen—don't trust nobody, don't believe nobody. I'll let you know what you need to know when you need to know it."

A loud fading honk, like a semi passing close by, then the click of the connection being broken. I stared at the phone, utterly at a loss. This was the kind of crap that only happened to people who knew what to do about it. Nice innocent people like me didn't get "trust no one" phone calls at midnight.

Besides, this midnight warning didn't make sense; I only knew of one cop guy—Garrity. Hmm…What did I really know about him? Quickly, I typed "Dan Garrity" into the search box.

The first entries were the usual APD stuff. Some articles about his recent promotion, a press release or two about his work with computer fraud. Nothing personal, no blogs or weird fan fiction sites, just a slew of professional accomplishments.

And then a series of articles with a familiar name paired with it—Trey Seaver. I clicked on the first entry, an archived *Journal-Constitution* from almost two years before.

And that's when I saw the word "fatal."

It's a hard word to move beyond. But there was Garrity's name, highlighted in blue, and the text of an article that I assumed at first to be about Trey's collision with the eighteen-wheeler.

But when I saw my brother's name, I looked twice. And I saw that the word after "fatal" wasn't "accident" or "crash."

It was "shooting." And I knew what it was that Garrity had been hiding from me.

Chapter Seventeen

Come Sunday morning, I was feeling a twinge of guilt at not telling anyone about my mysterious phone caller. In fact, I couldn't figure out why I didn't want to. Rico, however, had an idea.

"It's something you have that they don't," he said. "You're spiteful that way. Always gotta have something in pocket."

He'd called me as I was getting dressed, his voice rough with exhaustion and a night of talking too loudly. And he was right—I did like to hoard my secrets. After all, I wasn't telling him what I'd discovered about Trey the night before, and I told Rico everything.

I took the phone outside to a secluded area off the lobby where the valets hung out on their breaks. They were a wholesome-looking bunch, young and well-scrubbed. They all smoked. I tried to stay upwind, but the spiky bite of secondhand smoke found me anyway, curling into my nose. I shoved two pieces of gum into my mouth and took a seat on the edge of a planter.

"Hey, can you trace a call backwards, from a phone number?"

"Depends. Residential, cell phone, payphone?"

"I don't have a clue."

"Of course you don't. But yeah, I can give it a shot."

"I knew you could. You busy this morning?"

"Got nothin' but time."

"Cool." I hopped down off the planter. "How about giving me a lift? My car is still at Phoenix, and there's this field trip I'm dying to take."

I waited for him in the lobby. When he arrived, the two women sitting opposite me checked him out like he was some rap singer they should have recognized. Or perhaps a criminal from a wanted poster.

He did look startling. Baggy black pants flowing over high-top Converses. A red Falcons jersey with a black 69. Gold hoops in each ear, a diamond stud in his nose, and a goatee, neatly-trimmed and black as his eyes, which were hidden behind dark sunglasses this morning.

I jumped up and grabbed him in a bear hug. Up close, his skin looked darker than usual, more café than au lait. I waited for the Hollywood smile, but it was low wattage.

I pulled off the shades. His eyes were red-rimmed and bleary. "Jeez," I said. "How much sleep did you get?"

He snatched the glasses back. "Three hours, and that's roundin' up." He sat down, spread his legs. "So what's the plan?"

I shouldered my tote bag and grinned at him.

He sighed loudly. "Oh crap."

◇◇◇

We took his car, a leased Chevy Tahoe that wolfed down a third of his take-home pay. He'd recently converted the sound system to MP3, so I no longer had to kick through a pile of CDs to make room for my feet. He had one of his mixes playing, the bass cranked up so high his car was practically bouncing off the line. The bank employees walking down Peachtree stared, like they knew exactly who we were.

"Go left," I said.

We inched down Peachtree for a half mile or so, past the commuters, past the newspaper men hollering the *Journal-Constitution* headlines. I saw a panhandler talking on a cell phone while another slept under a blanket of wrapping paper.

Rico followed my directions without question, heading south until we hit the old part of the city, where the lofts of Cabbagetown rose over the MARTA railway line.

"Great," he said, "we're going to the zoo. You know I hate the zoo."

"Not the zoo."

"Unless the pandas are out. I'll go see the baby panda."

"Maybe later. Turn left."

Rico squinted ahead. "Oh man, I hate it when you do this to me."

"Do what?"

"Drag me into your ghost shit."

We pulled in front of the arching brick gates of Oakland Cemetery, eighty-eight verdant acres dotted with some of Atlanta's most elite dead people. The azaleas had yet to burst into full glory, but daffodils dotted the walking path in profusion. Two runners and their dogs stretched at the entrance as a docent gathered a group of tourists.

I shook my head. "I told you, ghosts don't usually haunt cemeteries—not enough residual energy."

He continued reluctantly through the gates, parking just past the visitor's center near an enormous magnolia. We got out with some door slamming on Rico's part, some kicking and muttering too.

He peered over his sunglasses. "White chicks and ghost shit. I do not get it."

As we walked, I opened my Beaumont folder. It now contained an article about the reburial of Charley's great-grandfather near the Confederate section. We followed my map to that area of the park, where I spotted the enormous stone lion I'd seen in the picture at Jake Whitaker's office. The Southern Cross fluttered crisply above the marble creature, its paws clutching a cannonball, its face contorted in dying anguish.

Rico stopped walking and took off his sunglasses. "Oh no, we are not doing *Gone with the Wind* ."

"At least it's not ghost shit."

"Look at this skin, baby girl, what color is this skin?"

I patted a massive bicep and grinned. "Hot chocolate."

"Shut up." He put his sunglasses back on. "You better have a good reason for dragging me to the Great Cracker Burial Ground."

"Stop being deliberately offensive, you know I hate that. I'm looking for somebody."

"Clark Gable?"

"No. Somebody who was buried here last year. Or reburied here actually."

"So this *is* ghost shit."

I ignored him. The Oakland Preservation Society representative I'd spoken with that morning had been very helpful—when I mentioned the lion, she knew exactly which grave I was talking about. Even though the last plot had been sold in 1865, families occasionally put one up for sale, and the Oakland staff maintained a list of interested buyers, like Mark Beaumont. She'd demurred when I'd asked how much it had cost.

"Over there," I said.

Shadrick Turner Floyd's grave nestled under a dogwood. It wasn't in the Confederate section proper, but in a private plot next to it. I got out my cell phone and took a picture.

"It's a pretty spot," I said. "You can see the lion, the obelisk—"

"The MARTA," Rico replied.

To prove his point, a train rumbled by. Private Floyd didn't have as prestigious a plot as the late Maynard Jackson, the city's first African-American mayor—his grave was sited catty-cornered with a prime view of the Atlanta skyline—but it wasn't bad.

"They imported him from Charley Beaumont's hometown in…" I peered closer at the tombstone. "Tennessee, apparently, not far from South Carolina-Georgia border. Found the remains in a cotton field. The Daughters of the Confederacy contacted Charley about it and here we are."

"I thought she was from Miami."

"Apparently she has these redneck credentials that she only drags up if it's politically useful."

"Why is it politically useful to drag your dead great-great-grandfather all the way to Atlanta?"

I pointed at the photograph accompanying the article, a twin of the one in Jake Whitaker's office, looking once again upon Senator Harrison Adam's beaming robust face.

"This, you cannot spin wrong. Somebody's gonna be pissed at you no matter what opinion you hold about the Confederate flag. But this…" I gestured toward the grave. It was well-manicured and tidy, with tasteful purple irises. "This is history."

"It's a stunt," Rico replied. He plopped down on a bench and examined his fingernails. "The Beaumonts dug up this man and dragged him from West Bum-Fucked to be buried here, just to get some good press so their boy will get elected."

"Looking like."

"What could this possibly have to do with the real live dead girl, the one in your brother's driveway?"

"I don't know yet, but I'm gonna find out." I pulled at his elbow. "Come on. I gotta get my car back."

Rico drove me back to Phoenix. He put me out at the main entrance, and I shoved three squares of gum in my mouth. He gave the building the skunk eye, then rejected my invitation to come inside.

"Just call me later. I'll have that number looked up by then, unless it's something tricky." He examined me over his shades. "You quit smoking again?"

"Yeah, a week ago. Why?"

"Because you haven't lit up once all morning. And you just ground out that gum wrapper with your shoe."

I looked down. "Oops."

The parking garage felt more deserted than usual. My footsteps echoed damply, and I didn't see another person. I spotted Trey's Ferrari right off—he'd parked it in a faraway corner and left it there, like a cowboy might tether his stallion before heading into the saloon. But no people.

My car was exactly where I'd left it, next to the elevator. Above it, I saw the empty spot where the security camera had been until someone had smashed it, that someone most probably being Dylan Flint. No security cameras meant no security. My paranoia quotient ratcheted up a few notches.

I quickened my pace, got out my keys. Suddenly, my little red Echo looked as sweet and welcoming and safe as a fortress.

I unlocked the door and climbed in. I was fastening my seatbelt when I saw the flyer on the windshield. My first thought was annoyance. My second thought was surprise. And my third thought? There wasn't one. Fear will do that, short circuit your thoughts.

Because it wasn't a flyer. It was a simple round target, black and white and clean as a whistle. Except that the center was a picture of me, with the middle shot clean through. Ragged edges, massive hole, probably something large caliber, something lethal.

A bull's eye.

Chapter Eighteen

Yvonne pressed her lips so tight her nostrils flared. "You can't see Mr. Seaver without an appointment."

"What if it's urgent?"

Her mouth remained immobile. "I'm sorry, but—"

"Just ask, okay? Let him decide."

Her expression never changed, but she reached for the telephone with excruciating slowness. As she spoke with Trey, I heard a voice I recognized coming down the hall—Landon. He was dressed in a very nice navy suit, the kind you'd wear to the funeral of someone important you didn't know well, and he wasn't alone.

A woman huddled close. She looked about my age, and she was sobbing. Landon draped his arm around her shoulders and spoke to her in low soothing tones, all the while steering her toward a conference room. He didn't see me, and I caught only snippets of the conversation, but I did catch one thing clearly— her name was Janie.

Janie. Now where had I heard that before?

Just then I heard the ding of the elevator, and Trey got out. He was dressed once again in his black suit and tie combo, and the blue flash was back in his eyes. He reached me just as Landon closed the conference room door.

"Who was that?" I said.

"Who was who?"

As he spoke, I noticed movement over his shoulder. The woman came out of the conference room, still crying. I watched as she ducked down the hall to my left, toward the restrooms. Janie. Aha—my mysterious caller had warned me not to trust Janie.

Trey eyed me with curiosity. Not yet reading me, but damn close to it.

I slipped the folded-up target into my tote bag. "How about I meet you in your office?"

"Why?"

"It's personal."

"But you said—

"I need to go to the bathroom first, okay?"

His eyes sharpened. He was on point now, his curiosity quickening into suspicion.

"Feminine stuff," I said.

I could sense the gears clicking and meshing in his brain, but he didn't argue. It's a rule: no man, no matter how screwed up, dares to question the phrase "feminine stuff."

Even if he suspects you're being technically truthful, but deliberately evasive.

She came out of the stall five minutes after I came in, her face white and her eyes red-rimmed. She was about my age and plump in a cheerleader way—lots of bosom, a generous behind, and curly brown hair clipped back in a high, tight ponytail. In her high school yearbook, she would have been Friendliest, maybe even Cutest. Now she smelled like cigarettes, and despite the denim skirt and matching vest and long-sleeved pink t-shirt, she looked middle-aged and worn out.

I waited until she'd started washing her hands before I spoke. "Janie?"

She froze, then reached for a paper towel. "Yes?"

"I'm Tai Randolph. I'm—"

"I know who you are. You're the one who found my sister." She threw the paper towel in the trash, and I noticed the silver cross, hanging from a chain around her neck, dangling over her heart. She put her hand to it, fingered it nervously. "What do you want?"

"Can we talk? Not here, of course, and maybe not even now—"

"Now is fine, if you know someplace I can smoke. I'm dying for a cigarette."

"Ummm, hang on a second."

I stuck my head out the restroom door. The coast was clear. "Follow me," I said.

◇◇◇

We sat on the edge of the fountain out back, downwind from the spray. The place smelled like warm concrete and not-too-distant exhaust, but the steady hum of traffic mingled with the sound of splashing water in an oddly harmonious way. Janie tapped out a Virginia Slims and offered the pack to me.

I shook my head firmly. "I don't smoke."

"Wish I didn't." She fished a lighter from her skirt pocket. "Mama says it's gonna kill me one day. 'Course she told Eliza the same thing, and look what happened."

I just nodded. What could you say to that?

Janie continued. "'Course Eliza didn't listen to much of nothing. I tried to tell her this was a bad idea."

"What was?"

"Leaving South Carolina. She went from big city to big city, limping home between stops to cry and get money. Atlanta was her latest, like it was some fresh new start, like it was different. And then that damn Bulldog—"

"Bulldog?"

"Yeah, that's what he called himself. Bulldog. Old boyfriend from high school. He's the one got her into trouble back in Jackson. That's where we're from, even if Eliza stopped admitting it." She frowned, took a long drag on the cigarette. "He couldn't get it in his thick skull that she didn't want anything to do with him anymore, so he tracked her down here."

"What kind of trouble did he get her into?"

"High school stuff."

"Like what?"

Suspicion flattened her expression, and she kept her eyes focused on the traffic just beyond the shrubbery. "It doesn't really matter now, does it? All I know is, if there was trouble around Eliza, it would be that creep causing it."

"White guy, built like a fire plug, crew cut, beady little eyes? Driving a blue pick-up truck?"

"Yeah, that's him. I told the police about him and they said they'd get right on it, but they didn't seem too interested, if you ask me. I don't think they care about Eliza one bit. Just another dead girl to them."

I wondered how many run-ins she'd had with uninterested officials of one stripe or another. And I understood, but what I really wanted to talk about was Eliza's life back in South Carolina, especially the trouble Bulldog had supposedly gotten her into, but I sensed that Janie was clamming up on me.

"You know what?" I said. "Maybe I'll take you up on that cigarette."

She offered the pack and I took one, holding it to my nose. Ah, the crisp warm tang of tobacco, seductive and tantalizing. God, I'd missed it.

She held out the lighter. "Thought you didn't smoke?"

"I don't." I fired it up, went easy on the first drag. It was like sucking in the fumes of heaven. "I gave it up a week ago. But I need one right now."

"Why?"

The tip of the cigarette glowed red, grayed to ash. "The thing is, my involvement with your sister's case is more than the fact that I found her. As it turns out, my brother knew her too. And even though neither of us had anything to do with her death, the cops are still suspicious."

Janie nodded. "Go on."

"So I understand what it's like to fight a bunch of nameless, faceless people who don't know you, who don't care. I'm not a cop or a reporter or a lawyer. I'm not one of these Phoenix people. All I want is information."

"Let me guess," she said dryly. "You want me to give you some."

"I promise I'm not out to ruin her reputation. I just want to know the truth."

The cigarette smoke clouded her face in a gray haze. "What makes you think I care about her reputation?"

That caught me off guard. "I guess I just assumed. If I had a sister—"

"She wasn't really my sister, just this brat my older brother dropped off right before he took off with some slut from out of town. Everybody tried to pretend otherwise, you know. Called her my sister. And then last year, the son of a bitch died. And now she's dead too. So nobody has to pretend anymore, least of all me. I'm an only child now."

Janie ground her cigarette out on the pavement, twisting her foot with more effort than purely necessary. "Eliza started off bad, I mean, right off the bat. Spoiled. Whiny. She never worked for a thing her whole damn life. But she was the baby, and she looked just like my stupid brother, so everybody cut her slack all the time. In the meantime, I'm out busting my butt, working to put myself through school, taking care of Mama after Daddy died, 'cause it wasn't like my brother ever helped, but did anybody ever care? No. 'Cause that's what I always did.

"And Eliza goes from one bad relationship to another. I tell her to stay away from the stuff, to stay away from Bulldog, but does she listen? No. She tracks down my brother, and he fills her head full of nonsense about how she's better than us, and she believes him. She hits the road, and I don't hear from her again until she's gotten messed up with these Atlanta people."

What Atlanta people? I thought. What stuff? But I didn't get to ask. Janie was on a roll.

"So now she's gone and got herself killed. And what's Mama tell me? You better keep your sister's name clean, she says. We don't need no more trouble. Like it's my fault all this crap happened in the first place."

Janie put her palms flat against her thighs and looked straight at me. "And she's right, we don't need no more trouble. And I guess it's my job to make sure we don't get any more. But you know that Bible story, the one where the prodigal son runs off and wastes his whole life and then when he comes back, his father throws this big damn party for him while the good son, the one who *did* stick around, who *did* do what he was supposed to do, that son gets the shaft. You know that story?"

I nodded. "Yeah, I know that story."

She shook her head. The tears were back again. "I always hated that story."

Then she wiped her eyes. Her voice hadn't changed the whole time—it was still rock steady. "And now you want a story too, and I just don't know what to tell you."

"Tell me you'll help me find out what happened." I hesitated. "Look, if there's dirt, it's gonna come out, and the cops don't care one way or the other. But I do care, and if you'll help me, maybe I can find something under the dirt that can spare your family—and my family too—any further grief."

She sent this look my way. "Uh huh. Like you care about me. Like you're not just saying that to get what you want."

I started to protest. "I didn't—"

She waved me quiet. "Oh, don't say you didn't mean it. Of course you did. But you know what? Maybe you're right."

She stood, wrapped her arms around her waist. "Let me think about it. I'll let you know tomorrow." She looked off toward the horizon, like she was trying to glimpse South Carolina there. "I just don't want any of this getting back to Jackson. That's my home. I don't deserve to have to deal with it there. I've dealt with enough already."

I stood too. "Here's my number," I said, scribbling on a scrap of paper I found in my pocket. "I'll do my best, I promise.

She examined my face. "I guess you will." She jabbed her chin toward the building. "I gotta get back in there."

"Can I ask you one more question?"

"What?"

"This Bulldog person. What's his real name?"

She told me. I started to write it on my hand, then hesitated..

"Could you spell that middle part?"

Rico called as I made my way back to the lobby. "Got your phone number—it's a payphone on Cheshire Bridge Road. Looks like it's next door to a strip club."

No surprise there—that area was nothing but naked dancing and sex toy emporiums. "Another question—how hard would it be for a civilian to get juvie info?"

"You mean stuff that's been sealed? Depends. You got a Social?"

"No."

"Then it gets trickier, but I'll try. What's the name?"

I told him.

"Spell that middle part," he said.

Chapter Nineteen

Trey looked up from his paperwork at my knock. I sat in his client chair, facing him, my tote bag in my lap. I realized I was clutching it like a life preserver and released my grip. Trey waited, politely.

"You wanted to see me," he finally said.

"Yes."

He waited some more. This was the part where I gave up the goods and threw the whole mess in his lap—the phone call at midnight, the target on my car, the grave in the cemetery, the sister in the courtyard—and let him sort it out. It was what he did. His resumé said so.

So why wasn't it coming out of my mouth? I trusted him, didn't I? I'd said as much to Garrity last night. But then I'd gone snooping, and then I'd found that article, the thing that Garrity wasn't telling me…

Trey was patient. He picked up a pen and held it poised over a blank yellow pad. The office was silent.

I clutched my bag tighter. "There's something—"

A knock interrupted me. A woman stood in the doorway, arms folded. "Tai Randolph," she said. "They told me you were here."

I turned to face her. She was tall and rectangular, like the prow of a dragon ship, an effect intensified by ice-gray eyes and a platinum chignon. Her voice reverberated deep and womanly, and she wore a black pantsuit cut like one of Trey's. Her nails were a flamboyant extravagance, however, as pink as frozen raspberries.

Trey stood. "Marisa. I wasn't expecting you until later."

So this was my mysterious benefactor. Up close, she was all artifice—the porcelain skin the result of an expert make-up job, the hair a shimmering monotone, the eye color too perfect to be anything but contacts.

She gestured my way with a manila folder. "Your brother has mentioned that you were interested in a job here, as one of our research assistants."

I noticed my name typed on the label. My dossier, I guessed. "Eric's sweet. But I've got a job."

"The gun shop, yes. He mentioned that. We were hoping you would change your mind."

She tossed the folder in Trey's inbox, and he promptly filed it in one of his meticulous drawers. Probably under T for Trouble. Cross-indexed under P for Problem.

"Eric is a fine employee," she continued. "We're very happy to have him here at Phoenix."

"Eric is something else, that's for sure."

She smiled without showing her teeth. "I hope he has a long and successful career with us. I really do."

I didn't miss the implication. Apparently the only thing standing in my brother's way was me, which meant that for his sake, I'd better behave.

She turned to Trey. "I need to see you when you're done."

"Certainly."

"With a full report."

"Of course."

She put a hand on his shoulder, casually, like a friend might. His expression didn't soften. They were bookends, these two, equally civilized, equally dangerous. Marisa might sport a French manicure, but she could kill too, without breaking a nail or smearing her lipstick. For all I knew, she was the one sticking threatening notes on my car—it would suit her purposes if I stayed still and scared.

She retracted her hand. "Tell me, Tai, what brings you here this afternoon?"

"I came to pick up my car."

"Trey was helping you with that?"

"No, he…" I took a deep breath. "I just wanted to thank him, for last night. It's been a rough couple of days."

"I can only imagine." She said it with a shake of her head. "Please let Trey know if there's anything else we can do for you. He knows to keep me informed."

She said this with a meaningful look Trey's way, and then she was gone. Trey sat back down. He looked a little dazed.

"That was a threat," I said. "A very pretty one."

"It was a reminder." He adjusted his in-box so that all the edges were straight once again, then returned his attention to me. "You said you needed to see me?"

I held the bag in my lap. Trey was a fortress too, like Marisa, all veneer and protocol. He'd do whatever she told him too—that was part of the rules. Suddenly all I wanted to do was get out of his expensive ergonomic client chair and go someplace real and gritty, with dirt and randomness.

I stood, shouldered my bag. "No. It's okay. I can handle things."

Trey's eyes were placid, but there was that definite edge in there, like the glint of a switchblade. The lie was written all over my face. And yet, once again, he didn't call me on it. He just nodded.

"I'll walk you down then."

Back at the shop, I scrubbed the linoleum until my elbows hurt, then attacked the cobwebs. I opened the front door and flooded the place in late afternoon light. With clean windows, the shop looked friendlier, warmer. I could see it tricked out with cherry-stained bookshelves, maybe a thick bright rug. A plant, something hardy and unkillable.

"So this is it," Garrity said from the doorway. "When you told me the address, I couldn't remember ever coming here. But now I do."

He held a bag of food that smelled of roasted meat and chili peppers. He closed the door behind him and the bell dingled cheerily. "I hope you like Cuban food. I brought enough to share."

I hid the overflowing ashtray behind the coffeemaker. "Good. We can eat, and you can tell me about the shooting."

"What shooting?"

"The one involving Trey."

Garrity sighed. He put the bag on the counter and turned to face me. "So you know."

"I know that Trey resigned afterward, that there was an official investigation and that he was cleared of all charges. I know that you were a witness, my brother too. But that's all I know. I got overwhelmed and gave up around one o'clock. You feel like filling me in on the rest?"

Garrity stared out the window. He was trying hard to be indifferent about this, and I was trying just as damn hard, but failing miserably.

Minefields. God, I hated them.

"It was maybe six months after the accident," he began. "Trey was hard as hell to work with. He was in PT, OT, all kinds of therapy. He'd get frustrated at the least thing, then veer back to calm, but it was this scary calm. He still followed orders, though, still had the skills. So he kept his gun and his badge.

"And then one night we were on our way home and stopped to get some gas. Off duty. Unfortunately, this prick decides to take the register and pulls out this piece, waves it around. Trey draws and fires. Drops him in one, I mean, right through the heart."

"I take it that's not procedure?"

"Oh, hell no. You tell them to drop their weapon, give them a chance to end it peacefully."

I made a noise. "I think I like Trey's way better."

Garrity's voice rose. "Look, did the jerk deserve to die? Maybe yes. But that wasn't the way to do it, because the moment he shot him, Trey became a liability."

I put down my broom. "So what happened?"

"There was a review, of course. Your brother was called as an expert witness—that's how he and I met. Based on my testimony, OPS ruled it justifiable use of deadly force. No indictment. The other people there—the clerk, this kid in line behind us—they testified to the same thing I did, that the punk was getting ready to fire, and that by acting when he did, Trey probably saved our necks."

"Well, was he?"

"What?"

"Was the guy getting ready to fire?"

Garrity didn't look at me. "That's what I testified to."

"That doesn't answer my question."

"It should."

I moved to stand beside him. "So what happened to Trey?"

"He resigned. He was a disaster waiting to happen, and we all knew it, even Trey. But your brother had connections at Phoenix, and they agreed to take him on."

"Phoenix hired him with that kind of history?"

"Your brother explained that the injury only affected certain functions, like making judgment calls or understanding emotional contexts. Trey actually got better at other things—long-term memory, focus, linear analysis."

"So Eric fudged the facts to get him a job at Phoenix?"

Garrity made a face. "Hell no, he just explained that as long as Trey works within certain boundaries—lots of rules, highly organized structures—he's capable of some amazing shit."

"Like the lying thing?"

"Like that, yeah. So now his job is premises liability, knocking holes in other people's security systems and then fixing them. It's all simulations, though, so nobody ever gets shot for real, and he's so damn good at it, it's scary. Plus, the Armani routine impresses the hot shot clientele."

"That's the second time you've used the word 'scary.'"

"If the shoe fits." He shot me a sideways glance, and then his mouth softened at the corners. "I'm not trying to frighten you; I'm just being honest."

I pulled off my blue rubber gloves with a thwack. His every word rang with deliberate honesty. Why then was every secret of mine still in that tote bag? I railed at Eric for keeping things from me and then proceeded to do the same thing. Were we really that much alike? Was I that calculating?

I wiped my hands. They were pasty and shriveled, like they'd been submerged in brackish water. "Is he going to get better?"

Garrity shook his head. "No. He learns how to handle things better, so he improves in some ways. His brain adapts. But the injury is permanent."

I remembered the way words eluded him sometimes, the way he repeated things. The way he stood too close. But I also remembered the shelves of books on neuroscience. Trey hadn't given up. He was still fighting.

Garrity laid out containers of food, yellow rice and pulled pork. "Listen, I may not be his partner anymore, but I trust him with my back. He has bizarre rules coming out his ears, but his main operating procedure is the one he learned in Catholic school—do unto others as you would have them do unto you."

I picked up one of the forks. "So I'm supposed to trust him because a bunch of nuns taught him the Golden Rule?"

"Yeah, that's the gist of it. And you might want to lay off brandishing weapons at him. You do *not* want to trigger that Special Ops training."

◇ ◇ ◇

Once Garrity left, I cleaned until I couldn't see straight. I thought about crashing on the sofa bed in Dexter's office, but then I remembered the photo of me with the bullet hole through the center, and my stubborn streak vanished.

The Ritz received me once again, as plush and predictable as Phoenix. My gritty hair and sweat-drenched clothes earned me horrified glances from the other guests, as if I were wearing convict stripes and leg irons.

The desk clerk displayed no such aversion. "Ms. Randolph?"

I turned around. So much for surreptitious. "Yes?"

"A gentleman left a package for you." She pulled a manila envelope from under the counter. I immediately recognized Rico's heavy scrawl across the flap: CONFIDENTIAL—FOR TAI RANDOLPH ONLY!

I thanked her and took it to my room, where I opened it while the bath ran, hot and steamy. It contained several printed pages, official documents on William Aloysius Perkins AKA Bulldog. I examined the first one, not sure I was seeing what I was seeing. But when I figured out what I was looking at, I knew Janie and I were having another talk, even if I had to corral her in a bathroom again.

Chapter Twenty

The phone rang at six the next morning. It was Trey.

"Marisa has called a meeting. You need to be here."

"Me? Why?"

"Because she said so. Nine o'clock."

I rubbed my eyes, still thick with exhaustion. "You're an abomination."

"Nine."

"Yeah yeah. I'll be there."

On the way across town, I stopped at a convenience store and got a pack of cigarettes, then threw away all but two. One I smoked on the way to Phoenix, the other I wrapped in tissue and left in my wallet, an emergency ration for whatever weirdness the day planned to throw in my face.

Yvonne waited for me in the lobby. I was expecting another lecture about my lack of appropriate badgewear, but she fixed me with her sweetheart eyes. "Third floor."

The room was deserted except for Trey, who occupied one chair on the long end of a rectangular table. He had a slew of paperwork in front of him—charts, graphs, summary reports.

I sat beside him. "You have any idea what this is about?"

"No."

"Me, either. She didn't say anything yesterday."

"Who?"

"Marisa. Who'd you think I meant?"

"Janie Compton." Trey fixed me with a hard stare. "She mentioned that you spoke with her yesterday, in the bathroom. You didn't tell me this."

I started to reply, but before I could formulate a reasonably innocent explanation, another guy joined us. He had a nice smile, but his distinguishing feature was a mop of double-helix brown hair that tumbled over his forehead, very nearly obscuring his eyes. He stopped in the doorway, hands on hips.

Then he grinned. "Hey, Trey, how's it going?"

Trey's head snapped back. "What are you doing here?"

The guy shrugged. Unlike every other dapperly suited employee, he was tricked out in khaki pants and an orange shirt. No tie. I glanced at his shoes. Black athletic sandals.

"Looking for Landon," he said.

"No, I mean what are you doing at Phoenix. You were fired."

"Landon pulled the suspension."

"You weren't suspended. You were fired."

"Landon reconsidered."

Suddenly, I realized who this guy was. I snapped my fingers. "Simpson!"

The guy grinned. He had an exuberant smile, open-mouthed. "All my friends call me Steve. Right, Trey?"

Trey was having none of this. "Because of your blatant incompetence—"

"Oh please! I was getting coffee!" He flung a finger in my direction. "How was I supposed to know *she* would show up?"

"You disregarded our objective and jeopardized my safety."

"Cut the crap. You're just mad 'cause you got made."

Trey stood up, dropping his shoulders and shifting his body weight. I recognized it for what it was—going into a fighting stance—and Steve actually took one step forward and all I could think was, Trey is about to mop the floor with this guy.

But then Trey closed his eyes—one second, two—and when he opened them again, that flat impassive blue was back. He exhaled, relaxed his hands, and sat back down, burying his attention once again in his paperwork.

Simpson grinned some more. "Tell Landon I was looking for him." And then he looked at me. "Nice to meet you, Tai Randolph. Been hearing a lot about you around here." Then he winked at me and ducked out the door.

I let out a breath. "What in the hell was that about?"

Trey didn't look up. "I thought he was terminated. Apparently he's not."

"He's the computer guy you were working with at Eric's, right?"

"Technical specialist."

Trey gathered his file folders into a neat stack, adjusted the edges with precise focused concentration. He had a pile of index cards that he placed right next to two mechanical pencils.

"Tell the truth," I said. "You were going to beat him to a bloody pulp."

A swift glance my direction, then back to his legal pad. "No, I wasn't."

"Yes, you were."

"No. I wasn't."

"But you wanted to, didn't you?"

He stopped rifling through papers and placed both hands flat on the table, one neatly atop the other.

"Yes," he said. "Yes, I did."

Marisa arrived thirty seconds after nine o'clock in a suit the color of white chocolate. She took a chair at the head of the table, Yvonne at her heels. Landon hung at her side, their voices a hushed tête-à-tête. When he saw me, he cut her a sharp look. She shook her head and opened her portfolio.

"It's been a hell of a morning," she said, "so let's start with the latest. Detective Ryan called. He wants to set up interviews with all of you."

Trey stopped writing. "Is this because we were all at Beau Elan on Thursday?"

I stared at him. Somehow he'd neglected to mention this choice fact in our conversations. So much for teamwork.

"So we're suspects now?" Landon said.

"Not suspects," Trey corrected. "Suspicious. There's no evidence to make us suspects at this time."

I raised my hand. "Um, excuse me, but—"

"You've been a suspect since you got into town," Landon interjected.

I shot him a look. "Don't start with me."

"It's immaterial," Marisa said, putting a halt to the squabble. "Right now, I want to make it clear that all of you must be cleared of suspicion as soon as possible."

Trey cocked his head. "The video should be proof enough."

Marisa's eyes flashed his way. "What video?"

"The video from the surveillance camera at the Beau Elan entrance. It records every vehicle entering or leaving. Of course the police have the original now, but we kept back-up footage at the office."

"And what will this footage show?"

"Our arrival at Beau Elan at approximately twelve-thirty that morning. Charley Beaumont arrived at five, left at six with Landon when the police arrived. Approximately. Simpson and I finished and left for Phoenix at six-thirty. Approximately. The video will provide specific time codes."

"Where were you?"

"In Jake Whitaker's office."

"With Jake?"

"No, I was alone. Jake was elsewhere on the property."

I wanted to follow up on that idea, but Marisa had her own agenda. "So you were in that office all afternoon?"

"Yes."

Marisa was writing everything down in her portfolio. "Charley will corroborate this story?"

"She can, yes."

"And what about Steve?"

"He was connecting the video feeds to the security system. Which meant that he was either working in the crawlspace or in the van."

Landon wrote something down in his notebook. "I'll talk to him. He did the work, so I'm sure we can establish his alibi."

Marisa nodded at Yvonne, who sent around a set of folders, each one labeled with a name—including mine. But before I could open it, Marisa rapped sharply on the table.

"Each of you has the case notes so far in front of you," she said, making a little steeple with her fingers. "I've received three phone calls in the past fifteen minutes from reporters asking me to verify if Mark Beaumont has indeed hired Phoenix to investigate Eliza's death. Which he has. "

Trey spoke up. "The police—"

"—are doing an excellent job, yes, but Mark feels it's his duty to contribute. He's giving a press conference in one hour, and we're going to be there."

I lifted the edge of my folder, tried to peek inside.

Marisa kept talking. "I don't mind admitting that we are out of our league here. We specialize in protecting our clients from such crimes, not mopping up afterward. But this is what Mark wants."

And, I thought, what Mark wants, Mark gets.

Trey's eyes snapped up from his paperwork. "But I don't do investigations."

"You do now."

"But—"

"No buts. They know you at the APD. You're a hero down there, and we need that kind of connection right now."

He looked back down at his notepad and said nothing, but his right hand toyed with his pen, tap-tap-tapping on the clean lined paper.

Marisa continued. "One more thing. Mark has requested that Janie Compton be included in any briefings that we offer him, as a special courtesy. Which is why Tai is here."

I looked up from my folder. "What?"

"Janie has requested that you be involved in our investigation every step of the way, as her special liaison."

"She did?"

"Yes, she did. If you're interested."

"Of course I am. Thank you."

"You're technically research now, which makes you Trey's responsibility."

Trey looked up at this. "What?"

Marisa smiled. "Her job is keeping Janie Compton happy. Your job is to make sure she does that."

Trey exhaled slowly. Then he looked back down at his folder. I slid a glance Landon's way. He had his jaw set so tight you could have chipped flint with it.

Marisa continued. "In fact, that leads me to my last and most important point. We are in the center ring now, people, the main attraction." She looked at Landon. "As for Steve Simpson, I rehired him on your say-so. Any further failings from that camp and your head will roll. And for God's sake, clean him up. If I see him in the halls, he'd better be wearing a suit and have real shoes on his feet."

Marisa stood, laid her palms flat on the table. "Because you'd better understand something, all of you. Mess this one up, and I will have your balls for breakfast. Now get going. I look forward to reading the preliminary reports this afternoon."

And then she gathered her materials, Yvonne opened the door, and the two of them exited stage left. Landon pulled out his cell phone and began a low, terse conversation, his eyes on me the whole time. Trey stared at his paperwork.

"Correct me if I'm wrong," I said, "but did you just become the boss of me?"

He underlined something with a highlighter. "It's not a chain of command relationship. I'm more of a coordinator."

"Does that mean you get to tell me what to do?"

"Yes."

He stood up abruptly. I scooped up my folders and stood too, clipping my new ID rather clumsily to my sweater. It read LIAISON in neat block script.

"Does it mean I finally get to question suspects?"

"No."

He cocked his head and frowned at me. Tucking his files under one arm, he reached out with both hands and straightened my ID badge one millimeter. His knuckle grazed my chin.

I kept my mouth shut. And I didn't say what I was thinking, that regardless of his rule, if suspects presented themselves, I was going to question them. Even if those suspects were the Beaumonts themselves. And no pathetic, photoshopped, slipped-under-the-windshield threats were going to stop me.

Chapter Twenty-One

The corporate headquarters of Beaumont Enterprises rose like a steel beanstalk right at the corner of Ponce de Leon and Peachtree, only a few blocks from the Fox Theatre, which still carried the architectural echoes of its former life as a Masonic lodge. The streets and sidewalks mingled separate tributaries—joggers, bicyclists, tourists asking for directions.

Mark Beaumont held court in a top-floor office that had a distinct members-only feel to it. The decorating scheme was earthy, with cinnamon drapes and cocoa carpeting in a vaguely Aztec-looking pattern. His walls, however, functioned as a wall-to-wall press release: thank-you plaques from prominent organizations, smiling handshake shots with various mayors.

And in the center of the commotion, Mark himself. Dressed for press, he sported conservative navy slacks and a photogenic blue shirt. A gaggle of similarly attired men and women surrounded him, each one vying for his attention.

Trey got it, however. Instantly. Mark saw him approaching and headed our way, hand outstretched. People moved aside for him, made clear the path.

"Trey," he said, smiling. "Marisa told me you'd be here." He nodded in my direction. "You're in on this now?"

"I hear I have Janie to thank for it."

His face sobered. "God, I can't imagine what she's going through now. All I can do…well, I'm doing all I can do. I just hope it's enough."

At that moment, a young woman touched his elbow and offered him a clipboard. He took it, and they spoke for a few seconds in low discreet tones. Trey's eyes roamed the room, slowly, and I was willing to bet that he had every face memorized in about four seconds.

I cleared my throat. "Mr. Beaumont?"

"Mark, please."

I smiled. "Mark. Where can I find Janie?"

"She's right through there, in Charley's office." He clapped Trey on the shoulder. "Come on. Let's get started."

Trey turned back to me as he melted into the crowd. "Stay close."

I felt a prickle. "Why? You think something's going to happen?"

"No. But I might need you. Or you might need me." He said this like it was the most obvious thing in the world.

Which maybe it was.

"I'll be right here," I called. But I was talking to his back.

I saw Charley first, seated on a rust-colored loveseat, one arm draped along the back. She'd pulled her hair into a chignon, all piece-ey and messy at the nape, and wore a jacket and pants set in the same hue as the furniture. Janie sat beside her. She'd dressed up too, in a floral dress with a sewn-on vest, her curly hair subdued with thin gold barrettes. She'd put on make-up, but her eyes were red and she was fidgety. She'd twist her fingers together, fiddle with her crucifix, then lay them deliberately in her lap, smoothing out the material. I couldn't tell if nerves gripped her, or a nicotine fit.

I moved to her side of the loveseat. "Thanks for letting me in on this."

"We had a deal, remember?" Her eyes dipped, taking in my ID. "They got you all official pretty quick like."

Charley spoke up. "So you know Kent?"

It seemed odd to hear someone calling Landon by his first name. "We've met."

"Kent's been with Mark ever since we moved here. But he leaves the grunt work to Trey and what's-his-name, that curly-headed one?"

"Steve Simpson."

"Right. That one. They were all working at Beau Elan on Thursday, but Kent was with me that afternoon. He said I might have to testify to that. I told him not to worry, that Mark would make sure he didn't have any trouble from the authorities."

I raised an eyebrow at that one, but said nothing. I knew Landon had connections—even Eric had asked him to pull some strings—and it was fast becoming obvious that his connections didn't mind being used.

Janie indicated the outer office. "So which one's Trey?"

"Mr. Tall, Dark, and Handsome in the black suit."

She squinted in that general direction. "I haven't seen him before."

"He stays behind the scenes mostly."

Charley made a noise. "I'll say. I don't think he likes natural light."

She said it with meanness at the edge, and I felt my backbone straighten involuntarily. She watched me, waiting for a response.

Janie watched me too, but without the predatory gleam. "You want to find me later? Maybe we could talk some more?"

She said it nonchalantly, but I detected the hint of something significant behind her words. I started to ask her what was wrong, but before I could, there was a knock at the door.

Landon stuck his head in. "They're ready to start."

Behind him I saw Trey. Janie got up, Charley too, and I followed them out. Then I saw it, at the door. As Charley passed Trey, she stopped and looked up at him. He met her eyes, direct and unblinking. No words, no gestures, just this singular moment of eye-to-eye contact, a split second, nothing more. Then she turned her head and kept walking, her jaw tight.

Trey looked at me. "Are you ready?"

Chapter Twenty-Two

The press conference was everything I expected it to be. Landon started with a little speech about Phoenix. Then the Beaumonts took the podium, explaining their reasons for offering the reward, for standing up for one of their own. Janie stood silent through it all, hidden behind the principals, clutching at her cross.

Mark Beaumont brought the proceedings to a close. "It comes down to what we do for each other. Eliza mattered, and I'm here, with these fine women and men, to make sure that she keeps on mattering."

Not especially profound, but the applause rose rich and thick around Mark as the nucleus, the center of the spin. One of the reporters—this rangy disreputable-looking kid—moved forward and fired off shot after shot just as Charley took Mark's hand. She looked nervous in the staccato bursts of light, and I wasn't surprised when one of the security guards took the guy firmly by the elbow. He fought it briefly, flashing a nasty grin toward the stage, and then allowed himself to be led away, still popping off shots with one hand.

When it was over, Landon and Trey escorted the Beaumonts back to their offices. I was about to follow when I felt a hand at my elbow.

It was Janie. "Get me out of here before I blow and start using the f-word," she said.

◇◇◇

We went across the street to a wine and chocolate shop that also sold coffee—she sucked down a cigarette on the walk over. I resisted the urge. But I did get two cappuccinos and a gigantic chocolate muffin before joining Janie on the patio. By then, her hands weren't shaking quite so badly, and she'd stopped fidgeting.

She took the top off her cup. "Thank you. That was starting to get to me." She stirred her foam with her finger. "I mean, I'm really grateful to the Beaumonts for everything they're doing. But I just want to get Eliza and go home."

The sidewalk teemed with people lured outside by the clear undiluted sunshine. But the bright air carried an unexpected bite, especially in this part of downtown, shot through with crosscurrent breezes that ambushed you at every corner. The tourists huddled under the Fox marquee with their Starbucks and street maps. The dog walkers kept their arms folded and practically dragged their Chihuahuas and terriers down the sidewalk.

I offered Janie some muffin. She shook her head. She was still pretty, and I could see the high school girl she must have been once, before she had to grow up and be responsible for everyone around her.

"They told me we could have an open casket. Mama will be relieved." She said it emotionlessly. "Do you have any news?"

"Maybe." I thought about the intake report Rico had delivered to me, the one he'd marked for my eyes only. He'd found it filed away at a data collection service when it was supposed to have been expunged, something he said happened all the time. "Did you know William Perkins—I mean, Bulldog—when you were in high school?"

"No, not really."

"Do you remember if he ever went away for a while?"

She frowned. "Went away? You mean like moved?"

"I mean like juvenile hall."

She licked the milky coffee from her finger. "Like I said, I didn't know him that well."

I pulled out the file Rico had sent me. "I've got some information that says he spent six months in a juvenile correctional facility. Of course, he went on to get a grown-up rap for some petty robbery, possession, meth especially. On probation now."

"So?"

"So it's the juvie charge that's got my interest." I tapped the papers. "Breaking and entering. The report mentions two people committing the crimes, one of them a girl. She'd be lookout while he ransacked the place. She fled the scene when the cops arrived, though, and Bulldog never spilled her name."

She stared at the report like it was a snake, or a bear trap, something unpredictable and dangerous. In the lot beside us, the stop-go drone of jackhammers intensified into a cacophony.

"How did you get this?" she said.

"Does it matter?"

She lowered her voice. "Do the cops know?"

"They can't. It's sealed."

"So how did you get it?"

"Like I said, it doesn't matter."

"Of course it does! If the cops see this, they'll think she was going to rob your brother's house."

"Maybe she was. Doesn't mean she deserved what happened to her."

Janie glowered, like she wanted to argue.

"Just tell me," I said. "Is it true?"

She sat there for a second, then exhaled. "Yeah, it's true. She always felt like she owed him for that one, and he made sure she kept feeling that way." Janie shoved the papers back at me. "He did it, didn't he? He killed her."

"I don't know."

"I told her to stay away, but she wouldn't listen. He kept telling Eliza he was a better man when he was with her, and she believed that. She liked that."

Don't we all? I thought.

"But she mainly kept him around for the drugs, you know? She said she was kicking the stuff, and I believed her...but then I found out otherwise." She looked me right in the eye, and I saw effort behind it. "They found drugs at her apartment, some meth, some pot. The manager at her place told the cops he'd been suspicious, but that he hadn't wanted to say anything."

"You mean Jake Whitaker?"

She shrugged. "I don't remember his name."

Suddenly, I was thinking about Whitaker, how he'd lied when he said Eliza was well-liked. And I remembered something else that had been bothering me.

"This may sound off the subject, but how well did Eliza know Mark Beaumont?"

"She'd met him at one of the staff events, said he was real nice. He even sent her this Christmas card one time."

"So they were close?"

Janie looked at me like I was a little cracked. "He's Mark Beaumont. She's a receptionist. Everybody got Christmas cards."

"But he's doing all this—"

"Yeah, well, I appreciate it, I really do." She unfolded her napkin, wiped her mouth, folded it again. "But it's not really about Eliza, you know?"

Yeah, I knew. The construction noise across the street abruptly ceased, and a startling silence fell. It was disconcerting, like being in the middle of a party when suddenly the only voice you can hear is your own. A mockingbird trilled from the shrub beside me. I guessed it had been singing all along.

Janie didn't speak. It wasn't until I reached for my bag that she said, "There's something else."

I waited. She stared at her napkin. "I went to the bank to clear out her account. Mama thought we could use it for the funeral. Anyway, Eliza had been getting money, a lot of money."

"How much?"

"A thousand here, more or less there."

"For how long?"

"Ever since she moved here, six months or so. The police found a shoebox full of cash on the top shelf of her closet." Janie cast her eyes sideways, like she was afraid of being overheard. "I know what that looks like, all that money. I know what the police are thinking, especially since she got hooked up with Bulldog again."

"Was she involved with any other shady people?"

"You mean like that stripper friend of hers?"

"What stripper friend?"

"I don't know, Bambi, Tricksie, something like that."

A stripper. I remembered the other thing Rico had discovered—that my mysterious caller had called me from a pay phone right in front of a strip club.

Janie's eyes went shiny, but her composure didn't crack. "The cops wouldn't let me have any of her stuff, not the cards I sent her, not her computer. I went over there to get something for her to wear. She had textbooks for this psychology course and some flowers in a vase in the kitchen, one of those bouquets you get at the supermarket. I keep thinking, if she could have found something to get serious about…"

I imagined the scene, a life cut short in midstream, the rest of the world running on around the absence, eventually washing over it. I thought about my old apartment—the sheets that hadn't been changed, the half-eaten roll of cookie dough in the fridge, the risqué e-mails from my ex-boyfriend.

She pushed her coffee away. "I've got to clean it out eventually. Of course I do, it's always me. And she's family, flesh and blood, I ain't denying it. But you tell me, what the hell do I do with all this?"

"I don't know, Janie." And we just sat there for five more minutes. And I was telling the truth—I didn't know what to do next, especially not with my envelope full of illicit information—but I hoped that I would figure it out, and soon.

The jackhammer started again. Something always did.

Chapter Twenty-Three

I waited until Trey and I were pulling out of the Beaumont Enterprises parking deck to spring it on him. "Hypothetical situation. Pretend I have some information that I technically shouldn't have."

"What kind of information?"

"Juvenile records."

His eyes snapped my way, then back on the road. "You can't get information like that without breaking the law."

"I didn't break the law."

"You said this was hypothetical."

"Hypothetically hypothetical."

We hit a red light and he turned to face me. "Say it again."

I looked him straight in the eye. "I didn't break the law."

He watched my mouth, focused on my eyes.

"You're reading me."

The light turned green, and he returned his attention to the road. "You're doing it again. Technically truthful but—"

"Damn it, I just want to know what I should do!"

"You can't use illegally procured information in a criminal investigation."

"How do you know it's illegally procured?"

"I know that juvenile records are sealed. Therefore—"

"I know, I know, you're Captain Rules. Got it."

Trey stopped arguing. There was a wrinkle right between his eyes, and one hand rested on the wheel, the other on the gearshift. His fingers were fidgety. Tap tap tap.

At the next light, a familiar figure crossed the street in front of us, cell phone pressed to his ear, camera around his neck. He looked like one of those gaunt models in certain blue jean ads, with pale tight skin and black hair spiked above his forehead, and he was so engrossed in his conversation that he didn't look our way.

"Hey," I said, "isn't that the guy who was taking pictures at the end of the press conference, the one they threw out?"

Trey's eyes followed him. "Yes, it is. The security guard didn't get a name."

The car behind us honked and Trey drove forward, slowly. I whipped around in my seat and watched the guy get into a black Ford Explorer with tinted windows. He roared away from the curb with a lurch, still talking on his cell phone.

I caught the license plate—D MAN—and I smiled. "Wanna bet it's Dylan Flint?"

Trey watched in his rearview mirror as the SUV rolled down the street. He nodded sagely, but otherwise showed little interest.

I stared at him. "You're not following him?

"Why would I do that?"

"Because he was following us on Saturday!"

"That doesn't mean—"

"Then call somebody! Tell them he's headed down Peachtree…Damn it, which Peachtree is this again?"

"It's not. It's Ponce de Leon."

"Doesn't matter. I've got an idea where he's headed." I dragged his folder out of my tote bag and waved it at Trey. "He has a photography studio near Centennial Park. We can catch him there."

Trey shook his head. "I don't think—"

I held out my hand. "Rock, scissors, paper."

"What?"

"You know this game, right? Winner chooses. On the count of three…"

He held out his hand. I counted, went with paper, which I then placed on top of Trey's closed fist. The light turned green.

"1212 Luckie Street," I said.

◇◇◇

From the street, Snoopshots didn't impress—a small shop front displaying sun-bleached photographs of brides and grooms, their faces sharp and averted like they were fleeing the scene of a crime. It was deserted, in stark contrast to the tan and sandstone squares of Centennial Park, which teemed with tourists. On the nights The Tabernacle held concerts, the street was a chaos of scalpers and music-drunk urbanites. But on this afternoon, the whole block felt like a throwback to Luckie Street's less lucky—and much less lucrative—pre-Olympic days. Trey parked, but kept the engine running.

I opened my window and took a picture of the front door. "I remember now—his daddy owns this whole building. Converted it to lofts during the boom. I'm guessing our boy doesn't pay much rent."

"It's closed," Trey pronounced.

"Looks that way." I put my cell phone in my bag. "So what do you think the best way around back is?"

I tried to open my door, but it was locked. Trey reached across me and laid his hand on top of mine.

"No," he said.

We froze that way for five solid seconds, neither of us moving a muscle. A family of four passed Dylan's shop, obviously lost. They all wore New World of Coke visors and carried dark blue plastic bags from the aquarium. The little girl licked a red, white and blue snow cone. The mother's eyes darted back and forth, like a minesweeper.

"Fine," I said. "But can we at least wait a few more minutes? Just in case he shows?"

Trey removed his hand from mine. He sat back and switched off the engine. "Five minutes. Then we go back to Phoenix."

So I watched the doorway. He watched his watch. After exactly five minutes, when there was still no sign of our quarry, Trey shifted the car into first and made a U-turn. I didn't protest. Dylan Flint wasn't showing, and I didn't really want to go snooping. All I wanted to do was go home.

Unfortunately for me, I didn't have one, not yet anyway.

The first thing I did when I got back to the Ritz was take a bath. A long one. I draped a washcloth on my face and ran the water as hot as I could. The bathroom filled with steam and all I could hear was the rhythmic plop plop of the water dripping from the faucet.

My brother was still in the Bahamas. Of course I had other concerns, namely that Dylan Flint was stalking me. And that a convicted criminal had been stalking Eliza and possibly my brother and was now MIA, which meant he was probably stalking me too. Janie had dumped about two pounds of backstory in my lap, along with a mess of inconsistencies, and some unknown woman was making creepy phone calls outside a strip club. And the Beaumonts—the freaking Beaumonts—with their cheese straws and press conferences and conveniently Confederate kinfolk. And then there was Garrity, and Trey, and Marisa, and Landon, and some redhead named Gabriella. . .

I turned off the water with my toe and sank under the surface.

The call came thirty minutes later, just as I was toweling off. I was expecting Rico. I got surprised.

It was my mystery caller again. "We need to talk. Meet me at the Waffle House out front of Boomer's. Midnight. And come alone."

I made a noise. "Look, I don't know what kind of idiot you think I am, but I don't show up at midnight when some stranger tells me to 'come alone.'"

"Bring a friend then, just no cops. I smell a cop, you'll never see me."

"No cops. Just a friend."

"Midnight," she said, and hung up.

My phone said it was five-thirty. I dialed Rico's number. He answered on the first ring. "What's up?"

"Hello, friend."

Chapter Twenty-Four

Rico wore a red flannel shirt and Doc Martens, and he'd turned his baseball cap around the right way for a change. No medallions. He kept the nose ring though.

I shook my head. "This is your idea of blending in with the Waffle House crowd?"

He shrugged. "I do the best I can."

Across the parking lot, Boomer's Adult Entertainment Emporium indeed boomed. I could hear its thumping rhythm even over the prehistoric grind of the eighteen-wheelers constantly coming and going. Rico held the door at the Waffle House, and we went inside. It smelled of cigarettes and syrup and hot strong coffee. A booth of upstanding male citizens gave me The Look as we passed, and I pulled my jacket tight in front.

"Don't bother," Rico whispered. "They're not looking at your chest, they're deciding you're a race traitor. Here, let's take this booth. It's by the exit."

I sat down, grabbed the least sticky menu. "It could be my chest, you know."

The waitress took our order, giving Rico a slow smile in the process. He returned it with equal smolder. I kicked him under the table.

"What is up with you? You're not turning hetero on me, are you? Because you can't do that, you know. I can't be a girl detective without a gay best friend."

"Nancy Drew didn't have no gay best friend." He looked around the restaurant, then leaned across the table. "Where's your mystery chick?"

"She said she'd find us."

He stirred his coffee. It was only a prop to him, just like the pecan waffle he'd ordered and then ignored. I pulled out my cigarettes, then put them back and got a piece of gum instead.

Rico jutted his chin. "Don't look now, but I bet that's your girl."

I looked anyway. A young woman walked to the cash register and ordered a coffee to go. She looked barely twenty, a tawny-skinned creature with a mane of ebony hair almost to her butt. She carried herself like a dancer—head up, stomach in—and her body was lush and full, with a thrust of cleavage. She slanted her gaze our way.

"Uh huh," Rico said. "Bingo."

The woman sat down next to me without a word of greeting. I recognized her as the woman who'd been lying by the pool when Trey and I had visited Beau Elan. She looked very different now, with tight shiny clothes and heavy but expert make-up. She also smelled of strawberries.

Definitely the stripper friend, I decided. For some reason, all strippers smelled like strawberries.

"No cops?" she said. Her voice held a slightly Hispanic lilt.

"No cops. Just Rico here."

Rico's favored her with his slow molasses smile. She hesitated, then smiled back. And then we got down to business.

Her name was Nikki. She was a friend of Eliza's. And she had some very definite ideas about who killed her.

"That bitch sister of hers," she said. "She hated Eliza, and she hated me worse. Said I was a bad influence."

I didn't argue since I remembered Janie saying those exact words. "Were you?"

"Shit, no! I didn't get Eliza back into the drugs—that was Bulldog. She used to buy from him in the parking lot over at Boomer's until the manager called the cops. But Dylan was the real problem."

"Dylan Flint?"

"Yeah." She rolled her eyes. "Jerk off. She met him at some club one night and thought he was the shit. I told her he was using her, but she didn't care."

"Using her for what?"

"To get the stuff." She rummaged in her pocketbook and pulled out a pack of Marlboros. She didn't ask, just lit up and blew out a fierce stream of smoke. I chewed my gum harder.

"She was selling drugs?"

"No, trading drugs. He took pictures of her."

"What kind of pictures?"

"What kind do you think?" She looked at me like I was an idiot. "She sent them to Playboy. Playboy did not call back. She didn't seem to care, though, just cooked up some new shady something."

"Which was?"

"I dunno. She hauled that boy's ass everywhere, to all these parties. I'd go too, and he'd take our picture with all these rich white people, and she'd laugh her ass off. It was stupid."

"So why do you think Janie killed her?"

Nikki shrugged. "She hated her. Isn't that enough?"

And that, I thought, is a lie. There was something Nikki wasn't telling me.

"You have no idea?"

She shrugged again. "Sister shit, I dunno. You done askin' about it?"

Rico watched our conversation from his side of the booth. He'd been silent the whole time, letting me ask all the questions. It was unusual behavior for him, so I wasn't surprised when he finally joined in.

"You got the sister, the creepy photographer dude, the meth man," he said. "Anybody else hanging around your girl?"

She sucked on her cigarette. "That manager. Always sliding up to us at the pool. Eliza told me she caught him looking in some woman's window once. But he was easy to work for, didn't crack whip, you know what I'm saying? So she didn't worry about him too much."

Rico nodded. "I hear you. That it?"

"Yeah, that's it."

"So why you got us here? You feeling particularly civic tonight?"

She stubbed out her cigarette, blew one last flume of smoke into the air. "The cops asked me a bunch of questions and told me a whole lot of nothing back. Don't return my calls. They still haven't pulled Bulldog in. That fool could show up at my place any minute now."

She looked at me. "Then I saw you and that other guy, the one in the suit, saw you write your phone number down. I waited until the manager wasn't looking and took it. I figured you weren't a cop, you might be willing to let me know stuff and not expect me to put myself out there, you know what I'm saying?"

I knew what she was saying. "Yeah. I'm willing. But if you want me to tell you stuff, I need some way of getting in touch. This 'meet me at the Waffle House' crap is crap."

She shrugged and gave me a business card. Sinnamon, it read, available for private parties, lingerie shows, etc. My grits had congealed into one solid mass, and the eggs were cold. I pulled off a piece of Rico's untouched waffle and dipped it into the butter.

"You were her friend?" I said.

Nikki didn't look at me, but she nodded.

"You cared about her?"

She stood abruptly, snatching at her purse as she did.

"Wait, one more question. I heard that Eliza had a bunch of cash in a shoebox. You know where all that money came from?"

Nikki shouldered her purse. "She told me she had a cake daddy. I didn't ask about it anymore."

She picked up her coffee and took it with her. The truckers at the first booth watched her rear end as she left. I looked at Rico.

He shrugged. "Even racists can appreciate a fine piece of dark meat."

I kicked him hard under the booth. "Stop trying to piss me off. You're still stuck helping me."

We left as soon as I picked all the pecans out of Rico's waffle and he explained what a "cake daddy" was, which was exactly what I thought it was. As we drove past Boomers, the club's lights striped the car interior with pink and purple neon bands. The crowd had thickened, and there was an Oldsmobile cop car pulled up at the entrance. I squinted at the figure standing right beside said cop car, hands on hips, looking mean and official.

Garrity. And he was staring right at me.

"Oh crap!" I turned my face away and hunkered down in the seat. "Get outta here!"

"What? Why?"

"Just do it! I can't let him see me!"

"Who?"

"The cop! I'm not supposed to be investigating, and he'll be pissed as hell!"

So Rico drove. I stayed on the floor. He turned the music up. "Hate to break it to you, baby girl, but I think you're busted. Cop dude's still watching, and you're right—he looks pissed as hell."

Back at the Ritz, I sat by the phone like a guilty teenager, waiting for Garrity to call and chew me out. But he never did. And since I wasn't about to call him, I went to bed around two, feeling like I'd temporarily dodged a bullet.

The call came at three-fifteen, and the dread returned. Only it wasn't Garrity—it was an officer with the Kennesaw Police Department.

"Ms. Randolph?" he said. "We've got a problem."

Chapter Twenty-Five

"What security system?" I said.

The Kennesaw officer looked perplexed. "The one rigged to the window. Nobody made it inside, though—the burglar bars did the job, and once the alarm started, your perpetrator fled the scene."

I took another deep breath. In the shop, a second officer took notes, his shoes crunching on the glass shards that used to be the gun shop's front window. Somewhere on my floor was a brick. And apparently none of this would have been discovered without the security system that alerted the Kennesaw cops.

Only one problem. Dexter didn't have a security system. And I hadn't installed one.

I explained this to the deputy. He scratched his forehead. "Well, there was one in there. A surveillance camera too, only it got busted. The perpetrator hit it with another brick. "

"If you're talking about the thing mounted on the wall behind the register, it's broken."

He looked at me like I was slow. "That's what I'm trying to tell you—somebody hit it with a brick and broke it. He had good aim too, whoever it was. Took it out in one shot."

I didn't try to explain. The old camera was for show only, a prop. Not that anyone could tell from looking at it—hence its current bashed-in state—but my real concern was the inventory.

"Was anything missing?"

"There doesn't seem to be. The alarm scared off the perpetrator, and the safe is untouched. But you'll want to check, of course."

He was right about that. There were a lot of things I planned to check out, just as soon as I got ahold of Eric, who still wasn't returning my calls.

Luckily, there was another person who was.

Garrity saw me and made his way over. He carried two cups of coffee, one of which he handed to me wordlessly. It was scalding hot and loaded with cream and sugar.

"You've got to stop calling me in the middle of the night," he said. "It never turns out well." He was dressed casually, but I saw the holster under the tan jacket.

I shrugged. "What can I say? You're my go-to guy these days."

He pulled the lid off his coffee and a tendril of steam curled into the air. "You have any idea who did this?"

"Nope. You?"

"Maybe."

He pulled a piece of paper from his jacket pocket. It was a photocopy of a BOLO on William Aloysius Perkins. I checked out the mug shot—it looked just like the sketch I remembered from my second interview. An ordinary face: dark buzz cut growing out, round eyes, small nose, soft chin.

"Bulldog," I said.

Garrity's eyebrows rose. "You know this guy?"

"Janie told me about him. She's convinced he killed Eliza." I handed the paper back. "Is he a suspect?"

"Right now he's wanted for questioning, but once they get him in a chair, I'm sure he'll spill. Not the sharpest knife in the drawer, you know what I mean? The manager at Boomers said he was usually riding the squirrel train."

"The what?"

Garrity looped a slow circle at his temple. "High, whacked out, hyped."

"You think he has something to do with this?"

"Maybe. There's been a lot of camera breakage going on—first Phoenix, now here. And this guy's got a history of B and E."

I hopped down and went to the back seat. "All of this is off the record, right?"

"For now."

I dug inside my tote bag and pulled out the manila envelope with Rico's illicit info inside. "Here. Have a look at this."

Garrity pulled out the materials and read a couple of lines. "Where did you get this?"

"I forget."

"You forget?"

"Yeah. I know that's odd."

"Not really. You wouldn't believe the kind of things people forget once they start talking to a cop." He shut the folder, but left it lying in his lap. "So Eliza was into B and E too. What do you want me to do about it?"

"I don't know. I promised Janie I'd keep it out of circulation, but now that it seems like Eliza's old partner is working my turf, I want it put in the right hands."

"Does this have anything to do with why you were at Boomer's earlier?"

His eyes would have been really beautiful, I decided, if he hadn't been forever narrowing them at me, like I was on the witness stand. "Is this still off the record?"

He agreed. So I told him the truth. Mostly. I left out the part where Nikki had been watching me, kind of de-emphasized the whole "meeting a creepy stranger at midnight" thing, but other than that, my version was right on the money.

He sipped his coffee. "That was borderline idiotic, you know, the kind of stupid thing—"

"You're one to talk. Boomers is a little out of the way for something that's not even your case."

"So? I'm a cop. You're a civilian. End of argument."

"I'm a liaison now, Detective."

He gave me the cop eye. "A what?"

So I told him everything about that—the ball-breaker of a morning meeting, my new position, Trey's near-pummeling of Steve Simpson, the fact that Landon and Trey and Simpson were all "suspicious" now, the sighting of the mysterious Dylan Flint.

When I was done, he shook his head. "Jesus. Marisa's got Trey on an investigation? He doesn't do investigations."

"His point exactly. She shot him down. I swear, you should have seen her, like you crossed Scarlett O'Hara and the Terminator."

"That's what they want, you know."

"Who?"

"Her clientele. Ever since 9/11, every CEO in Fulton County wants to know how to kill somebody with a spork, and they want to know how to do it without messing up their suit. Phoenix draws 'em like catnip. But I'll tell you one thing—I don't like it in there. Maybe I've just been a cop too long, but I can't shake the feeling that those walls have ears. And eyes. And who knows what else."

He dropped his voice, narrowed his gaze. "I don't even take a piss in there if I can help it."

We sat on my hood while the Kennesaw officers finished their look-around. Some of them had known Dexter, had bought from him. They'd introduced themselves, told me how sorry they were for my loss. Every single one was polite, well-scrubbed and white as cream of wheat.

I rubbed my eyes until I could see straight. "So tell me, Detective—what were you doing at Boomer's?"

"Off-duty curiosity. Bulldog used to sell in that parking lot. I wanted to see if he'd been around recently."

"Had he?"

"Not that the manager knew of." He made a serious face. "Have you told Trey about any of this?"

"I tried to tell him about the juvie records, but he went all stickler on me."

"Then you need to tell him a different way."

I was about to let him have it for that one—like Trey being Trey was my fault—when the Kennesaw officer tapped my shoulder. "Ma'am? I hate to interrupt, but does this mean anything to you? We found it behind some boxes under the window. Looks like your perpetrator dropped it through the burglar bars."

He showed me the target, a picture of me in the center, the bull's eye a blasted hole. I felt the blood drain from my face, and an involuntary tremor started in my hands. Tears sparked, blurring my vision. Garrity moved to stand in front of me. "Hey, hey."

"Damn it, I hate crying." I wiped my eyes. "But I'm running on two hours sleep, and now I'm being threatened—again—and I don't even know why, and I've got a shop full of guns that I can't even carry yet, and—"

"What do you mean, 'threatened again?'"

The officer handed me a tissue. I blew my nose. And then I explained.

◇◇◇

Once I calmed down, Garrity went off to ask the deputies some more questions. I huddled on my hood, arms wrapped around my knees. I felt empty, but it was a cathartic empty. No more secrets. I couldn't handle this mess by myself.

I watched him talking with the other policemen, making a tight official knot with them. When he returned, he wore a strange expression. "You said you knew nothing about the security system?"

"Right."

"And that the camera was just a decoy, hadn't worked in years?"

"Right again."

He sighed and ran his hand through his hair. "In that case, you really need to talk to Eric. And Trey. Because not only was that camera live, it was Phoenix issue."

Chapter Twenty-Six

The next morning came in the afternoon. I'd crawled into bed just before six and slept like I'd been drugged, finally dragging myself into the shower a little after noon. One café mocha and a half a cigarette later, I was driving to Phoenix with a mission in mind. My mission was thwarted, however, by Phoenix's own Cerberus at the gate—Yvonne.

"Mr. Seaver is out of the office," she said. "If you'd like to leave a message—"

"Where is he?"

"I'm sorry, but—"

A voice behind me cut the argument in half. "He's at the gym, teaching a karate workshop."

I whirled around to face Steve Simpson. To my astonishment, he wore a suit and tie and real shoes, and his unruly curls had been tamed into something like a hair style.

"What gym?"

"The one across the street. He'll be back in an hour. He always is."

I peered closer at Steve's tie. It was bright green, with dollar signs in the paisley pattern. "You're tech support, right?"

He looked suspicious. "Yeah. Why?"

"Forget Trey. You'll do."

◇◇◇

Steve's office was an extravagant mess. It smelled metallic and dusty, and stacks of DVDs and surplus computer parts covered every flat surface. There was no window, and very little fresh air. I didn't bother finding a place to sit.

"Did you install the security system in my shop? Dexter's Guns and More?"

Steve removed a six-pack of Coca Cola from his chair. "The one in Kennesaw? Yeah, I remember. Why?"

My temper flared. "Why wasn't I informed?"

"Hey, I just wire things, I don't do paperwork. You'll have to talk to Mr. Premises Liability about that."

Back to Trey again. I turned to go, and Steve called after me, "Don't run off. I have something you might be interested in."

I stopped. "You're throwing bait."

"Are you biting?"

"Depends. What do you have?"

He waggled a DVD. "Hot-off-the-press copy of the security camera footage at Beau Elan."

"The one they mentioned in the meeting, the alibi footage?"

"The same. I'm supposed to demux it and make copies for the higher ups, Trey included. Which he will share, of course. Because Phoenix agents are such sharing people—"

"Just show me."

"Shut the door." He slid the disc into his computer and patted the edge of his seat.

I sat thigh to thigh with him, wary but curious. "Why are you showing me this?"

"Consider it a favor."

"Meaning I owe you one?"

"Exactly."

He tapped at the keyboard. I squinted at the blur of static. "I don't see anything."

"Hence the demux. It's four channels merged into one, see? But watch this."

He tapped again, and the images sorted themselves into a neat foursquare grid. Each screen looked exactly like I'd expected—low-resolution footage of cars coming and going, date and time information scrolling in the lower right hand corner.

"This one tracks the front gate," he said and clicked on the upper right-hand quadrant, fast forwarding to twelve-thirty. Sure enough, there was the white Phoenix van rolling in. I couldn't see Steve, however, only Trey and Landon.

"I was in the back," Steve said. "Now nothing much happens until…"

The recorded images sped up, then Steve hit stop. He pointed at the screen. "See, that's Charley right there, in the Mercedes with the tinted windows."

Yes, absolutely Charley Beaumont, her black hair loose about her shoulders, her eyes hidden behind impenetrable sunglasses. She wasn't smiling. Her car window slid back up, and she disappeared behind the dark glass.

"This is about five. Now we just go forward an hour until… right there."

I watched as the same car rolled out of the gate. Only this time Charley wasn't alone.

"That looks like Landon."

"It is. She took him back to his car at Phoenix, where he left for your brother's house. Okay, go forward until six-thirty and you'll see Trey and me leaving in the van. Well, you'll see the van, no faces. But he can vouch for me."

I checked out the other squares. "So is there any footage of a black SUV?"

"Nope."

"What about a blue pick-up?"

"You mean Bulldog? No dice. The camera caught him sneaking past the gate Wednesday night, on foot, but nothing on Thursday. And it would have caught him, no doubt about that, whether he was in his car or on foot, because this is the only way in."

"No other way at all?"

Steve rolled his eyes. "So you've heard Trey's little rant, huh? I suppose he could have gotten in over the wall. But the area around Eliza's apartment is covered by the security camera there—that whole corner is. See?"

I had to take his word for it. All I could see was an expanse of lawn with people sunbathing.

"Jake Whitaker lives right across from her apartment."

"The manager? Yeah."

"What was he doing during this time?"

"He was with the landscaping people, creating urban gardening space." He said it with sarcastic little air quotes. "Why is it the people who can afford to do otherwise always want to grow their own tomatoes?"

I kept my eyes on the screen. "You came to that meeting yesterday just to piss Trey off."

"Maybe. I have a problem with authority sometimes. But I'm not a bad guy. White hat all the way."

"So why'd they hire you back?"

"Because I'm good. But mostly because they want to keep an eye on me. Why do you think they made you a liaison?"

I stood up, dusted off my backside. "Because Mark Beaumont said so."

"Yeah, but it's more than that, it's control. These people want their fingers in everybody's pie, especially Marisa. Boss Lady does not like surprises. Phoenix has something you want—access—which means you've got to toe the line now."

"I don't do that very well."

"Neither do I. But look at me, all suited up and proper today." He leaned forward, his elbows on his knees. "Look, tell Trey I said I was sorry. And if you need anything—"

"How about a copy of that disc?"

Steve smiled. "I knew you were going to say that."

As Steve promised, I found Trey in a back room at the gym. He wore a white t-shirt and black workout pants, and he was barefoot. A group of yoga-ready females sat on the cushioned floor in front of him, watching intently while he put one of their own into a chokehold.

"Relax your muscles," he told her. "I'm using your resistance against you."

The pony-tailed woman wasn't listening—she kept tugging at his forearm, which wasn't budging. She twisted about, making mousy girl noises, getting nowhere.

I rolled my eyes. "Bite him. That'll teach the son-of-a-bitch."

A dozen heads swiveled my way, Trey's included. He didn't break his hold, however, and his voice remained calm and authoritative. "Bend your knees first, then tuck your hips… yes, like that. Good."

She pushed his arm away with a feeble shove, and the entire class applauded as she returned to her spot. Trey finished up briskly after that. As the class filed out, each woman stopped to thank him personally. There was a lot of laughing and hair stroking, soft hands on his shoulder. Trey seemed oblivious to the whole parade, and eventually the room was empty except for the two of us. I noticed that his hands were wrapped like a boxer's, and that he kept them loose and ready, even though it was just me at the door.

"Did you need something?" he said.

"Yeah." I came into the room. "I need to know why there's a Phoenix-issue security camera in my shop that nobody told me about."

"What?"

"Don't play dumb. There's a freaking camera in *my* gun shop, and I want to know how it got there!"

"We installed it last week." He moved to the middle of the room where a weight bag dangled. He steadied it, then took a couple of easy jabs. "You know this. You signed the authorization paperwork."

"I did not!"

"Yes, you did. I have it on file in my office."

"Then it's a forgery."

"It's notarized."

I stomped onto the mat. Trey pointed at my feet. "You have to take your shoes off."

I pulled off one boot and threw it down. "This is ridiculous."

"It's to protect—"

"Not the shoes." I yanked off the other boot and joined him on the mat. "The situation. You just told me something that makes no sense whatsoever."

Trey returned to the weight bag. Up close, I could see the sheen of sweat on his forehead.

"I'll make you copies of the paperwork when I get back to the office," he said. "I suspect it will make sense then."

He moved lightly on his feet. Punch, punch, spin and kick. Precise and deadly.

"Not then, now. I want to see now."

"I'm busy now."

"Now."

He froze, hands up, and shot me a look—annoyance, tamped tight, but definitely percolating. That's when I remembered I was pissing off a killer. Of course there was another killer I'd pissed off too, one not as polite as Trey, whose current victim was a medium-to-large weight bag.

"You and your brother own the shop under a cotenancy agreement," he said. "Equal shares, equal access, equal right to alter property as long as said alterations—"

"This is Eric's doing?"

Trey returned to his workout. "The signed probate papers were all Phoenix needed, and Eric brought those in complete with your signature."

"Doesn't he have to ask me first?"

"No."

I kicked the weight bag, and pain arced across my instep. "Damn it!"

Trey frowned. "You shouldn't—"

"Don't tell me what I shouldn't do! I'm sick and tired of it!" I kicked the bag again, and again. "Why didn't you tell me? I thought you were supposed to be all about rules and shit!"

"I am, but—"

"You tell me you're here to help, you tell me you'll take a bullet for me, and then you go and—"

"I thought you knew."

I stopped kicking the bag. "What?"

"Eric said he was going tell you."

"He lied."

"No. He was telling the truth at the time." Trey steadied the bag. "But apparently he changed his mind."

Before I could reply, my cell phone chirruped at me in a happy way, letting me know I had a text message. I pulled out my phone. It was from Eric. It said that he was coming in that night, that I was welcome back at the house, that he'd see me later.

I deleted the message. "When did he have the camera installed?"

"Monday morning."

Before Eliza's death. Before he had any reason to believe that I was in danger and needed protecting. Not for my safety. So he could spy on me.

I put the phone away. "Trey, do I have the same rights to alter the property without alerting Eric?"

"Of course."

"So I could dismantle the whole get-up if I wanted?"

"You could. But there may be systems in place besides the obvious alarms and cameras."

"Wouldn't you know if there were?"

"I should. But then, I'm obviously not being told everything."

He said it without a hint of emotion, but I could sense the irritation running under the words. I'd learned a few things about Trey Seaver—he believed in rules and didn't like it one iota when other people didn't follow them.

"So will you come to my shop tonight and help me figure out what's what?"

"Simpson is the technical expert, not—"

"Will you?"

He unfastened his handwraps, exposing bare knuckle. "Certainly."

Chapter Twenty-Seven

Trey arrived exactly at seven, just as he said he would, back in his official suit, but tieless. His leather shoes crunched on broken glass.

"Garrity told me about the break-in," he said.

"Yeah, it's a mess." I showed him my new broom, still wrapped in plastic. "Just getting around to cleaning it up."

But Trey wasn't paying attention. He placed his briefcase on the counter and popped it open. "I'll perform a basic sweep first, then decide if more intensive measures are called for."

He scanned the shop, making notes on his ubiquitous yellow pad. He frowned a lot. The place did look rough—wooden slats nailed where the window used to be, gravel and crushed glass and the detritus of a dozen law enforcement shoes, the whole scene washed sallow by the fluorescent overheads.

Trey pointed with his pen. "The windows were wired to an alarm, but not the doors. I don't understand."

I did. Eric was less concerned with keeping me safe than with keeping tabs on me. I would have tripped a door alarm and spoiled his plan. My temper ignited again. When I finally got my hands on him…

Trey pointed at the ceiling. "What's up there?"

"I don't know. Crawl space?"

"I'll check it later." He moved behind the counter to examine the now-defunct surveillance camera. He fingered the tangled wires and broken black plastic like an archeologist perusing a pottery shard. "This is a wireless system. When it was operational, it could be accessed through an Internet connection, both archived and real-time footage."

"Meaning?"

"Meaning that registered users could log in and view the shop at any time, from anywhere."

I dropped the broom and joined him behind the counter. "That means we can see what happened the night it got smashed!"

"No, we can't. The account is password protected."

"You can't override it?"

"I could, but that would make this a Phoenix situation. I'd rather keep it a favor. There are fewer complications that way. And less paperwork."

I looked to see if he was making a joke, but his delivery and expression were both deadpan. I understood his point, however. As rules went, not involving Phoenix unless absolutely necessary was fine with me.

But I was dying to see that footage.

He pulled a file folder from his briefcase. "Here's another copy of the installation paperwork. I sent two sets with Eric. You were supposed to get yours last week."

I glanced through the folder. Nothing unexpected. "What if the Kennesaw cops themselves asked you for the footage? Could you override the password then? Without, you know…paperwork?"

"That would require a subpoena, which would make it an official Phoenix matter. With paperwork."

"So until Eric coughs up the password, we're stuck."

"Yes. Stuck."

He fiddled with the camera for a few more minutes, then examined the rest of the shop, including the crawlspace. Working methodically from a checklist, he inspected the closet in Dexter's office, the gun safe, the light fixtures. He checked the telephone for bugs twice, even though I assured him I hadn't even gotten service yet. He ran his finger along the door jambs and took copious notes.

I contributed by unwrapping my broom and staying out of his way. Garrity was right—Trey could spot eleven different ways to break into a place without even trying hard. He was fascinating to watch, like a cat burglar in action.

He declined my offer of coffee, preferring his ever-present bottle of Pellegrino. I made a huge pot anyway, dark as road tar. While it perked, he explained the system.

"It's a hybrid," he said, "hard-wired except for the security camera. Door and window contacts in place, as well as glassbreak detectors and one motion sensor over there." He pointed toward the safe. "No surveillance devices. But I did find the control panel in the closet upstairs, the key pad behind the front door."

"That little gray plastic box thingie? I thought that was part of the air conditioning."

He shook his head. "That's how you control the system. One touch arm and disarm, one touch perimeter. It shows you which devices are engaged, which are not."

"What's engaged right now?"

"Nothing. The window was, but it was deactivated after the break-in."

"Can I change any of this?"

"I can—I have the installer code. And then I can create a user code for you."

I could have hugged him. "I owe you for this, Trey. Big time."

He shut his briefcase. "You owe me nothing."

"I do too. You're my hero."

He busied himself at the keypad and didn't say another word. But I thought I saw a twitch at the left corner of his mouth.

While he worked, I poured myself a cup of coffee and opened three packages of sugar into it. Every now and then, I'd glimpse the holster under his jacket and remember, this is a man whose hands are lethal weapons and here I am, all alone with him. At night. In a deserted shop full of guns and ammo. And yet I felt comfortable with him, cozy even. At that moment, I trusted him more than my own brother.

I hopped up cross-legged on the counter. "If I asked you a hard question, would you tell the truth?"

"It depends."

"Do you think Eric's involved in Eliza's death?"

Trey tapped a number sequence into the keypad. "He has a solid alibi."

"Not for the murder per se, just…involved."

"He's certainly involved—he knew Eliza, he planned on meeting her. The evidence suggests she was killed while trying to talk to him. That doesn't make him guilty of any wrongdoing, however."

"Was Eliza pregnant?"

He looked up abruptly. "What?"

"Pregnant. I'm stretching here."

"I haven't seen the official report. According to what Ryan and Vance told me, however, the evidence indicates drug use, but no mention of pregnancy."

"That's what Janie told me too." I rummaged under the counter and found a half-eaten box of chocolate chip cookies. "What about her bank account, the deposits, the money in the shoe box? Any idea where that was coming from?"

"No."

"I can't figure it out either. I mean, you look at the money and her history with Bulldog, and it looks like she'd decided to start selling drugs."

"An acceptable hypothesis."

I dipped a cookie into my coffee. "But that doesn't explain her involvement with my brother. He's a lot of things, but drug dealer isn't one. Or drug taker for that matter."

Trey didn't reply. He pressed numbers and examined the lights that lit up in response, over and over, like he was practicing a magic trick.

I dusted cookie crumbs from my hands. "I'm guessing she was blackmailing somebody. But who's done something blackmailable?"

Trey frowned. "Blackmailable?"

"It's a sort-of-real word, stay with me here. And what about Dylan? We know that his SUV was at Phoenix on Thursday morning—you saw it—the same day the security cameras got busted up. And we know he was following us on Saturday, and that he showed up at the press conference yesterday, but we have no clue what he was up to."

"We have a small clue." He closed the keypad cover. "You're on his blog now."

"What!"

"Look and see."

I bounced off the counter and over to Dexter's computer. A few keystrokes later and there I was, framed by the Ferrari's passenger side window, looking like a slightly frowzy movie star. I recognized the shot—it had been taken on Saturday, the day Dylan followed us.

I stared at the image, sunglassed and remote. "I swear, no matter what I find out, it just confuses me more."

"This is a complicated case."

I looked across the room at him. Even under low wattage, his eyes were distractingly gorgeous. But the expression there was utterly professional, patient and polite and unwavering. He'd been nothing but above-board with me every step of the way, this man who opened doors, who said "please" and "thank you." This man who had driven all the way up to Kennesaw as a favor for me, a woman he barely knew, because it was the decent thing to do.

And then I remembered all the times I'd snooped in his desk, eavesdropped on his conversations, quizzed Garrity about his personal life or accused him of being a liar and held him at sword point…

A guilty knot congealed in my gut. "I'm sorry."

"For what?"

"For everything. For disrupting your class. For yelling at you. For making a complicated situation even more complicated." I exited Dylan's blog. "Did Garrity tell you about the target with my picture in the middle?"

"He did."

"Did he tell you it wasn't the first time?"

Trey nodded. "He thinks someone is threatening you."

"Or trying to scare me, I don't know which."

"Why would someone do that?"

"Your guess is as good as mine. But I'd say it's because I'm getting close to something somebody doesn't want me close to. And if it continues, I'm going to start packing heat, even if the state of Georgia says I have to do it openly."

I expected an argument, but didn't get one. Trey looked thoughtful, but then went back to his legal pad without a word. I moved closer.

"Does it really work? What you were showing that woman in class?"

"I wouldn't teach it if it didn't."

"Could you show me how? Until that carry permit comes through…"

He made one final mark and stuck the pen behind his ear. "Of course."

◇◇◇

And that was how I ended up in a chokehold, with Trey standing behind me, one arm looped around my neck. I had my fingers deep in his forearm, but it was like tugging at a steel bar. My brain ratcheted into panic mode.

It's just Trey, I told myself, he's not really trying to throttle you. But my body was having none of it. My body knew he'd killed before.

"Damn it," I hissed. "This wouldn't happen if I had a gun!"

"Turn your head into the crook of my elbow so you can breathe. Lower your hips so that I'm off balance."

I did as he said. But I was still breathing hard and fast, every muscle tensed for fight or flight. Even my teeth were clenched.

Trey's mouth was right at my ear, his voice calm. "I'm using your resistance against you, see? If you relax, you take away some of my power. Stop fighting so hard. Go loose."

My body rebelled, but when I did as he said, I felt the shift in his stance. Suddenly, he was struggling to support me.

"See, there's leverage now. You can drop and roll, drop and get your weapon, drop and…stop."

"Stop what?"

"Are you expecting anyone?"

I heard it then—the slam of a car door, the crunch of footsteps on gravel. Then silence.

Before I could react, Trey yanked me across the room and practically threw me behind the counter. "Get down. Stay there."

"What are you doing?"

"Quiet."

He moved beside the door, back flat against the wall, his gun held right below his belt. I hadn't even seen him get it out. Then he hit the overheads, plunging the shop into darkness.

That's when it became real, when the dark descended. Light-headed with fear, I crouched on the freshly swept floor. Time slowed, every second bright with adrenalin, amplified. I searched the floor for a weapon and my hands closed on the broom handle. Great. I was going to die in a room full of guns with a freaking broom in my hand.

And then I heard a familiar voice. "Tai? What's happening? Open up!"

Trey switched on the light and opened the door. Eric stood on my doorstep, a vision of moral outrage in navy slacks and baby blue dress shirt.

"What the hell's going on here?" he demanded.

Chapter Twenty-Eight

I marched up to him, broom in hand. "You don't get to show up at...whatever time it is."

"Nine forty-seven," Trey supplied.

"Yeah, nine forty-seven, with *no* warning—no call, no text, no nothing—and demand that I tell *you* what the hell is going on!"

Eric took off his glasses and stuck them on top of his head. "I own this place as much as you do. And I *did* text you!"

"You said you were coming back to Atlanta—you didn't say anything about driving up to Kennesaw."

"I thought you'd be at the house. Only when I get there, the guest room is empty and your stuff is gone. So I check the Ritz, and they tell me you checked out. This was my next guess."

Eric shut the door behind himself. He looked just like his usual J. Crew self, and he wasn't at all tan. I'd expected him to be tan.

"I'm not pleased about this," he said. "You shouldn't be here this late at night."

I waved my broom at him. "*Now* you decide to be concerned? You vanish for five days—"

"I didn't vanish."

"—leaving me with a murder in my lap and the police breathing down the back of my neck. You sic Phoenix on me, only you don't see fit to tell me. You install a security camera—which you also don't tell me about and which I only discover because somebody took a brick to it."

"A what?"

"A brick." I pointed. "Why do you think the front window's boarded up?"

He glanced at what used to be the window. "Oh my god, what happened?"

Trey moved forward. Now that the threat was over, he'd tucked the H&K back in its holster. "Now that you're here, we can find out."

We gathered around Dexter's desk. Eric sat. He pulled up the log-in screen and typed his password. The archived footage was grainy, but after fiddling with the resolution, it cleared. Unfortunately all it showed was a sweatshirt-hooded figure, wrapped in shadow. Thick, hunched, brick in hand. Blurry face covered, hidden in the dark.

"Two-eleven am," Trey said.

It didn't show whoever it was slipping the threatening target under the door. That must have come afterward.

Eric slumped back in his seat. "This is news to me."

"What, you weren't checking things out with your little spy set-up?"

At least he had the decency to look chagrined. "I was going to tell you when I got back."

"Why didn't you tell me when you installed it?"

"Think about it. If I'd said, hey, let me get you a bodyguard, or hey, let me install this security system, you would have done what you always do—argue."

"You're acting like Dad."

"And you're acting like a child."

That tripped my switch. "Don't you dare—"

But Trey cut me off. "I'm sorry. I have to go now."

In the heat of the argument, I'd forgotten he was in the room. Eric looked as abashed as I felt. He stood up and shook hands with Trey. "I appreciate your keeping an eye on her for me."

Trey shook his head. "That's not why I was here." Then he looked at me. "Is there anything else I can help you with?"

I smiled. "No, you've done plenty. Thanks for coming."

"You're welcome. The access codes are beside the cash register." He slipped his yellow pads into his briefcase and left without looking back. I soon heard the Ferrari rip into the gravel and roar into the street. Zero to speed limit in two point seven seconds.

Eric looked at me. He shoved his glasses further into his dirty-blonde cowlicks. And then he got that patient "this is for the best" look. "Tai, there's some things you need to know about Trey."

"Like the fact that he cared enough to come out here tonight and help me undo what you did?"

"It's complicated."

"Screw complicated, Eric, I'm more interested in the things *you* haven't told me."

Now he looked surprised. "What do you mean?"

"Oh, come on! It's the question everybody's been asking." My voice shook despite my efforts to control it. "Were you involved with Eliza Compton?"

He exhaled slowly. "Don't you think the police checked me out? And don't you think they'd have pulled me in for questioning ASAP if they'd found anything? I barely knew the girl."

"You knew her enough to change your plans to meet with her—secretly, out of the office—and then lie about it."

"She needed help."

"Which had nothing to do with the fact that she was a young, attractive woman?"

He made noise of disgust. "Oh, please. She was alone and desperate and scared."

"About what?"

"I don't know! But I do know that I had nothing to do with it! And you should know that, too!"

Tears blurred my vision, and I wiped my eyes with the back of my hand.

"You could have explained that to me instead of leaving me to deal with all this crap by myself!"

"What did you want me to do, turn around and come back here?"

"That's exactly what I wanted you to do!"

Eric waved me off. Under the bleak fluorescence, he looked washed out and utterly alien. Not even familiar, much less my own flesh and blood.

"I didn't have time," he said. "This workshop wasn't something I could abandon just because some girl I barely knew died across the street from my house. Life goes on, Tai. The grown-ups go with it."

It was all I could do not to fling cold coffee on him. "You don't get to lecture me about being a grown-up, not after what I went through with Mom."

"What do you want, a medal?"

"I want you to take some responsibility!"

He laughed, a grating nasty sound. "That's rich, coming from you. You've never stayed in one place for more than a year, never had a relationship for more than six months. Face it—even when she was dying, Mom was the one taking care of you. And now I'm the one stuck taking care of you."

"I can take care of myself!"

"You can't even keep a job!"

"I have a job, thank you very much!"

He dug one hand into the hair on his forehead. "Are you insane? You're an arms merchant for a bunch of rednecks. There's a goddamn rebel flag hanging on the wall! Do you have any idea how embarrassing this is to me?"

"You work for a company full of gun-toting corporate tools, and you have the gall to be embarrassed by Uncle Dexter? Like rich people with guns are cool and poor people with guns are trashy and dangerous?"

"One of those trashy dangerous people killed a girl five days ago! Have you forgotten?"

"Of course I haven't, you idiot, but all you do is lecture me about being an embarrassment and then go back to pretending that Eliza's death doesn't affect you!"

He wasn't listening, was just ticking off on his fingers. "I gave you a bed under my roof, I tried to get you a decent job, I—"

"I don't need your bed, or your roof, or your goddamn decent job!"

"Where else do you have to go?"

"Here."

He got steely quiet. "There's a killer out there, Tai."

"Lucky for me I got a whole bunch of guns."

"You don't even know how to shoot."

If I'd had a gun in hand, I might have shot him just to prove the point. "You don't know anything, big brother."

I threw him out. I was trembling, and my chest felt hollow and crumpled. Despite my best efforts, the tears came hard and fast, blurring the lights into hazy globs. I lit up a cigarette. Then I blew my nose and double-checked the deadbolts. Then I engaged every device I saw on the keypad, including the motion detector. And then I got a .38 revolver from the safe and filled it with bullets. Dexter had a pull-out sofa in his office. It was brown velour and smelled like gun oil and stale popcorn, but it was the bed I had made, and for better or worse, I was going to lie in it.

◇◇◇

The gun didn't help. Neither did the security system. I stayed awake most of the night, all the lights on, dozing in fits and starts. Which is why I was fully awake when my cell phone rang at six in the morning.

It was Janie. "They found Bulldog."

"They did! Where?"

"Meth lab in Smyrna. Son of a bitch got himself blown up last night. You feel like driving me out there so I can ID the bastard?"

Chapter Twenty-Nine

Gravel crunched beneath the tires as we pulled into the storage facility, past the barrier that kept out the news crews but far away from the smoking heap at the end of the driveway. The security zone, Garrity had informed me.

"Tell them you're bringing in the identifying witness," he'd said, "and they'll let you in. Do exactly as you're told, and I mean exactly. A meth lab burnout is not the place to go snooping."

I didn't need to be told twice. The air at the site reeked of ash and chemicals, even from our parking spot. Janie looked grim and determined. She wore her crucifix, but her fingers went nowhere near it, as if she didn't want to be reminded of all that "turn the other cheek" stuff. When the patrol made her put out her cigarette, I thought for a second she might refuse. But she dropped it into the dregs of her coffee and got out of the car. I was not invited to go with her.

It was a slice of hell, that place, heavy with the stink of ammonia, like a radioactive litter box, and thick with clotted oily smoke. A hazmat-suited agent crouched next to an overturned oil drum, waving a Geiger counter at it.

But I did see one thing I recognized. A beat-up blue pick-up, swarming with uniforms. Janie was led to it. She stared at it, nodded, then spat on the ground.

Back in my car, she reached for her cigarettes. "They wouldn't let me look at the body, said it was too dangerous right now.

They said it didn't matter anyway, that I couldn't ID him if I tried. I asked if it was bad, and they said yes. Three people, all of them burnt to death. Crispy critters, one of them said. Didn't think I could hear him. Somebody told him to hush." She blew out smoke in a burst. "But I wanted to see."

"They didn't find any ID on the body?"

"All burnt up. The truck, though, that's his. No doubt."

We were back in the city by the time the morning commute had started its sluggish crawl. The radio reported the usual litany of accidents and road work and stalled vehicles. I was regretting my fashion choices. In an effort to look like a liaison, I'd put my hair up and worn this purple pantsuit I'd gotten at J.C. Penney. Now I was regretting it—the armholes were too high, and it itched. But I looked official. Somewhat.

"The fire took out the whole block of units, twenty at least. Went up like that." Janie snapped her fingers. "You get a bunch of tweakers playing with fire, next thing you know, the whole neighborhood's burning like hell itself."

I thought of the smell, the ash, the odor that surely signaled death. The landscape, toxic and wasted. And somewhere in there, under a sheet, the charred corpse of a murderer.

"I wanted justice," Janie said, and ground out her cigarette. "But this will do."

◇◇◇

Phoenix was jumping when we got there. Yvonne steered Janie toward Landon's office, casting suspicious looks over her shoulder as she did. I shoved my ID into my tote bag the minute she got out of sight and headed straight for Trey's office.

Marisa was already in there, clad in a charcoal skirt and jacket, accented with pearls a shade darker than her blouse. One eyebrow arched as she gave my pantsuit the up and down.

"Interesting color choice," she said.

I smoothed the fabric. "It's aubergine."

And then she pummeled me with questions. I answered as best I could. Trey took notes. He watched me as I gave my recitation, jotting down information in his neat precise hand. Not reading me, just paying attention.

Marisa stood by his desk. "If this means what I think it means, then our part in the investigation is over. This changes everything."

I understood. After all, every piece of evidence I'd seen was pointing to Bulldog as Eliza's killer, so now that he was a pile of disreputable ash, further speculations seemed a moot point, as did the reward the Beaumonts had offered.

She directed a look at Trey. "Which means I need you this Friday at the Adams reception."

He stared at her. "But I completed the security plan two weeks ago."

"Things have changed. I need you in person."

"Landon—"

"—is a personal guest of the Beaumonts, you know that. You were the only person who wasn't going to be there this weekend, and now you are."

Trey shook his head. "I don't do that kind of work anymore. There are too many variables."

"That's why I need you. We're dealing with rent-a-cops, local cops, other people's bodyguards. I need somebody I can trust in the middle of all this."

"We planned—"

"Not for this, we didn't. You did the zone breakdown, the contingency protocol. All I'm asking you to do is be there and be available."

He didn't reply. But he didn't drop his eyes or look away either.

"This is a major event for major players," she said. "None of us wants it ruined by some stupid rumor."

I was confused. "What rumor?"

She waved a hand dismissively. "It's going around that there was something between Mark and Eliza Compton. The blogs are all over it, talk radio too. Probably that little photographer creep we ran off."

Dylan. Of course.

Trey kept his eyes on his yellow pad. "Is there evidence?"

"Of course not. What evidence could they have for something that doesn't exist?"

"Evidence can be misinterpreted."

"Then it's not evidence," Marisa continued, "it's nonsense, and if Mark takes the energy to deny it, he'll just look defensive."

"I still don't understand why I have to be there this weekend."

"I want you there because Mark wants you there, so you will be there. Period. Cocktails start at six, dinner at seven-thirty."

Trey exhaled loudly. Marisa ignored the huff, dropped a file folder on his desk. "Black-tie. I know you've got a tux."

"I do not."

"So get one, now. Put it on your expense account." Marisa indicated me with a nod. "Take her with you."

This caught me off guard. "But Janie—"

"We'll see that she gets back to her hotel, don't worry. You stay with Trey."

She glared at me as she said this. I remembered Simpson's words: *they want to control you.* Setting me up with the resident Boy Scout probably seemed a great way to do it. I didn't argue. Trey was a maze of rules, but I was beginning to get the hang of how they bent. And bend they did.

Trey stared after her, tap-tapping his pen on the edge of the desk as her heels click-clacked down the hall. His expression was blank, but the little wrinkle between his eyes was fast becoming a furrow.

I perched myself on the edge of his desk. "So tell me, where does one go to get a tux in this town?"

He slid the folder into a drawer. "Gabriella's."

I stifled a grin. The woman in the photograph Charley had confiscated from Trey's office, the stunning redhead at his side during the Mardi Gras ball. In Marisa's efforts to keep me out of the thick of things, she'd thrown me right into the briar patch.

I leaned over and rubbed the spot on Trey's forehead. He looked puzzled, but he let me do it.

"Stop worrying, Mr. Seaver. Otherwise we're gonna have to Botox you."

Chapter Thirty

Gabriella's Day Spa and Boutique lay behind Lenox Square Mall, not three blocks from Trey's condo and within walking distance of the Ritz. It was hardly impressive from the parking lot, especially in the monochromatic gray drizzle, and there was a closed sign on the door. Trey ignored it. I followed suit.

Inside was a surprise. Small but lavish, it smelled of sandalwood incense and beeswax candles. We stood in the boutique area, surrounded by tiny cocktail dresses and pointy-toed heels on marble columns. The spa area lay to the right, through an arched doorway. I heard female voices beyond it, saw some votives shimmering around a soft gold loveseat.

A woman stuck her head around the corner. Her red hair was piled on her head in careless ringlets, and she had enormous green eyes, round like a cat's.

"Trey!" she exclaimed.

She hurried over, and I noticed that even though she wore white pants and a matching baby tee, her feet were bare. She took his hands in hers, and he let her do it, even let her press a kiss to his cheek, but his face registered no emotion at the contact. She, however, looked positively enraptured.

"You must be Gabriella," I said.

"And you must be Tai. I've heard so much about you."

Her voice carried the vowels of someplace European. France, I decided. I slid a look at Trey, but he was examining this red dress, running one finger along the beaded neckline.

"I need a tuxedo for Friday night," he said.

"So I'll see you at the reception after all." She took his arm. "Don't pout. Come on back and we'll double-check your measurements. It looks like you've been overworking your deltoids again."

"It's the Krav."

Then they disappeared behind this burgundy curtain, leaving me alone. I examined the red dress that had caught Trey's eye. It was gorgeous, all right, a glittering length of red beading and tiny sequins with a thigh-high slit like a bolt of lightning. I fingered the price tag, whistled under my breath.

I could hear the two of them talking behind the curtain, but I couldn't catch what they were saying, so I moved closer. It wasn't eavesdropping, per se, just paying attention to a conversation of which I wasn't a part. I heard her laugh, softly, heard his monosyllabic reply. I took another step toward the curtain.

That's when I saw the photograph.

It was just lying there behind the counter, half covered with other mail. I reached over—casually, like I was looking for a pen or something—and brushed the envelope aside so I could get a better look.

It was the exact same shot that Mark had brought to Trey, the one Charley had confiscated. Lying next to it was the envelope from Snoopshots. Apparently Mark Beaumont wasn't the only one who'd gotten Dylan's sales pitch—he'd obviously sent the same shots to Gabriella, hoping to impress her with his photographic genius.

And then I noticed something else, something I'd missed the first time.

I snatched up the photos and marched the whole lot right into the dressing room. Trey was standing very still while Gabriella ran a tape measure across the back of his shoulders.

I shoved the photo at him. "That's her, standing outside of the frame."

"Who?"

"Eliza." I tapped the image. "See? That hand there, on Charley's waist?"

Trey looked where I was pointing. "How do you know that's Eliza?"

"The silver cuff bracelet. She was wearing it when she died. I remember it vividly."

"Let me see." Gabriella stood, peered over his shoulder. "That's a bracelet from my silverwork collection."

"So you knew her?"

"The girl who was killed? Eliza? Not very well. She came in here sometimes, but she rarely bought anything."

"Except this bracelet."

Gabriella looked at me pointedly. "It's from my more accessible line."

"You mean it's the only thing somebody like Eliza could afford?"

"Yes. She seemed to enjoy looking, though, and she asked a lot of questions about my clients, especially Charley."

"That didn't seem odd to you?"

She shrugged. "People ask about Charley all the time."

"But you remember this girl in particular. Why?"

"Because this girl asked very personal questions. Other people bring in magazines and say, I want this, or, do you have shoes like that? But this girl wanted to know about Charley, not the clothes. And for a while she showed up right after Charley did, within minutes."

"Did you tell Charley any of this?"

"Of course. She didn't seem concerned. In the end, the girl stopped coming here, and I stopped worrying."

While she spoke, she continued to take Trey's measurements, running her pink tape measure around his waist, across his chest. There was familiarity in her touch.

"And now the girl's dead," I said.

Gabriella tucked the tape in her pocket. "Yes. But what does that have to do with Charley?"

"It has everything to do with Charley! Eliza was obsessed with her in way that goes far beyond some celebrity crush! She's got her hand on Charley's waist, for crying out loud!" I turned to Trey. "Now will you believe me when I say there's something fishy going on with the Beaumonts?"

He handed the photo back to me. "There's a logical reason—"

"Of course there is! Charley took *this* picture from *your* office because she's trying to cover up a link between her and Mark and this girl. I can't believe you don't see it!"

"Hundreds of people are linked to the Beaumonts."

"But why her, why here, why at this party? She was a receptionist, how could she afford a Mardi Gras party that cost two hundred bucks a ticket?"

"I don't know."

"Did she bring a date?"

"I don't know."

"You were there! Didn't you see her?"

"There were 587 people at that event."

I started to argue, but then I remembered the other photographs in my hand. I took them over to a cushioned bench and dumped them out. If Gabriella was annoyed that I'd been going through her stuff, she didn't say anything—she just joined me as I sifted through them.

"You got these from Dylan Flint," I said.

"Yes. I wasn't the only one. Several of my friends who were at the Mardi Gras ball got the same package."

"Didn't you think that was strange?"

"I've seen much stranger promotions than dropping off samples of one's work."

The photos looked identical to the ones Dylan had sent Mark Beaumont. They contained Mark and Charley and Senator Adams, my brother and the mayor. And then, in the background, another familiar face, only this time he wasn't holding a toilet brush.

"Jake Whitaker," I said.

Gabriella twisted her mouth in a tight knot. "Him."

"You know him?"

She examined her fingernails like Rico did, fingers curled in a loose fist. "That night at the ball, he wouldn't leave me alone. And then he showed up here the next morning."

Trey's head snapped back. "You didn't tell me this."

She waved him quiet. "It was only once, and I made it clear this was a place of business, and that if he had none, he needed to leave. He hasn't returned." She switched her cat-eyes back to me again. "Why all the questions?"

"Yes," Trey echoed, "why all the questions?"

I tapped the next photograph. "This is why."

It showed Eliza, her face half-turned away from the camera, her eyes bright and cunning. She had on a shiny purple dress, and standing right at her elbow…

Nikki. She wore a black cocktail dress and looked directly at the camera, but Eliza's gaze was fastened elsewhere, on someone not in frame. I would have bet my emergency cigarette that it was one of the damn Beaumonts, uncaptured by the lens, visible only in Eliza's hungry, fascinated eyes.

Trey tilted his head to examine it. "Who is that?"

"It's Nikki, this stripper friend Janie keeps talking about, from Beau Elan."

"Why is she important?"

"Do you remember those rumors Marisa mentioned, about Mark and Eliza? I was blaming Dylan and his stupid blog, but what if Nikki started them? Or Jake Whitaker. He was there, she was there, they were there. Maybe this didn't start at Mardi Gras—maybe it started at Beau Elan."

Trey's expression switched to mildly interested. "Go on."

"So maybe Mark and Eliza really were having an affair. Maybe Jake really does know something. After all, you said he was lying about her being nice."

"But Marisa says—"

"Like Marisa knows everything. The point is, this is something we need to pursue. And I know exactly where to start."

"I don't think—"

I held out my hand. "Rock, scissors, paper."

He frowned. "Again?"

I stuck my hand out. He did the same. And on three, I laid my flat palm over his closed fist.

"Paper covers rock," I said. "Again."

He didn't argue, just looked at the photographs in my hand, then addressed Gabriella. "Do you mind if we keep those?"

She shook her pretty head. "Of course not. If it will help."

"It will." He checked his watch, then looked at me. "We leave in eight minutes. Get your questions ready."

Chapter Thirty-One

Jake Whitaker spread his hands. "I really don't see how I can be of any more help to you."

By "you" he meant me, the person sitting in the client chair in front of his desk. Trey was standing off to the side. He and Whitaker had circled in that alpha male way, then ignored each other. Which had been fine with me. It meant that I had Whitaker's full attention.

"You neglected to mention you were at the Mardi Gras ball Tuesday night. Or that you visited Gabriella's the next day."

"I met her at the party and she was hot—what can I say? I still don't see what this has to do with Eliza."

Trey glanced our way. Sharply. I took note, but kept talking to Whitaker. "Did Eliza ever tell you why she liked hanging around at Beaumont parties?"

"Are you asking me about those rumors?"

I played dumb. "What rumors?"

He ignored the dumb. "Because if you are, I'll just put your mind at ease. I didn't start the rumors, I don't believe the rumors. I never saw them together that way."

"You're talking about her and Mark Beaumont?"

"Of course. What are you talking about?"

"There were rumors of a more illegal activity than fooling around with your married boss."

He leaned back. He was looking professional today—dark gray slacks, winter-white oxford shirt, muted red tie. He'd shaved, which made him look smarter and more wholesome, emphasizing that former quarterback thing he had going on.

"You mean drugs," he said.

I fixed him with a look. "Did you know she was using?"

"Sure."

"What about dealing?"

"I suspected so."

"So why didn't you tell us?"

"It wasn't any of your business. Had I had problems with her? Yes, especially recently. She was late a lot, she seemed unfocused and weird sometimes, and she and that redneck ex-boyfriend liked to argue in public. Did I see any reason to share this information with you? No."

"Did she seem to be getting any special attention from the Mark? Or Charley?"

"No."

Trey moved to stand in front of the photograph of the Beaumonts over the information table. Jake's eyes flicked in his direction and then back to me.

"Did you notice her paying them any special attention?" I said.

He swiveled in his chair. "She had stars in her eyes, maybe. I told her she was out of her league, but she didn't listen."

"So you have no idea why anybody would want her dead?"

"Are you asking in some cute way if I killed her?"

"Not a bad question. Did you?"

Now he was mad. "No, I didn't. I was meeting with the landscaping guy all day Friday. He verified it, ask the cops. Does that satisfy you?"

He wasn't looking at me when he said this—his eyes were focused just above my shoulder. Trey moved into my peripheral vision.

"I'm satisfied," he said. "You're not lying."

Whitaker took the comment in stride. "Nice to know I'm not a liar."

Trey shook his head. "I didn't say that."

◇◇◇

By now, the rain had intensified, and the breeze cut with a cold edge. We walked back to Trey's car, sharing his umbrella.

"Well," I said, "that wasn't helpful at all. I guess I thought he would let something slip, so we could call him on it and then he'd confess everything."

"Everything?"

"Hypothetical everything. Like in the movies." I sighed. "But if you say he wasn't lying…"

"He wasn't. But he was being evasive."

I stopped walking. "About what, which part?"

Trey shook his head. "Just generally evasive. Technically true—"

"—but deliberately evasive, yeah yeah, I know the drill. Do you think—"

"Stop."

"Stop what?"

"Stop talking."

He moved in face-to-face, inches between us. And the rain was pattering on the umbrella above us, and we were all alone beside the car, and I thought, omigod, he's gonna kiss me, right here, right now, and I couldn't decide whether or not to close my eyes.

"We're being watched," he said. "Don't look."

"Don't look where?"

"At the stand of trees by the mailboxes, a hundred feet behind you. There's a maroon Buick LeSabre with the engine running and a man in a gray sweatshirt standing beside it. It's William Perkins."

"Bulldog! But he's dead!"

"No, he's not."

"Are you sure?"

"I'm sure."

The urge to look was almost irresistible. "What do we do?"

"You get in the car and lock it." He pressed the Ferrari keys into my hand. "Do you have your phone?"

"Yes."

"Call 911—tell them what's happening." He handed me the umbrella. "Stay on the line. I'm going to keep an eye on him."

I started toward the Ferrari. But I couldn't help it—I looked—and when I did, the guy was staring right at me. He had the hood of his sweatshirt pulled down around his face, but he was Bulldog, without a doubt. Same small eyes, same round mouth, same little goatee. I froze, he froze, and then in a burst of motion, he made a mad dash for the maroon car.

Trey sprinted around to the driver's side of the Ferrari. He already had the engine running by the time I scrambled in.

"Give me the phone," he said.

I yanked at my seatbelt. "Screw the phone, just go!"

"I don't think—"

"That's Bulldog, Trey!"

"But—"

"Presumed dead, wanted killer—"

"I just—"

"Wanted killer, Trey!"

He slammed the car into first and accelerated with stunning velocity. Up ahead, Bulldog reached the Beau Elan exit. He plowed over the speedbumps and burst through the lowered arm of the security gate without hesitation. The Ferrari took the speedbumps painfully, then screamed onto the street, cutting off a pick-up and swinging into the far left lane.

I clutched the seat. "Are you sure you know what you're doing?"

"I assure you, I'm well-qualified—"

"Shit! Red light!" I closed my eyes and we slid through it. Horns honked behind us, brakes squealed. I opened my eyes. "That was not cool!"

Trey didn't reply, just kept his eyes straight ahead, his jaw set. He pressed a button on the console.

"What are you doing?"

"Calling Garrity."

Up ahead, the Buick did a shimmy at the next intersection and made a sudden left across traffic. Trey followed. In abrupt horror, I saw movement at the corner and realized that someone was about to step into the crosswalk.

I waved frantically. "Watch out! Old lady!"

We rocketed through the light, and I whirled to look behind us. "Shit! You hit an old lady!"

He glanced in the rearview mirror. "I did not. She just fainted."

The Buick tore up the street, the Ferrari right on its tail. Bulldog had no chance of outrunning us. His only hope was to lose us, and he seemed to think that lots of impulsive, dangerous turns across several lanes might be the key.

I caught the reading on the speedometer. "Omigod, slow down!"

"I could concentrate a lot better if you'd—"

"He's headed for the interstate!"

Trey yanked the wheel. I screamed again. I wanted to watch the road, but I couldn't tear my eyes from him. He kept his shoulders down, his hands easy at the wheel, but his eyes were narrowed and focused, like a wolf. I recognized the look.

"You're getting off on this!"

He exhaled sharply. "Perhaps."

"That is *not* the correct answer!"

"It's the adrenalin."

"I don't care what—"

I heard sirens behind us just as Garrity's voice came in over the speakers. "Hey, what's up?"

"I'm in vehicular pursuit," Trey said, eyes scanning the rearview mirror. "William Perkins."

"That's impossible!"

"Not impossible. Tai is supposed to be calling 911."

"School bus!" I screamed.

Trey snatched the wheel right and then left.

Garrity's voice ratcheted into panic. "Oh, sweet Jesus. Where are you?"

"Ashford Dunwoody Road, headed south toward 285. And I've got a tail." Trey's voice had an edge. "Can you help me, please?"

"Hold on."

We hit a bump. The glove compartment flew open, and a flurry of papers tumbled into my lap along with a set of rosary beads. Suddenly, a massive red bloom of brake lights materialized in front of us.

I grabbed his arm. "Road work!"

But Trey had already switched lanes and was downshifting so fast his hand seemed a blur. We slammed to a stop like we'd hit a wall.

Ahead of us, the Buick fishtailed, then slid sideways into the blocked lane, sending orange cones popping into the air. One police car swept past us, but another pulled in right behind. Bulldog scrambled from the car and took off into the chaos of the construction, two officers in pursuit.

Garrity's voice returned through the speakers. "Huge ticket, my friend. Quadruple digits. You might even be arrested."

But Trey wasn't really listening. He leaned back in the seat, closed his eyes. Then he exhaled slow and deep.

"Want a cigarette?" I said.

The officer behind us got out of his car and came to the window. Trey lowered it.

It was a young guy, one of those corn-fed, earnest rookies. Surprisingly, he didn't have his gun drawn, but his hand did hover nervously at his side. He bent and looked inside.

He smiled real politely. "Hey there, Mr. Seaver."

Trey cocked his head. "Did I know you?"

"No. Dispatch gave us the ID."

Garrity, I thought.

Trey motioned toward the glove compartment. "License and registration?"

The cop seemed apologetic. "Yes, sir. I guess so, sir."

Chapter Thirty-Two

So he did get a ticket, a massive one, and we did have to go to the station. Garrity's station. He met us at the door. He did not look happy.

"I'm going to do what I can about this," he said. "In the meantime, in my office, both of you."

Trey immediately complied. I hung back a little. "Go easy on him."

Garrity stared at me. "Don't worry about him, my friend. It's you that needs to worry."

"Me? What did I do?"

Garrity just pointed. "Now."

His office was tiny and cramped, his desk a landscape of papers and envelopes. Trey stood by the window, watching the parking lot. I moved to the desk. There were only two pictures on it. One was a studio portrait of a smiling toddler wearing a Braves hat. The other was a candid shot. I picked it up.

In it, Trey was smiling for the camera, his mouth open like he was either laughing or about to say something. He was wearing a distressed leather jacket and a dark green Izod shirt, and his hair fell over his forehead, messy and long on top. Garrity stood to his right—they had their arms around each other's shoulders. I imagined beer and peanuts, a house band playing eighties cover.

Trey saw what I was holding. "You remember this?" I said.

He shook his head. "No."

I put the photo back on Garrity's desk. "I think I would have liked you."

"I think I would have liked me too."

Just then Garrity came in. His voice was clipped. "Trey, you wait out front." Then he looked straight at me, and I didn't like the look one bit.

"This won't take long," he said.

I sat opposite the desk. Garrity, however, remained standing, propped against a file cabinet. I couldn't stand the suspense.

"Did they catch him?"

"They caught him."

"Good, I can't wait to hear—"

"You just had to say 'wanted killer,' didn't you?"

I spread my hands. "It was Bulldog! You know, Bulldog, presumed dead, murder suspect?"

"Which was all the more reason to let the cops handle it."

"What cops? We were all alone!"

He wasn't listening. "It wasn't worth the risk."

"Oh, please, Trey's a crackerjack behind the wheel."

"Yeah, well, it didn't help him last time, did it?"

"That's bullshit!" I shook my head. "Trey is not some invalid—"

"Who are you to be telling me what he's like? I've known him for ten years, you've known him, what? A week?"

For some reason, this infuriated me. "You're just mad because you don't know him anymore, and you're wondering if maybe you never did."

Garrity stared at me. His voice was calm. "Trey was in a coma for five days, on a respirator for most of them. Catheter, feeding tube, the whole nine yards. People came, and then they left. Real quick."

I saw tears, hard ones, like diamonds. "I'm sorry, I didn't mean—"

"But I was there every single day. And I made deals with God—bring him back and I'll stop smoking. Don't let him die and I'll give ten percent to the church. You find God real quick in ICU, let me tell you."

He blinked, and the tears disappeared. "The only thing is, I don't know if my prayers were answered or not, because he didn't die, but he sure as hell didn't come back."

He was waiting for me to argue, and I started to say something, then decided I had no right. So I got up and walked out. I paused at the threshold. "I'm sorry. So sorry."

He didn't reply, so I headed for the lobby to find Trey, closing the door softly behind me.

Marisa was waiting for us back at Phoenix. She wasted no time on small talk. "Agent Davidson with the GBI needs copies of the revised TSCM plan ASAP. He's in your office. I didn't tell him that you were busy being booked and printed."

Trey didn't flinch. "I was not."

She held up her hand. "Whatever. Revamp them based on the new data sheets and get them to him, and me. You've got a meeting with Landon at four today. And I need a 302 on this morning's little adventure before you leave."

"Of course."

Then she turned to me. The hairs on the back of my neck stood up.

"The same goes for you. Get a report to Trey by three-thirty, follow the 302 format."

"The what?"

"Three-oh-two. You're supposedly good at research—look it up. I've cleared space in the secondary area for you. And you need to return calls from Jake Whitaker—he's still can't find your number and left two voice mails for you here."

I knew Nikki was to blame for the missing phone number, but I didn't say anything about that. "I'm on it."

She waved Trey toward the elevators. "Get to work. If you're done playing Thelma to her Louise, that is."

Trey obliged. Marisa watched him go—for a moment I caught the slippage of the mask, the taut white fear at the corner of her eyes, underneath more layers of foundation that I cared to count. Then she turned smoothly and headed for her office. Even in heels, she moved with an invisible book on her head.

◇◇◇

Secondary area, as it turned out, meant surplus room. I flopped in the chair, this faux leather number, and inspected my temporary headquarters—eight by eight, no window, one bleak spare desk. On the plus side, it did have a working computer with external Internet access—Phoenix's intraoffice system was off limits, however. I started to pull up my e-mail, then hesitated. I picked up the phone instead.

Rico wasn't answering—again—so I left a message. "Bring lunch, whatever you want, my treat. Just one little favor in return."

I told him what I wanted and then tried Eric. More voice mail. So I called Jake Whitaker, who was practically apoplectic with anxiety.

"I heard what happened this morning—that Bulldog person was here."

"Apparently so."

"I thought he was dead."

"Apparently not."

"The cops said he was trying to get into Eliza's apartment." A nervous silence. "You don't think he was after me, do you?"

Not the question I expected. "Why would he be after you?"

"Because he thinks I know something."

"Do you?"

"No! But who knows what that lunatic's thinking."

I tried to sound soothing, but Whitaker was having none of it. I promised I'd let him know something as soon as there was anything to know, but that didn't mollify him and he hung up abruptly.

Okay, I thought, that was interesting. Why in the world would Whitaker think Bulldog might be after him? Before I could figure out that puzzle, however, my phone rang.

It was Garrity. "Look, what I meant to say was, be careful. Please. And then I meant to say that I was glad you were working with him, at some point that should have been in the conversation."

"Before or after you lectured me?"

"Probably before. Listen, you have to be careful. You say stuff like 'wanted killer' and every damn rule goes bam, right out the window."

"But it was an emergency!"

"No, arterial bleeding is an emergency, not chasing down suspects. And you don't want Trey breaking his rules for anything less, trust me." A pause. "So do you want to hear what they got from Bulldog or not?"

"Let me grab a pen."

His story was short, but oh, was it interesting. Eliza had called him a month or so ago, wanting some pot, a little meth. He'd ponied the stuff right up, and—he'd admitted—moved to Atlanta where he tried to renew the romantic relationship. She kept putting him off, which just made him more persistent. This was why he'd been following her the Wednesday she went to Eric's house, why he'd followed her back to her place. Only she'd refused to talk to him.

"Big surprise there," I said.

"Yeah, well, Bulldog saw her talking to your brother and freaked. He admitted that he got loud, maybe a little rough with the hands."

"The fight that Jake Whitaker heard."

"Right. He denies being the one to play rough with her the night of Mardi Gras, though. He said she had the bruises when he saw her."

"You believe him?"

"No. Anyway, Eliza threatened to call the cops, so he left the premises. Sort of. His idea of leaving the premises was to hang around the gate waiting for her to appear again."

"No wonder she didn't go meet Eric for dinner. There was a nutcase outside."

"Yeah, that'll put a damper on your social life."

"But psychotic or not, his version of events makes sense."

"Oh, yes," Garrity agreed. "Lots of sense. Only one problem—they found her purse in the floorboard of his truck, everything in it but the cash, along with what's looking like the murder weapon."

I almost dropped the phone. "Get out!"

"Nope. Thirty-eight revolver. Some blood on it—still waiting for the DNA on that, but it's her type, and it's consistent with the bullet they pulled from her skull, according to the ME anyway. No fingerprints though. Looks like someone wiped it."

"Who's it registered to?"

"Nobody. It's a throwaway."

"So is he admitting anything?"

"No, but he'll crack soon enough. He's too stupid to maintain a story for long."

"He was smart enough to keep from being blown up," I reminded him.

Garrity made a noise. "Lucky enough, you mean. He'd stepped across the street to get some beer and cigarettes when the place went up. Stupid people shouldn't mess with meth—they incinerate themselves eventually."

"Any chance it was deliberate?"

"Interesting you should say that. Bulldog's claiming that he's being framed and that the explosion was a deliberate attempt on his life."

"Is that possible?"

"Sure. Blowing up a meth lab is cake—a second grader could do it. Plus the gun is the alleged weapon until the forensics come back. No matter—he's denying any knowledge of how it got in his truck."

"Just like he's denying killing her?"

"Just like. And just like he's denying having anything to do with you either, not the break-in, not the threatening pictures. Says he doesn't even know who you are."

So much for my prime suspect. From the looks of things, I had plenty more to choose from, however. "Do the Beaumonts know about this development?"

"Chances are good they're gearing up for a press conference as we speak."

"Maybe not."

Then I told him about Mark Beaumont's decision to downplay things for a while. I also mentioned that Trey had been drafted for Senator Adams' reception that weekend in an effort to keep it as low-key as possible while still maximizing the its political potential.

I looked up to see Rico standing in my doorway, waving a Varsity takeout box. I motioned him inside.

"But if they're pinning this on Bulldog, then my back-stage pass is about to expire. I'm only good as long as the case is unsolved."

Garrity took a beat. "I meant what I said earlier. Be careful with Trey."

Suddenly, I knew what it was that was constantly zipping between them. I'd thought it was some man thing, but it wasn't. It was fraternal, yes, but more like a big-brother-little-brother relationship. And Garrity was the big brother—protective, anxious, always trying to hide it.

"I'll be very careful," I promised, "but it's a moot point. Marisa's got him desk-bound."

"Not surprised. But you know what? It's nice to know he's still got a little vroom-vroom in him."

"The Iceman Melteth."

"Maybe. Just maybe."

Chapter Thirty-Three

Rico placed a bag on my desk. "Nice suit."

I preened for him. "You like? It came in real handy during the morning car chase and my subsequent trip downtown. My third."

He laughed. Then he stopped laughing. "You're serious?"

"As the proverbial heart attack. And speaking of…" I peered into the bag. "All right, chili dogs."

So we sat in the secondary room, and I filled him in on my morning. He ate delicately, fastidiously even, whereas I managed to blop ketchup on my pants. I papered myself with napkins and kept eating.

"Where's Hot Guy?" Rico said.

I licked my lips. "Grounded, like me."

"No wonder you're in a hurry with this little project." He pulled a portable drive from his pocket. "All the people you don't trust are tied up somewhere else."

"Don't be ridiculous. I trust Trey."

Rico looked surprised. "That's new."

"I guess it is. But it's true." I licked my fingers. "Did you bring the program?"

"So now we change the subject. Yes, I've got it." Rico bellied up to my computer. "I've got to be at Lakewood in two hours. Some of us do more than tool around in Ferraris for a living."

I smiled. Then I rolled my chair beside him and peered over his shoulder as he got to work. "You know the club scene, right?"

"Sure."

"How's Dylan Flint fit into it?"

Rico kept his eyes on the screen. "I see him a lot, especially at the new places, usually riding somebody else's coattails past the velvet rope. But he's popular—that sex tape thing is serious juice."

"Any idea why he'd be hanging around the Beaumonts? Or a place like Phoenix?"

"Looking for dirt. Remember when Bobby Brown got arrested at the steak place over in Dekalb? The next day pictures are all over the place, including Dylan's trifling little blog."

"Yeah, well, I'm on the trifling little blog now."

"Doing what?"

"Tooling around in a Ferrari. I don't get it, Rico. Why in the world would he try to be a real photographer on the one hand and mess around with crap like that on the other?"

"Because it means he's in. He's in because he notices you and you're in because you're noticed—I deal with this shit all the time." He sucked in a long slow breath. "It's crack is what it is. Messes up your head."

I kept thinking about the glimpse of myself on Dylan's website. I did look exotic through the window of a Ferrari, sunglassed and untouchable. More fascinating than I really was, mysterious even. Rico read my thoughts.

"Don't go getting all up in that, girlfriend. It's poison." Then he looked at the rest of the photographs spread out on the table. He tapped the one of Eliza. "That the dead girl?"

"That's her."

"Who's everybody else?"

"Eric you know. That's Senator Adams and a bunch of his friends. Eliza, with Nikki from the other night, and Trey, once again in Hot Guy mode. And that's Gabriella, massage therapist to the stars."

I looked at Trey's face, at Gabriella's. His expression was utterly neutral. But in her dressing room, I'd seen something shifting between them. Tectonics at work, I suspected, deep buried things.

Rico frowned. "Do you think they're a couple?"

I sighed. "I have no idea. I haven't asked him. It's not like we're dating—or any other 'ing' words for that matter, so—"

"Not Hot Guy. Them."

He tapped the photograph. Eliza and Nikki. And it all suddenly fell into place.

"Omigod, you really think so?"

"It's pretty obvious."

"But nobody's said anything!"

"Nobody would. This Eliza girl gets shot to death and dumped in a driveway, the collective antennae go up, you know what I'm saying?"

I knew what he was saying. "But why stay in the closet in Atlanta? This place is almost as out as San Francisco."

Rico shrugged. "If I worked for someone like Mark Beaumont, Mr. Family Values Conservative himself, I'd sure keep it on the QT. Hell, yeah, I would."

I thought of Janie and her crucifix, the way her fingers sought it, toyed with it. There were lots of reasons to keep such things to yourself besides employment.

"Do you think the cops know?" I said.

"Maybe yes, maybe no. Either way, I'm thinking there's a lot of stuff that a lot of people aren't telling. This computer's clean, by the way."

A happy green light was flashing on the screen. Rico's program had found nothing suspicious—no viruses, no worms, no key loggers, nothing that would allow someone to creep in when I wasn't paying attention.

"So nobody's spying on me?"

"Nobody at all."

"So I was being paranoid?"

He grinned. "You know what they say about paranoia. But nobody's snooping on this particular computer. It's safe. I'll check the one at Dexter's shop the next time I'm there. Assuming you've taken that racist piece of rag down."

"No more Confederate flag. I promise."

Rico finished up quickly after that, and I walked him to his car. When we reached it, he turned and looked at me seriously, which was an unusual expression for him.

"You be careful. There are people out there who don't play, you know what I'm saying?"

I didn't reply for a moment. Then I stood on tiptoe and kissed his cheek. "You be careful too, Rico."

He looked at me for a long second, then the gravity melted from his face. He made a fist and punched it at my chest, fast, like a snake striking. I put my hands up and smacked it away.

He grinned. "Look at you, getting all dangerous and shit."

Chapter Thirty-Four

The first thing I did was try Dylan Flint at his Snoopshot's number, but he wasn't answering—again. I left a message asking him to please get in touch with me, then spent the rest of the afternoon with a bunch of manila folders and a note pad. And it gave me a lot to think about.

If Eliza was lesbian, she'd been hiding it, which meant she thought it was something to hide. Which put a whole new spin on Jake Whitaker's comments. Was this the reason he didn't believe the rumors about her and Mark? Was that what he'd been being "technically true but deliberately evasive" about? It made sense, especially considering some of the things Nikki had said about him, like how Eliza had caught him peeping into windows.

Still, I knew that people were too complicated to jam into rigid sexual categories. Even Rico had had a girlfriend once, back when we were in high school, when he was still Richard Worthington and I was still…confused.

I smiled at the memory. I'd learned a lot since then. Of course, none of that mattered. I needed smarts beyond what I'd gotten in Sex Ed 101 to explain Eliza. I didn't have time to ponder the possibilities, however. It was two-thirty, and I had a 302 to complete.

Whatever the hell that was.

◇◇◇

Trey showed up in the copy room an hour later, 302 report in hand. I had just slipped mine into the feeder, and the copy machine was humming itself to life. I hopped onto a work table. "Got a quick question for you, Mr. Seaver. Did you know Eliza was lesbian?"

"No." Trey's expression sharpened. "Do you know that?"

"It's a theory at this point."

The machine coughed and clunked to a stop. Trey knelt and opened the doors to find about seven million little lights blinking at him. He started turning knobs and rollers, threading his fingers into dark hot metal places.

"A theory requires evidence."

"I'm getting to that. But first things first—Garrity called."

"I know." He pulled out a mangled, blackened piece of paper and handed it to me. "He called me first."

I threw the paper in the trash. "Then you know that story. Factor in this—I called Whitaker. He said that the police told him that Bulldog was trying to break into Eliza's apartment."

Trey fished the paper out of the trash and put it in the recycling box. "Had broken into. He was hoping to retrieve the drugs he'd sold Eliza, but he couldn't find them."

I snorted. "Did it not occur to him that the police would have confiscated any drugs when they searched the place?"

"He thought she might have hidden them well enough that the police had missed them."

"Had they?"

"No."

I put a hand on his elbow. He looked at it, then looked at me. "This lesbian thing is a big deal, Trey. A very big deal."

"If it's true."

"I know of only one way to find out."

The copy machine whirred and spat out my report, along with its duplicate. Trey fed his in next. I was expecting it to wheeze and rattle, but the contraption practically purred as it got to work.

"And that would be?" he said.

"We need to talk to Eliza's friend Nikki. I think they were lovers."

Trey shook his head, but I interrupted whatever he was about to say.

"Just come with me and talk to her, okay? Call it personal protection, call it whatever you have to, but I need you there to tell me if she's telling the truth."

"I'm in a meeting until six."

"When you're done then. I'll go back to the shop, change into something less corporate agency, then pick you up on the way."

He collected his report from the tray and tucked it into a file folder. I noticed that it already had a label on it, neatly typed.

"Look," I said. "Even if you don't come along, I'm just going to do it anyway, and then who knows what will happen. You might end up bailing me out of jail tonight. Or worse. I mean, I'm not an idiot, but I'm no investigator either."

"Fine. I'll do it. You've made a compelling case that you're in need of professional supervision. But we're doing this on my terms."

"Okay."

"We stay together at all times."

"Okay."

"My role is not investigatory—I am there as your personal protection as per the original contract extension, not as an official representative of Phoenix."

"Okay."

"And whatever we learn remains confidential until the proper paperwork has been processed. Is that clear?"

"As a bell." I extended my hand. He shook it solemnly.

"I'll pick you up at the shop," he said. "Stay in the suit."

At Boomers, the first of the after-work crowd had reported for action—ties loosened, inhibitions too, oiled by the two-for-one drink specials. Boomers was kind enough to keep its website up-to-date with the dancers' performance schedules, and I'd noticed that Nikki was due to go on stage in an hour. Only she was using her professional name—Sinnamon.

Trey flashed his ID, and the bouncer called back to see if she'd see us. We then had to go through the strip club den mother, who seemed even less enthusiastic than the bouncer. But in the end, Nikki said we could come on back.

We found her in a crowded dressing room putting on her stage make-up. She sported a platinum wig, plus fishnet hose, five-inch heels, and a tiny white blouse and seersucker skirt.

"You got something to tell me?" she said.

Trey stood politely at my side, hands folded. All around us, half-naked women pulled on thongs and shimmied into break-away tops. He didn't even glance their way.

"I was hoping you had something to tell me," I replied.

"Like what?"

"Like how you and Eliza were lovers."

She reached for a bottle of water and unscrewed the cap, her expression unchanging. Trey studied her, his eyes focused on her mouth. She didn't acknowledge his attention.

"None of your damn business," she said.

She turned her back on us and went back to applying her make-up. The dressing room was a buzzy cacophony of female sounds and thumping bass from the stage. I met her eyes in the mirror.

"You were at the party with her, the Mardi Gras Ball."

Another shrug. "So? I told you we went to those things."

"You didn't mention this specific one, which makes me curious, especially since Dylan was there too, taking pictures of you and Eliza and the Beaumonts. What were they up to?"

"I told you, I don't know. We got into a fight, and she left with him."

"What was the fight about?"

"She kept dragging me around the room, following the Beaumonts around. She said she wanted pictures with them and wanted me in them, too. I told her that was stupid, she told me I was stupid, and I told her if she liked those people so much, she could get them to take her home."

Nikki stroked mascara on in thick swipes. Her eyes grew darker and more recessed the more she talked.

"Why didn't you tell anybody about the two of you?"

"What the fuck good would that have done? It wasn't like they were ever gonna make her one of them. She was redneck white trash. That's all she was and all she was ever gonna be."

"Was that why she was so infatuated with Charley, because she used to be white trash too? Did she think that would make her sympathetic?"

"Give me a break. Neither of them had nothing to do with her. She thought they shit gold, though. Everything she wanted to be."

She stood up then. She was an Amazon. Impenetrable.

"You think Eliza would be dead if she was some rich woman like Charley Beaumont? She was broke, and she was a nobody, and the only thing she had going for her was that she was white, and I ain't got that. And you wonder why I ain't told anybody about me and her?"

She pushed past me to leave. Trey had been standing there silent the whole time. She looked up at him. "You got any questions, Mr. Suit and Tie?"

Trey cocked his head. "Did Eliza's sister know about your relationship?"

Nikki cocked her head back. "Yeah."

"How did she feel about that?"

"That tight-assed bitch?" Nikki made a noise of disgust. "She told me I was gonna burn in hell, and Eliza with me. That's what she thought about that."

The ride back to Kennesaw was rather subdued. Trey didn't speak and neither did I. I just watched the city roll by, the procession of organic food shops and cigar emporiums and adult movie stores. And always the road work, the perpetual bustle, the endless growing pains of a city forever too big for its britches.

I gathered my things. "So this turned out to be a successful trip, right?"

"My role was to keep you safe. I accomplished that."

I didn't argue. He liked proper categories, naming things. I found that I appreciated it too. It kept me honest. Mostly.

"We make a good team, me and you," I said.

"We're a team?"

I thought about that. "Yeah. A team."

"Okay."

I looked over at him, sitting there all neat and polite and—it hit me with a pang—so singular, so alone with all he was and all he could never be. I felt a keen sensation of loss, almost familiar now, and I suddenly wanted more than anything to hug him, and if he'd been anybody else in the world, I would have done it.

But he was Trey. And he was separated from me by a gulf far wider than a few feet of leather upholstery. I watched him drive away and thought of empty spaces.

But I also thought of bridges.

Chapter Thirty-Five

The next morning, I woke up with a stiff back and a stuffed-up head. The photograph of Uncle Dexter looked spiteful in the half-light, like he knew I was taking down his Stars and Bars.

I was feeling conflicted. Not out of any Confederate loyalty—I didn't much like the thing myself. But taking it down felt like an insult to Dexter, not unlike the way Atlanta had razed what antebellum architecture the Yankees hadn't burned to a cinder, erecting in its place a post-modern skyline, gleaming and reflecting, a city of mirrors. Atlanta called itself the city too busy to hate. It was a heady fiction.

"Sorry, Dexter—it has to go," I told him, and rubbed the ache out of my neck.

But it would wait. I had other things to attend to first, namely cleaning myself up and hauling it to Phoenix. So I dressed rapidly and closed the shop, setting every alarm Trey had showed me. The late morning sky loomed low and gray, like a ceiling of dirty ice, and I shivered as I walked to my car. Please, I thought, let this day be easy.

It was not to be. Standing square in my path was Dylan Flint, spiked hair and all. He yanked off his sunglasses. "You're gonna pay for this!"

"For what?"

"You know what! You think you trash my place, I'm gonna get scared and back down? I'm not afraid of you or your boyfriend."

He'd moved in close, and I realized for the first time how very young he was, barely twenty. His pale face popped with cold sweat, and he looked like he hadn't slept, hadn't bathed, hadn't even changed clothes in a while.

"I have no idea what you're talking about."

Passersby stared and kept walking. I tried to sound patient and logical, but fear cracked my voice. This guy was a wing nut of the first order, and I was mostly alone with him, with all my guns locked up in the shop. And he was infuriated.

"That's bullshit! I heard the message you left. You were checking to see if I was there so you could break in!"

"If I had been going to break in, do you think I would have left a message?"

"I know what I know! And I don't need pictures to prove it!"

"Prove what?"

He sneered. "Maybe you should talk to your boyfriend, ask him what he's been doing hanging around with Charley Beaumont when her husband's out of town."

"You mean Trey?" I took a deep breath. "He's not my boyfriend—and she's his client." Then it hit me. "Is that why you were following us around Saturday? You thought I was the other woman?"

The sneer twisted, and he laughed. "Stupid lying bitch."

And that did it. I gripped my tote bag tighter and widened my stance. What was it Trey had said to his class? Balance was my greatest strength. I felt it suddenly, the sturdiness that comes from standing on two feet, owning your space.

"Look, you moron, I don't know why you're here, but I know one thing—you're in big trouble."

"You don't know shit!"

"I know you kept Eliza around so she'd score drugs for you. You got the shakes, dude."

He wiped his nose with the back of his hand. There was a folder in my tote bag that described the signs of meth addiction—agitation, paranoia, rage. He was a veritable poster boy.

"Is that how she paid you off for showing up and taking pictures at the Mardi Gras party? A few hits of this or that?"

"The cops want to talk to me," he said. "And I'm thinking of doing it."

"Why? What was so hot about those photographs you took?"

He clammed up again and stared at me with this smug look, but fear twitched behind the bravado. Dumb, simple fear.

I shook my head. "You have no clue, do you? All you knew was she could get you some attention from the Beaumonts, maybe throw some dope in the mix. Good times. You make up all kinds of rumors—Charley and Trey, Mark and Eliza, me and God knows who—and hope something will stick so somebody will pay."

"You just keep thinking that."

"Why'd you bust out the parking garage cameras at Phoenix on Thursday?"

"What?" His mouth twisted. "I didn't do that!"

"Trey saw you there that morning, don't deny it."

"I was just taking pictures!"

"That's all you've been up to, huh? You haven't been hanging around here, have you? Tossing a few bricks? Slipping a few threats under the door?"

He started to say something, then clammed up. "I ain't gotta tell you a goddamned thing, bitch!"

That did it. "Listen to me, you moron, and listen good. You may not realize how deeply over your head you are, but I do, and I am telling you, getting your photographs nicked is the least of your worries. Whatever it was Eliza was involved in, somebody killed her to shut her up."

"If anybody needs to shut up, it's you."

"Are you threatening me?"

"Just layin' it on the line."

He stepped forward as he said this. I held my ground. His hand went into my face, and I smacked it away, hard. His sunglasses went flying, and he curled his fingers into a fist...

And then he froze.

"Is there a problem?" Trey said.

I jumped as Trey moved to stand beside me. He was in full corporate agent mode and looked calm, but he exuded hazard the way that knives did, on a purely visceral level.

Dylan didn't back away. "What's the matter, girlie, can't fight your own battles?"

I suddenly want to yank off his arm and beat him to death with it. "Back up, Trey. You don't want to get blood on that Armani."

Trey didn't budge, of course, but then, he didn't need to. Dylan was already backing down. "I'm talking to the cops. And then you'll be sorry, all of you!"

He jabbed a finger at us, one last pathetic attempt at menace, then disappeared around the corner. I picked up his sunglasses and examined them. Tommy Hilfiger. Nice. I pocketed them and turned to Trey.

"Where did you come from? I don't see the Ferrari."

He nodded toward a gray sedan parked across the street. "Company car. I'll be working at Lake Oconee most of the day, and Marisa insisted I take it."

"Was she being generous or does this have something to do with the car chase yesterday?"

"The latter, I suspect."

Now that the confrontation was over, I was shaking from the adrenalin spike and plummet. I steadied myself, but Trey noticed. He extended a hand, then just as quickly retracted it.

"Are you okay? Perhaps you should—"

"I'm fine."

And I was. Mostly. There had been a shift during the confrontation, a moment when I'd felt aggressively powerful, but calm. Now I was cold—the wind had kicked up and the clouds had clotted and lowered. But I remembered that feeling.

"Dylan was seriously pissed about a break-in. You know what he's talking about?"

"There was a burglary at his studio—his photographic and video equipment were taken, photographs and videos too. His computer was destroyed, but not before someone hacked his website and deleted it."

"He mentioned having photos of Charley Beaumont." I took a beat. "And you."

Trey looked puzzled. "She's a client. Of course there are photographs of us together. Why would he mention that?"

"Because he thought he had photos of Charley Beaumont and her illicit lover."

It took Trey a moment to make the connection. "But we're not lovers."

He said it so easily, with such disarming confusion, that I wanted to believe him. Could a human lie detector spin a falsehood as easily as he could spot one?

My next question was even more delicate. "Phoenix did this, didn't they?"

Trey didn't reply. But his index finger started a restless tap-tap-tap on his thigh.

"Come on, Trey. Did Phoenix trash that boy's place and steal his stuff so that he'd stop making trouble for the Beaumonts?"

"The Beaumonts are our clients."

"That doesn't answer the question. Is Phoenix responsible for this?"

"You could ask Landon. He'll give you the same answer he gave me."

"Which was?"

"Of course not."

"Was he lying?"

Trey looked directly at me. "Landon is usually lying about something. It's part of his job."

He turned abruptly and started across the street. I followed after him. "Dylan also admitted he was at Phoenix on Thursday, when the cameras were busted out, but denies doing it. Likewise on busting out my camera and planting the threats."

Trey opened the door to the sedan. He was avoiding my eyes. "I'll be in-field for the rest of the day. Call me if you need me."

I put a hand out as he went to get in, and he froze, my hand on his midsection.

"What were you doing here?" I said.

"Dylan came looking for you at Phoenix. It made sense that this would be his next stop." He finally looked directly at me. "Please be careful. Even though Perkins has been caught, it's still dangerous."

I removed my hand. "You worried old Dylan will get me in some dark alley?"

"No, I'm almost certain this will be the last we hear of Dylan Flint. But I'm afraid he's not our only concern."

"What do you mean?"

"I mean that I'm apprehensive, and I don't know why. And I usually do." He got into the car. "Marisa told me that Janie has asked to see you. Please call me later and tell me what she said. And Tai…"

It was the first time he'd ever called me by name. "Yes?"

"I meant it. Be careful."

I finished my emergency cigarette in the Phoenix parking garage, brushed my hair, and got ready to face Yvonne. To my surprise, she smiled as I walked to the front desk.

"You have to wait here," she said.

"But Janie asked me to come, I'm supposed to—"

And then Landon walked out of the conference room. He was smiling too. My stomach sank.

"You just missed Janie," he said. "She went to the hotel to pack. Now that her sister's killer is behind bars, she going back to South Carolina."

I shouldered my bag and turned to leave. Landon glided into my path.

"Not so fast. I heard you had a run-in with Dylan Flint."

"I heard you did too, or so Dylan seems to think."

A flicker of surprise rode across his eyes, but he covered it, quick. "I don't care what he thinks, and neither does anybody else."

"Somebody cared enough to trash his place."

Landon tsk-tsked. "It's a crime-ridden world out there."

"Which makes it so great that Phoenix is there to protect and serve." I delivered this morsel with a thick coating of sarcasm, but Landon didn't bite. His smile deepened, which further unnerved me.

"Now that justice has been served and Janie is returning home, your services are no longer required. We'll have the paperwork ready for you tomorrow, along with a check from the Beaumonts, a final thank-you."

I didn't move. He swept a hand toward the doors. "Go home. And don't even think about running to Marisa. After I told her you dragged Trey to Boomers last night, she finally decided you're more trouble than you're worth, no matter what Eric says."

I stared at him. He tsk-tsked.

"Of course I know about your little adventure—Trey submitted a 302 on it this morning. Filed it under personal protection."

Of course he did. I fumed, but said nothing.

Landon continued. "So Marisa terminated your personal protection order as well. Case closed."

"That's debatable."

"Maybe. But this isn't. You have to leave now. Come back tomorrow morning for your termination package."

"Keep it," I said, and turned to go.

"Not so fast." Landon held out his hand. "Your ID."

"I lost the cheap piece of crap. Stick that in your termination package."

Chapter Thirty-Six

I found Janie in her room at the Ritz, a twin of the one I'd abandoned for Dexter's pull-out. She invited me in absent-mindedly, and went back to the half-filled suitcase flopped open on the bed. Outside I heard sirens, an ambulance, a police car. The sounds of someone else's day gone suddenly bad.

"I just got back from Phoenix," I said. "Landon told me you're leaving."

Janie laid a white blouse in the suitcase. "They've released the body, so we can take her home now."

"That must be a relief."

"Yeah. We've just got to finish up here, and then we can get started with the arrangements." She looked at the clothes-strewn bed, then back at me. "I appreciate all you've done, though, over the past few days."

"I didn't do much."

"You listened, that was a lot. But it's over now, and the best we can do is get back to normal."

She was right, of course. But there was so much still unanswered, unhonored, unspoken. I sat on the edge of the bed. The room smelled of old coffee and fresh laundry, but a hint of smoke was in there too—I saw an ashtray by the bed, overflowing with butts. My fingers twitched.

"Janie, this may seem like it's coming out of nowhere, and I hate to pry into something so personal, but…" I steadied my voice. "Did you know your sister was a lesbian?"

Her eyes darkened and got hard in the center. "That's not something we're gonna talk about."

"But—"

"No buts." Her voice hardened to match her eyes. "My sister was murdered, and the man who did it is in jail. That's justice, and I'm grateful for it. The rest is between her and God."

"Is that what you two fought about?"

She shook her head. "Eliza's dead, and all that died with her. I don't care what questions you want to ask, I'm taking her home now, and we're going to do the best we can with the life she lived. It wasn't much, but she was family, flesh and blood, and that's what family does for family."

"But I'm not convinced Bulldog did it."

"I am. Eliza spent her whole life chasing some fantasy that she was better than who she was. You chase something long enough, you forget something might be chasing you. Eliza paid for that mistake with her life."

Her face was taut with emotion, her fists clenched so hard her knuckles whitened. Whatever parts of her had loosened over the last few days had tightened up again, and she wasn't about to drop her guard, not for me, not for anybody.

I stood. "I'm sorry, Janie. I appreciate everything you shared with me. I wish I could have done more with it."

Her mouth stayed hard, but her eyes relaxed, just at the corners. She reached up and fingered the ever-present crucifix.

"You did the best you could. That's worth something."

I left quickly, too heartsick to argue with her. RIP Eliza Compton. Daughter, sister, friend, co-worker. Murder victim, former thief, closet lesbian, possible blackmailer.

God, why do we even bother with tombstones? It's not like we don't lie enough without them.

My second stop was back at Beau Elan to find Jake Whitaker—I had a couple of questions for the antsy bastard before he got word that I was no longer legit. Despite what I'd told Landon,

I still had my Phoenix ID. One flash of the plastic at the front gate, and the security guard let me in without a quibble.

Inside Jake's office, the first thing I noticed was that Jake himself was gone. In his place, a young woman with a planed, no-nonsense expression and black bunned hair stood behind his desk. I recognized her as one of Mark Beaumont's staff.

She frowned at my ID badge. "I thought they were sending Mr. Seaver?"

That's when I noticed that everything on Jake's desk had been piled into two boxes. The woman stared at me, slightly puzzled but not alarmed.

I smiled. "He got tied up in a meeting, last minute stuff. He sent me instead."

"Fine, then. Here." She handed over a small box. "This is the back-up footage I found. I don't know why Mr. Whitaker had it in his desk. The originals are with the police, and you already have the archives at Phoenix."

I accepted it with a smile. "It's a mystery."

And then she handed me another box, this one sealed with duct tape. Her lips curled with distaste. "I wanted to throw this away, but Mr. Beaumont said to turn it over to you people. So here. Get rid of it."

I smiled again, broad and reassuring. "Don't worry. I'll take care of everything."

◇◇◇

I tried to call Trey, but got his voice mail, which meant that he was still in his meeting. I left him a rambling message. "Listen, Trey? Call me back as soon as you get this. Nothing's wrong, but I have to talk to you ASAP. I've kinda…crap, just call me, okay?"

I decided voicemail was not the way to mention my recent termination. Ditto on the contraband materials from Jake's desk. Driving out of Beau Elan with the illicit boxes sitting next to me was an exercise in patience. Had Jake been fired? Reassigned? And what kind of surveillance footage did he have hidden in his desk? I knew that the main records had been turned over to the police, the back-ups to Phoenix. What in the world would Jake be keeping just for himself?

My fingers itched to pry it open, even if I knew Trey would kill me in some hideous SWAT-intensive manner if I did.

So I called Rico. "Do you know where can I find someone— someone discreet—who can unplex some security footage?"

Rico sent me to his friend Doug at the Buckhead branch of the Fulton County Library. As its media specialist, Doug had studied at Dartmouth on their digital antiforgery project, and he had a treasure trove of sneaky smart software at his fingertips. According to Rico, he also possessed a strong subversive streak, and would be glad to help me sock it to The Man.

Doug sported mouse-brown bangs and sharp blue eyes intensified by black-rimmed hipster glasses. His voice was soft, and his eyes darted around a lot.

"Wait here," he said.

I handed over the DVDs. While he got his geek on, I found an empty study carrel. And I sat there, me and my illicit boxes and a tote bag crammed thick as underbrush with file folders. I'd been ditched by Janie, fired by Phoenix, yelled at by Garrity, deserted by Eric. And when Trey found out about my latest subterfuge…

I stared at the sealed box. Then I went to Doug's desk and borrowed a pair of scissors. If I was going to be lectured, it might as well be for the whole shebang.

I ran the blade along the flap and opened the box. And then I did a doubletake. "Oh my god."

My phone rang before I could examine the contents further. It was Trey.

"I got your message," he said. "What's the problem?"

"I'd rather explain in person."

"I can meet you at Phoenix."

I slammed the lid shut and shoved the box away. "This is not a Phoenix conversation."

"In that case, I'll be in Atlanta in an hour. I have to stop by Beau Elan first, but—"

"I'm thinking you don't."

"What?"

"I ran your Beau Elan errand for you. Call Jake's office. The nice lady will fill you in."

Dead silence at his end.

"Don't be mad. I have all the materials with me, safe and sound."

"Tai—"

"I'll meet you at your place and explain everything."

A long pause. "I'm counting on it."

He hung up just as Doug returned. His eyes loomed large and skittish behind the glasses.

"I got your footage loaded," he said, his voice low. "And I'm really hoping it's not what you're expecting."

Chapter Thirty-Seven

Seventy-five minutes later, I knocked at Trey's door. He opened it in two seconds flat. He'd obviously just gotten in, hadn't even turned the lights on yet. Behind him the evening sky melted orange and gold, deepening, burning.

I came in and closed the door behind me. "I can explain."

He folded his arms and waited. And I explained. He listened. As I talked, his mouth remained tight, but his eyes unsquinched somewhat.

"You should have called me."

"I did. You were in a meeting."

"Nonetheless." He looked me right in the eye. "I would have shared the information with you."

I met his gaze. "Landon wouldn't have."

"You're an authorized agent of Phoenix. Unless there had been some specific prohibition—"

"I got fired today."

Trey's head snapped back. "What?"

"Fired. They released Eliza's body to the family, so Janie's headed back to Jackson. Plus Marisa wasn't happy about our little detour to the strip club last night. So yeah, fired."

I flopped myself on his sofa, throwing my tote bag down beside me. My feet hurt, shoulders too. My body throbbed in one great big ache. Trey shook his head.

"I didn't see any paperwork about this."

"I'm supposed to pick it up tomorrow."

"But I'm supposed to see it first. I didn't even receive an e-mail."

"I guess you're *persona non grata* now, too. But here's a heads-up—my getting terminated isn't nearly as problematic as that surveillance footage."

I retrieved the deplexed DVD from my tote bag and handed it to him. He slid it into his computer and watched as his screen blossomed into a tight shot of someone's bikini-clad derrière. It was soon replaced by another bathing beauty slathering sunscreen on her ample breasts.

"What is this?" he said.

"Jake's private collection, I'm guessing. Looks like he positioned the security cameras to catch some interesting footage."

Onscreen, a woman tugged a sweatshirt over her head. The shot was obviously taken through a window, and just as obviously, taken without the woman's knowledge. I didn't recognize her, but I knew the next subject. Trey did too.

"Nikki," he said.

She lay in bed reading a magazine, wearing a thin t-shirt that barely skimmed the top of her thighs. Eliza sat at the foot of the bed, smiling, her mouth stretching, her eyes half-lidded. She leaned forward lazily...

Trey stopped the video. The two women froze on his computer, still shots from a life that didn't exist anymore.

"This isn't the worst of it," I said. "Look in the box."

Trey did. "It's a box of underwear."

"Women's underwear. Bras and panties and things with straps and hooks."

Trey picked up a red leather thong. "This was in Jake's desk?"

"Apparently he had several private collections, not just voyeur footage. I'm thinking if we ask around, lots of Beau Elan tenants will report missing lingerie."

Trey put the scrap of underwear back in the box. He seemed at a loss for what to do next.

"I am certain this is why Jake was sent packing," I said. "And I am equally certain no one will be pleased that I got my hands on it first."

"You're right."

"I'm not asking you to cover for me or get me off the hook. It wasn't your fault."

"No. It was the fault of the woman who released this to you without checking with me or Landon first. But I'll still get in trouble."

He stood up and made his way to the kitchen where he pulled a familiar green bottle from the refrigerator. He unscrewed it slowly, then took a deliberate mindful sip. I waited while he finished. It took three minutes and he didn't say one word the entire time. But when he was done, he placed the empty bottle on the counter and retrieved a second one. This one he brought to me.

"Are you mad?" I said.

"No."

I put the bottle on the coffee table. "Why not?"

"I'm not sure. Perhaps we're a team now, as you said. That comes with different rules."

I managed a laugh. "I'm not so good with rules, you know."

"I know. But you always have a good reason for breaking them. I don't always understand the reason, but you seem to, so I trust you."

The thought warmed me. "You do?"

"Of course. That's how partners operate. It's been a long time since I've had one, but I remember that much."

He was standing too close again—I had to tilt my head way back to look into his face. I thought of the MRI scans, the puzzle pieces of his identity. I'd seen his cognitive blueprint, and he was still unknown to me, perhaps unknowable. I thought again of bridges, and I decided the hardest part of building one must be deciding where to start.

So before I could analyze my actions, much less stop myself, I stood up and put my hand to his face. And then I pulled his mouth to mine and kissed him.

His mouth was warm and soft, and he responded with easy abandon. And it was good, soooo good, but in the back of my head, I was thinking panicked thoughts—oh, God, I started this, what am I doing, I'm too stupid for words, gotta stop—but the kiss was so lovely and so mind-blowing that I just surrendered to it like an addict.

He pulled away suddenly, his expression deeply curious. "Are you trying to seduce me?"

I laughed. "Yes, I think I am."

Without a word of warning, he put his hands on my waist and steered me backwards, then lifted me gently and settled me on his desk. And then he moved closer, and I looked him right in the eye. Something new burned beneath the cool detachment, and it made me feel powerful and reckless. I wanted him so much at that moment, wanted to lose myself in him, just for one moment. I reached for the top button on his shirt…

And his phone rang.

He didn't even look at it, didn't even blink.

I sighed. "You have to get it, you know you do."

He hesitated.

"Trey."

He fished the phone out of his jacket pocket and put it to his ear. "Seaver here."

His voice was calm. I, however, felt like crying.

"Yes," he said. "I can do that. Give me twenty, no, thirty minutes."

He slipped the phone back in his pocket. Then he put his hand to the side of my face and ran his thumb along my jaw line. I closed my eyes, waiting for his mouth, but nothing happened. I opened my eyes.

He was reading me. Like I'd lie to him, like I'd even try it. But still he watched my mouth, once again remote, once again the calculating machine.

"What do you want?" he said.

"I swear I don't know, Trey. I really don't."

He nodded. And then he abruptly pulled away and straightened his jacket, heading for the bathroom. His absence was a vacuum. The inevitable retreat, I thought, and I wasn't expecting it.

But then I thought, oh, sure I was. I'd been expecting it all along.

I pulled myself together and slid down from the desk, knocking over his pencil cup as I did. It created a spot of chaos in the otherwise unbroken neatness, the kind of precise disaster that tornados inflict.

Trey came out of the bathroom, a new tie loose around his neck. "Your blouse is unbuttoned."

"It doesn't matter, I'm going back to the shop."

"You're welcome to wait here until I return."

I shook my head and picked up my tote bag.

He nodded. "I'll walk you down then."

Shrugging into a new jacket, he opened the front door and disappeared into the hallway. I fastened myself up and followed him into the elevator.

"So what's the emergency?"

He knotted the tie into a neat double Windsor. "Dylan Flint's dead. Fish and Game pulled the body from the Chattahoochee thirty minutes ago."

"What!?!"

The elevator dinged. Trey stepped out and headed for the parking area. I scurried to keep up.

"What happened?"

"He'd been shot, three times. Once in the chest, twice in the back of the head. Patrol located his car at the Morgan's Fall boat ramp, keys in the ignition."

I didn't know what news I'd been expecting, but it hadn't been Dylan Flint shot to death and dumped in the Hooch. I followed at Trey's heels.

"So what are you doing now?"

"Emergency meeting with Landon and Marisa."

"Can I come?"

"No."

"What if I just follow you in?"

"No." He popped the locks on the Ferrari. "I have my orders—report to Phoenix ASAP. Alone." He paused. "This is not my decision. Please don't think it is."

He'd said "please" again. What was it with that word? It gave me this little frisson of intimacy, and I was suddenly very tired of fighting all the time, shadowboxing the universe.

"Will you at least call me and tell me what you find out?"

"When I can, yes."

He didn't start up the car; didn't shut the door either. He just sat staring straight ahead, one hand on the wheel, the other toying with the gear shift.

I took a step closer. "What happened tonight doesn't change anything between us."

He listened. His eyes slanted my way, but stayed somewhere at stomach level.

"Of course you know that," I said. "But I want you to know that I know it too."

He frowned, but still wouldn't look me in the face. "Did I do something wrong?"

"What?"

"Did I—"

"I heard you. I just…I mean…no, you didn't. Everything you did was right."

He took a beat to digest that, finally sliding his eyes up to meet mine. "Really?"

"Really."

He hesitated, then I saw the quirk at the corner of his mouth, the almost-smile. "Okay. That's very unusual. But okay."

I couldn't fight the smile. "You know what, Trey? Maybe I will stay until you get back."

He handed me the key, all serious now. "There's a deadbolt. Keep it engaged. I have a spare key, so don't open the door until I get back. Not for anyone."

Chapter Thirty-Eight

Back in his apartment, I remembered the number easily. I'd used it enough.

"I was wondering when you'd call," Garrity said.

"Dylan Flint's turned up DOA. You heard?"

"Ear to the ground."

"Murdered?"

"Looking like. But this is real early to be speculating who or why. I do have one piece of news, however, that'll make your little heart thump. Eliza's girlfriend came in this afternoon."

"Nikki?"

"Now how did you—"

"Doesn't matter. Just spill."

He spilled. According to Nikki, the last event Eliza and Dylan went to was the Mardi Gras party. Nikki reported that even though Eliza left with him afterward, the next morning she suddenly called off whatever deal they'd had, which pissed Dylan off royally.

"What made her do that?" I said.

"Nikki thinks it had something to do with the smacking around somebody gave Eliza late Tuesday night."

I remembered the bruises detailed in the coroner's report, the ones Bulldog denied inflicting. Eliza had obviously pissed somebody off that night, and if it wasn't Bulldog—and I was betting it wasn't—it was somebody at that party.

Garrity agreed. "Somebody who didn't like her showing up with Camera Boy."

"But what were those two up to?"

"Nikki had no clue. Eliza never said, not even to Dylan. The boy seemed clueless."

"If that's the case, why is he dead?"

"He certainly *thought* he knew something, and rumor has it he was gonna spill it to the cops. So maybe whatever secret he was close to was the kind of thing people get really paranoid about keeping."

"You think somebody shot him and dumped him in the Hooch to shut him up?"

"People've been dumped in the Hooch for less."

"Revenge is just a form of wild justice."

"That right?"

"So they say."

He exhaled. "Like I told you, ear to the ground. I'll let you know if we find out something. But right now, all we've got is a dead guy who stinks of coincidence."

"Dead girl. Dead guy. Burned-up meth lab."

"Yep."

"Rumors and rumors of rumors."

"Welcome to my world," he said.

"You're welcome to it," I replied.

After that, I went to the convenience store for some Winston Lights and a six-pack of Sam Adams, both of which I took onto Trey's terrace. It was misty weather, prophetic of rains to come. I sat on a chaise lounge underneath a narrow sliver of roof and took out my phone.

Then I called Eric. To my utter astonishment, he answered. His tone was matter-of-fact, and I kept mine the same as I told him the latest. He didn't seem surprised.

"Dylan was causing problems for a lot of people. At least the whole mess is over with."

"Sure it is," I replied, opening the cigarettes. "Tell me about Gabriella."

"You know I can't do that. I work with Trey, he's—"

"I wasn't asking you to talk about Trey, just Gabriella. Unless she's your client too, in which case, just screw it, I don't have a snowball's chance in hell of figuring any of this out."

There was a pause. "They met through the Beaumonts, and she took him on as a…project would be the best word. Self-described sexual healer, certified massage therapist. I think she does a little fortune-telling on the side."

I remembered the tarot deck in Trey's desk. "Of course she does." I searched the grocery bag for the lighter. "I cannot believe I am having this conversation."

"Frankly, neither can I. Why are you?"

"Because she's connected. I just don't know how."

His voice softened a little. "You sound upset."

"It's been a long day. I need sleep."

"So come home. We'll talk." A long pause. "There are some things I need to apologize for."

"It's okay—"

"No, it's not. We said some hurtful things to each other, and we need to process that."

Process. He wanted me to process.

"The thing is, I'm staying over here tonight."

"That shop isn't safe, Tai, it's—"

"I'm not at the shop."

"Rico's?"

"No."

Another pause, this one ripe with unsaid something. He exhaled softly. "Fine. Whatever you decide. We'll talk about it tomorrow. Are you going to the reception tomorrow?"

"I'm guessing I'm not welcome there." I lit the cigarette, pulled in a soft, deep drag. "You doing okay?"

"I'm fine. I've been staying busy."

"Staying busy is not helping me get to fine. I just keep veering farther and farther away from fine."

A curious pause. "Are you smoking again?"

" No." I tapped ash into an empty Pellegrino bottle. "Listen, I gotta go. But we'll talk soon, I promise."

When he was gone, I sat and stared at the phone for a long time, finishing one cigarette and starting another. The smoke felt lovely in my mouth, velvety and warm, as I watched the streetlights and the bruised purple sky beyond. The rain dripped on my hair, my face. I didn't wipe it away.

I didn't realize I'd fallen asleep until my head jerked. The sky had blackened to jet layered with yellow, the infamous Atlanta haze. I checked my watch. Twelve-fifteen. Trey wasn't back yet.

I slid open the terrace door and ducked inside the darkened apartment. A pencil crunched underfoot next to his desk. When I bent to pick it up, I saw his briefcase lying beside the door, dumped haphazardly on its side. Suddenly I noticed the disarray on his desk, the scattered papers.

"Trey?" I called.

No answer. I closed the terrace door and turned on the light.

I saw him on the kitchen floor, curled on his side, his head at the base of the refrigerator. I ran over and put a hand on his shoulder. He was shaking. Even worse, his breathing was shallow and fast, his arms wrapped tightly around his midsection.

I retrieved my cell phone and dialed Garrity's number. He'd barely answered when I started in on him.

"Trey is sick, really sick."

"What do you mean, sick?"

"He's lying on the floor, he won't answer me, he's shaking all over. Damn it, Garrity, I need his doctor."

"Hold on." I heard him rummaging through papers. He found the number and gave it to me. "I'll be right there, okay? Stay with him."

I hung up the phone. Like I was going anywhere.

I went to Trey and brushed the hair from his forehead. At my touch, his eyes flew open. They were glazed with pain and exhaustion.

"Go away," he said.

"Not a chance." I brushed back another piece of hair, and he reached up and knocked my hand away.

"I have to get up."

"Not now."

"Now." He pushed to standing and buckled, catching himself before he hit the ground. I grabbed him, and he put one arm around me, no argument this time. He was almost deadweight, but his legs still worked, so with one arm around his waist and the whole of his upper body leaning against me, I carried him to bed.

"Talk to me, Trey, what happened?"

He mumbled something. It was pretty incoherent, but I got enough to understand that there had been nausea and vomiting and other debilitating stuff.

I sat beside him. "I'll get a bucket or something. And some more towels. Be still while I call the doctor."

He babbled a weak protest, something completely incomprehensible, but I caught the last part as I got out my phone.

"It's too late anyway," he said. "Too late."

The doctor diagnosed him with probable food poisoning and said the same things doctors always said—watch for fever, keep him in bed, small doses of fluids when he could hold them down. She was calling in a prescription for promethazine, but it wouldn't do much good until Trey could keep it in down. The worst would be over in six hours, she said.

I called Garrity back and asked him to drop by the pharmacy. He arrived an hour later with the prescription. I took it from his hands without touching him and wouldn't let him in the door.

"Look, it could be food poisoning, or it could be a virus, in which case, I'm doomed. Which means that the least I can do is not doom you too."

Garrity gave me that cop look. "So what happened to make you think you're doomed?"

"Why are you asking me this now? You're breathing in pathogens as we speak. Go away."

He crossed his arms and looked at me, hard, but didn't step over the threshold. "Did you two—"

"No, and stop looking at me like you're the one who can read minds." I started to shut the door. He put his foot in it.

"We're going to talk about this," he said.

I shoved the door closed, locked it too. And then I went to take care of Trey.

Chapter Thirty-Nine

Eventually he fell asleep. It wasn't good sleep—he tossed his head and mumbled nonsense into the pillow—but if he was asleep he wasn't vomiting, and if he wasn't vomiting, he was getting better. I curled into a ball on the sofa and eventually fell asleep too, somewhere around four.

His phone rang at seven. I answered it in a daze. "Yeah?"

"Who the hell is this?"

I scrubbed at my eyes. "It's Tai, Marisa. How are you this fine morning?"

"I'm calling for Trey."

"He's sick."

"He didn't call in sick."

"He's *really* sick, like too sick to call in sick."

If she was the least bit curious at my being there, she didn't show it. "There's a press conference this morning—ten o'clock at Beaumont Enterprises. Tell Trey to bring back the files on the meeting last night."

"Listen to me—Trey is throwing-up-delirious sick. He's not coming in."

"Then you need to bring them. Wear something suitable for the camera, not that purple thing."

I sat up and my head throbbed. "You're not getting this, are you? He's sick, and I'm not leaving him. Besides, Landon fired my ass yesterday, so forget you or him or anybody else at Phoenix bossing me around anymore."

A long pause. "You have a point. Landon will be over to pick up the materials in an hour."

"I'll meet him in the lobby," I said, then hung up.

I heard Trey stirring in the bed and went to see if he was awake, but he'd just turned to his other side, wrapped himself around a different pillow. I ran my hand over his forehead. Still cool, which was a relief.

I sat on the edge of the bed. "You need to wake up, Trey. They all think it's over, but I know better, and you do too."

He didn't reply. Even though the night had been a cycle of garbled dream-talk and throwing up, every time I touched him, I felt this surge of tenderness, which completely unnerved me. It reminded me too much of taking care of Mom, the helplessness and the frustration. But he needed somebody, and there I was. Somebody.

So I got up and wet the washcloth one more time.

I figured I had about thirty minutes before Landon arrived, so I got to work looking for the files. Trey's briefcase was an uncharacteristic mess, as was his deck, so I rummaged through the drawers and found a stack of empty folders. And then I sat on the floor and started putting things back where they belonged. Or seemed too. I figured Trey would rearrange everything the right way once he woke up.

Going through his desk—this time with no ulterior motive—was fascinating. He'd managed to get his gun put away—that drawer was locked up tight, as usual. The tarot deck was still in the desk drawer, as were the usual prescription meds and emergency folders, plus the *GQ* magazine. Only now I noticed that it was over two years old, and that it featured a black Armani suit on the front cover.

So that was where he got his fashion sense.

I put it back in the drawer—interesting, but not pertinent. What I needed to do was get a handle on Trey's notes before Landon absconded with them.

The biggest part of the jumbled paperwork was mostly familiar, but I occasionally ran into new material, like the meeting notes from the night before. Eliza's file now had a sticky note on the cover in Trey's handwriting: *Blackmailable?* I smiled, but he had a vital point. All this time, we'd been looking at Eliza as a blackmailer, but what if she'd been the one whose secrets were on the line?

Of course, that didn't explain why she'd been hiding so much cash in a shoebox. Trey hadn't speculated further. He had, however, taken a yellow highlighter to the forensic analysis of the murder weapon. Another sticky note: *why not disposed of?*

Another excellent point. How stupid was it for Bulldog to stash the murder weapon and her purse in his truck? Why not toss it all in the Hooch? And why hadn't he used any of her credit cards? Admittedly, that would have made him easier to trace, but he hadn't impressed me as a big-picture kind of felon.

It was all damn confusing. I didn't have a criminal mind; how was I supposed to comprehend the whacked-out functions of such a thing? I couldn't even figure out Trey's head, and I had brain scans on that one.

Okay, I thought, what if Eliza *had* been taking hush money. And if the money alone hadn't convinced her, what if someone had dropped hints that her own secrets would be exposed to the Beaumonts?

And what if she'd decided that, finally, she'd had enough? That would explain why she'd come to Eric, asking questions about client confidentiality. It would explain her nervousness, her frantic pull between speaking out and safety. I remembered the bruises that had been inflicted on her two days before her death, long before Bulldog admitted to getting rough with her on Thursday night. Apparently, she'd been right to be afraid, but it hadn't been Bulldog alone who inspired that fear.

As for Bulldog, he claimed to know nothing about Dylan Flint. I was betting Dylan had known nothing about Bulldog. And the Beaumonts knew nothing about anything. They occupied their own rarefied penthouse far above such sordid goings-on, and yet everywhere I looked, the Beaumont name ran though the mess like a fault line.

I paged through the rest of Trey's notes and found another police report, the one on the discovery of Dylan's body. It gave me goosebumps. He'd been yelling at me on the sidewalk and dripping-wet-dead less than ten hours later. He hadn't made it in to talk to the cops.

Which made another fact even more alarming—Nikki had disappeared. When police went to question her about Dylan, her apartment was empty, with evidence of a hasty packing job. I felt a cold splotch of dread. Would they be pulling her from the river next?

The rest of Trey's stuff was mostly security data for the Senator's reception—floor plans, security rolls, perimeter break-downs, plus lots of promotional material, all of which featured a smiling Mark and Charley. I paged through the guest list, discovering a veritable *Who's Who* of Atlanta's monied elite. A separate roster catalogued Beaumont Enterprise employees who would be attending. I noticed Jake Whitaker's name—nothing surprising there, considering his penchant for sucking up. Still, I doubted he'd show, not after getting fired.

I also found a hefty file on Senator Adams, another knot in the incestuous tangle of Beaumont World. Everyone connected to everyone else by less than six degrees of separation—more like two and three-quarters. This wasn't the usual political fluff 'n' stuff, however. This was a well-researched dossier with a lot of background data, most of it irrelevant to the current situation.

Except.

And it was one hell of an except. I took up the highlighter and marked the name, then I underlined it. Then I drew an asterisk beside it. And then another.

And then Trey's phone rang. It was Landon.

"I'm coming up," he said.

"No, you're not. I'm coming down."

"Don't start."

"This isn't starting. Starting would be loading whatever gun I can find and waiting for your ass to show up at this door."

There was silence at the other end of the phone. He wasn't happy, but couldn't find a way around the situation.

"In the lobby then. Ten minutes. And I want all of it. If there's a single sheet of paper missing, so help me, I'll—"

"Shut up, Landon. I'm not in the mood."

"Just bring it."

"Oh, I'm bringing it all right."

Landon had planted himself in the lobby like a bad-tempered hill. "This had better be everything," he said, looking through the folders.

"It is. Including this bunch of stuff here about you and Senator Adams, how he was your partner at the company you sold before you became partners with Marisa."

He looked at me hard, the folders fanned in his hands. "You say that like you're discovered something, Ms. Randolph."

"Why'd he leave?"

"To start his own law firm. Can't you read?"

"I read fine, especially the part about the illegal wiretaps. Your old firm was about to get into hot water thanks to Adams—spying on the wrong people, it seems."

"The charges were dropped."

"Lots of charges got dropped during the nineties—Atlanta was famous for it. People got rich from it."

"I wasn't one."

"No, Adams was the money, you were the talent. Mr. Air Force Special Services. Luckily, Marisa swooped in with her trust fund and bailed you out. Adams leaves, she's the new partner, the name gets changed to Phoenix, and everything blows over. And now he's running for governor."

"And this means what exactly?"

"It means you've got a personal stake in this campaign. Quid pro quo. Adams kicks a little influence your way, you toss a little top secret information his. A nice partnership."

Landon looked at me—pleasantly, it seemed. I'd never noticed how malleable his expression was, how like a layer on top of another layer on top of something hard and fixed and smooth.

"We don't have to like each other."

I crossed my arms. "Good thing."

"So cut the crap. Nobody appreciates it."

"Eliza might have."

When Landon spoke, his voice was not argumentative. "One thing everybody at Phoenix has in common—me, Marisa, Trey too, especially Trey—is that the work is the most important thing in our lives. Sometimes it's the only thing. And it's never personal. We do what we have to do."

He turned to leave, then paused. "Ask yourself this—if you'd been the one upstairs sprawled out sick, would Trey have stayed with you? Or would he have made sure you weren't dead, then left you there to fend for yourself while he did his job?"

He didn't wait for a reply. Which was just as well, since I didn't have one.

Chapter Forty

The minute I walked back into the apartment, I heard noises in the kitchen. Trey, I assumed.

Boy, was I wrong. It was Gabriella, dressed once again in her white baby-tee uniform, only this time she carried a picnic basket. Her hair fell loose about her shoulders, and she smelled of sandalwood.

I shut the door behind me. "Could have sworn I locked that."

"I have keys." She gestured toward the stove, where a small cast iron pot simmered. "Do you like miso soup?"

"I prefer donuts. You know, the ones with the little sprinkles."

She turned the stove eye on low and wiped her hands. "I came to get my tarot cards and check on Trey. I didn't mean to intrude."

"You're not intruding—I'm glad you dropped by. I've been wanting to talk to you."

She cocked her head, her green eyes clever. "Of course. Would you like to join me on the terrace? I'm dying for a cigarette."

So I stretched out once again on the chaise lounge, cigarette in hand. I was done by the time Gabriella joined me, having stopped at Trey's desk to gather her tarot deck. She brought it and her picnic basket onto the terrace, placing both beside her as she dropped into a half-lotus. Then she extracted a pack of Gitanes blondes from the basket and tapped one out.

"My least interesting vice," she said.

I offered her the lighter. She lit the cigarette and inhaled luxuriously, almost sexually. "You said you had questions?"

"A few, just to fill in some backstory. Like how you met the Beaumonts."

She pursed her lips to blow out a smoky tendril. "I was Charley's massage therapist—we met soon after she and Mark moved here. We became friends, and they invested in my shop."

"How did Phoenix get involved with them?"

"Phoenix is visible and well regarded, of course. But mostly because of Marisa. And her connections."

I remembered what I'd read about her in the files I'd returned to Landon, how she came to Atlanta with a stack of money and an impressive Old Charleston family tree. "She's not one of the Good Old Boys, is she?"

"No. She's properly respectful, but she is an outsider and always will be."

"Which is why she threw her lot in with Senator Adams. He *is* a Good Old Boy."

Gabriella smiled. "It was a risky investment. Less so now. Adams has an excellent chance of winning."

"Which means Phoenix wins too. And the Beaumonts." And Landon, I thought, since I was sure he'd brokered the Beaumont-Phoenix-Adams partnership. But I didn't share this with Gabriella, who dropped her still smoldering cigarette into the Pellegrino bottle from last night. She picked up her tarot deck and cocked her head.

"Have you seen the Beaumonts' new resort property, on Lake Oconee?"

"No. They're holding the reception there, I know that much."

"The boat dock is especially nice—slips for the yachts, a gorgeous view. It's the water that makes the place, you know, especially now, after the drought two years ago."

I waited for her point. There wasn't one. "So?"

She shuffled the cards in her hands, smoothly. Not like a poker player. Like a magician.

"If you do your research, you will notice that the wife of Senator Adams has a sister who has a husband on the water board of Greene County. Not yet, of course. He begins his term next year. But he has a reputation for protecting the commercial interests of property owners."

"Friends tend to have friends in high places."

"Yes, in high places you can always find some friends for sale." She was cutting and restacking the deck now. "This is the nature of business."

"What about Eliza? Was she starting to make noise about this business?"

She looked at me with puzzled amusement. "You think this is a secret? Don't be naïve. As for Eliza, I'm afraid I can't help you—I've told you everything I know about her. Ask Trey if you don't believe me. He knows I don't lie."

She pulled a card from the deck and laid it face-up at my feet. A woman on a throne, some clouds, butterflies.

"The Queen of Swords," she said. "Intensely perceptive. Quick and confident, independent and clear-thinking, sometimes rashly so. She has suffered loss, but has the strength to bear her sorrow."

I shook my head. "I don't believe in that stuff."

"That hardly matters." She pulled another card and laid it down at a right angle to the first. It was a man this time, also on a throne, also armed with a formidable piece of steel.

"The King of Swords. A card of power, of strength, of a man who holds life and death in the palm of his hand. He is firm in both friendship and in enmity, but often over-cautious. Usually solitary. And sometimes ruthless."

I regarded her carefully. She was playing me, yes, but I was curious enough to play along. "So what are you and Trey? Friends? Lovers?"

"Both. But only because he isn't in a relationship...is he?"

"You're the one with the cards, you tell me."

"That's not how it works." She turned over one more card. "This is the final outcome—The Magician, the card of creative archetypal energy. Whatever you choose to do, you will have the power to do it. Because there will be a choice, an important one—for both you and Trey."

She collected her cards and tucked them in her basket. "He's not what he seems to be on the surface. He's very brave, yes, but also afraid. Only fear could make someone so brave."

"I don't understand."

"You will. Mark my words." She stood and headed for the sliding glass door, her dainty slides clip-clopping with each step. "Tell Trey to enjoy the soup—it's good for his electrolyte balance. And you should get some sleep—you're going to need it."

"Why? What—?"

But she was already gone.

Chapter Forty-One

Trey slept through everything, which was just as well. When I checked on him, his breathing had deepened, dropping into a steady rhythm.

I left him to rest and flipped on the television just in time to catch the press conference. The gist was this: the APD announced that they had arrested William Aloysius Perkins, AKA Bulldog, and were charging him with the murder of Eliza Abigail Compton. Mark and Charley did a nice concluding piece about community, culminating in a big fat check to the Police Benevolent Fund with lots of hurrah-hurrah and general back-patting.

Mark spoke with solemn relish. "There will be justice now, not just for Eliza Compton—"

Wow, I thought, he finally got the name right.

"—but justice for all."

A smattering of applause. I shut it off before I got sick. Now that Bulldog was behind bars, everyone was eager to move on, case closed, let's get some Champagne. Forget that Dylan's body just got pulled from the Hooch, forget that Nikki was missing.

Life keeps going, Eric said. Yes, it did.

I collected all the tobacco-related trash on the terrace and took it to the kitchen. The miso soup simmered; other than that, the silence of the apartment was stunning. Combined with the stark black-and-white décor, the hard floors and empty walls, the place was downright spooky.

Gabriella. I had one brochure on her spa, four sentences from my brother, and a morning riddled with French cigarettes and tarot cards. Other than that, she was a cipher.

A cipher who was sleeping with Trey, my gut reminded me.

I shoved the butt-filled Pellegrino bottle deep into the trashcan. I had no right to feel territorial, and yet her presence nagged at me. I finished straightening the apartment, including putting the file folders I hadn't used back in Trey's desk. I noticed that he'd left his computer on, his Phoenix laptop. This didn't surprise me—he'd been uncharacteristically haphazard with his things the night before—but what did surprise me was that his desktop was up.

Gabriella had been after more than cards—she'd been on his computer.

I sat at the desk too, and my conscience gave a twinge. Not snooping, I told myself. Investigating.

Thirty minutes later, I'd examined all the files that had been opened recently—nothing suspicious, just lots of premises liability reports, a couple of other Phoenix forms. Boring stuff. And none had been opened in the last hour.

His web history was a different story. An e-mail program had been pulled up during the time of Gabriella's visit. I clicked on it and got a log-in page, password required. But there was no chance of retrieving the message, or even seeing where it had gone.

She'd trespassed on his work computer to send an e-mail? Or perhaps something more nefarious?

I fetched Rico's portable drive from my bag. From what I'd observed, running his security program was a simple matter of turning it loose and letting it do its thing. It ran a virus scan first, then a more intensive search for more dangerous malware. The second part of the procedure—fixing what it found—was more complicated. But then, I wasn't interested in correcting the problem. I just wanted to know if one existed.

While the program hummed along, I checked out Trey's desk—everything looked just like I'd left it when I reassembled it that morning. His gun drawer was locked, just like it had been the night before. I checked the drawers—papers, folders, pencils. The meds and the *GQ* magazine.

I picked up the magazine and thumbed through it. There was a single sticky note marking an article about formal wear. I thumbed through the rest of the pages, but found nothing else of interest. I did, however, notice an ad for Trey's watch, a Bulgari Diagono GMT. It retailed for $6,600. Right beside it were his shoes, Ferregamo classic black lace-ups: $595. I turned back to the front cover, to the model wearing Trey's suit.

Always Armani, Garrity had said, *or some other Italian crap I can't pronounce.*

I flipped rapidly through the pages. The first article featured his apartment, B&B Italia with La Scala marble in the kitchen and bath. I kept going, seeing his coffee table, his trench coat. I even found shaving soap, Acqua di Gio, and I knew if I could put my nose to it, it would smell faintly of the ocean.

And then I saw it, the *pièce de résistance*, stretched out languorously on a two-page centerfold spread—the Ferrari F430 coupe in all its sleek glory. *La Dolce Velocità,* the headline read. The sweet speed.

I held him in my hands, all of him, or rather, all of who he was now. No wonder Garrity was confused—Trey had reconstructed himself as precisely as from a blueprint, obliterating the previous Trey like razing a construction site. I realized my hands were shaking.

I didn't have time to ponder the implications, however. Rico's program had done its job. I examined the screen—a flashing green light. No viruses, which wasn't a surprise, since Trey had rather formidable firewall.

But then the second part of the program kicked in.

And that was a different story.

I'd just finished talking to Rico when I heard the bedroom door click open. Trey stood in the doorway, his dress shirt a wrinkled mess, untucked and unbuttoned.

"You were supposed to go home," he said.

Trey's *GQ* still rested in my lap. I slipped it nonchalantly into the drawer. "I was waiting to make sure you were okay."

He didn't move. "I'm okay. Go home."

I stood up and got right in front of him, then put the back of my hand to his forehead. He yanked away and scowled.

"Good," I said. "Still no fever."

"Go home."

"You are such a one-trick pony sometimes."

He was getting exasperated. "This could be contagious. I don't want you to get it. I want—"

"I know, I know, you want me to go home. But we need to talk first." I waved toward his desk. "Did you know you have a key logger program on your computer?"

That got his attention. "What? How?"

"Good question. I'm assuming you didn't install it."

He frowned and moved past me, sat down in front of the computer. Sick or not, he typed like wildfire. "What did you run?"

I moved to stand behind him. "One of Rico's programs. It's behavior-based, looks for things that are trying to hide, which makes it more effective than the signature-based stuff. Or so Rico says. I mean, virus scans and firewalls are nice, but they don't protect you against something that's recording your every key stroke."

"But this isn't possible," he said, studying the information I'd scrawled on a sticky note. "Rico. I know that name."

"He came to Phoenix once—big guy, piercings everywhere. He says it was most likely a physical installation since you're not exactly a high-risk user, and the program didn't find any Trojan horses."

"A physical installation isn't possible. I mounted the locks on these doors myself. They're grade one deadbolts."

"So it was someone who has a key."

I let the words fall. He shook his head.

"Only three people beside me have keys to the apartment— the concierge, Garrity—"

"And Gabriella."

He was still staring at the computer screen. "She wouldn't—"

"She would. She came over and dropped off some soup right before she went through your things."

He turned around. "How do you know this?"

"I saw her do it."

He fixed me with the look.

"Okay, not exactly." And then I told him the story—the picnic basket, the cigarettes, the tarot cards, the e-mail, the magazine with the sticky note inside. He stopped me there.

"She looked at the magazine several days ago, when she ordered my tuxedo."

"So? It's not any *one* thing that makes her look guilty, it's *all* the things."

"There's no evidence."

"Screw evidence, I thought you trusted me."

"I do."

"Then you should believe me without evidence."

"Belief and trust aren't the same thing. For belief, I need evidence." He stood up abruptly. "Go home now. I'll deal with this."

"You're still—"

"Go home."

He pushed past me toward the kitchen, where he got a bottle of Pellegrino from the refrigerator and unscrewed the cap. He took one tiny tentative sip.

"Go," he said.

I walked over to my stuff, slung my bag over my shoulder. "You want me to go home, you have to go back to bed."

"But—"

"That's my offer." I pointed toward the front door. "Home." I pointed toward his room. "Bed."

He turned around and went to his room without another word. I called after him, "Yes, and thank you, Tai, for saving me in my hour of need. Oh, you're very welcome, Trey, it's what I do. Saving people and all that."

His voice carried from the bedroom. "Go home."

"I'm going! Enjoy the soup your two-faced spying mistress brought you!"

I slammed the door on the way out. It felt really, really good.

I'd barely hit the lobby when my phone rang. I kept walking as I answered. "Now what?

"Thank you, Tai, for saving me in my hour of need."

My pace slowed from huffy to merely annoyed. "Whatever. Are you in bed?"

"Not yet. I decided to take a shower."

"Not a bad idea. For the first time since I've known you, you do *not* smell good."

A pause. "I mean it. I couldn't think of the words to say it, but I felt it. Thank you."

His voice was soft. It melted away the last scrap of resistance. "I know, Trey. Just be careful, okay? You're still pretty weak."

"You are too. You couldn't have gotten much rest."

I stopped at the exit. The concierge watched me with disguised disinterest.

"I can rest at the shop."

"Okay."

"Or I could come back up. But if I come back up, we have to talk about this Gabriella thing."

"Okay."

I sighed. "Fine. I'm coming back up. But I'm going to get you some crackers and ginger ale first."

Chapter Forty-Two

When I got back to Trey's, I put a six-pack of ginger ale in the fridge and a box of saltines on the counter. He was just getting off the telephone and was back in full Armani mode. He even smelled good again.

He poured a steaming cupful of tea. "Would you like some lapsang souchong? It's decaffeinated."

"We need to talk first. About you-know-who."

He looked down at his mug. The tea smelled like lemon and herb, and he held it cradled between his palms. I took him by the elbow and led him to the sofa. He sat with me, but didn't look the least bit comfortable about it.

"I'm not trying to interfere," I said.

"With what?"

"With your relationship with her."

He thought about that. "We don't have the kind of relationship that you can interfere with. She's—"

"It's none of my business what she is. I don't poach on other women's property."

"I'm not property." He said this with the slightest edge, but his expression was placid, as always.

"Look, I'm guessing she means something to you, but she's up to no good, Trey. And I'm betting it involves the Beaumonts."

Trey looked puzzled. "Why?"

"She and Charley are thick as thieves, and Charley's hiding something, I can tell. And that something involves Eliza." I ticked off the points on my fingers. "Landon's in their pocket, Marisa too. All of Phoenix. Senator Adams. Janie's a member of the fold now, and even the cops seem willing to toe the party line. I promise you, Trey, if you did one of your little circle graphs, you'd see them right in the middle, connected to everything."

"The Beaumonts are clients, not suspects."

"So what? Remember what Garrity said, everybody's guilty of something, and—"

"—it's a cop's job is to find out what. I know." He shook his head. "We're not cops."

"No, the cops seem to think idiotic drug-addled Bulldog is the guilty party."

"He admitted—"

"Oh, come on! The best the cops can do for motive is that Eliza refused to sleep with him. Or sheer confounded meanness, that's their other theory. And then he conveniently leaves her purse *and* the murder weapon in his truck before narrowly escaping death?"

"That's the official narrative."

"Which you are *not* buying, please tell me you're not."

He exhaled. "It has its weaknesses."

"Hell yeah, it does. That hypothesis is a goldmine of weaknesses. But here's one that isn't: Gabriella put a key logger on your computer, and she did it because she's up to something, and that something involves the Beaumonts."

Trey stood up and started pacing a tight line in front of the sofa. Six steps, then reverse, then repeat. "We have no proof. She was at my desk, yes, but you were too. Why shouldn't I suspect you?"

He had a point. "I hadn't thought of it that way."

"It's not an accusation, just a logical analysis."

"I suppose you didn't check your e-mail to see if she'd sent you something?"

"Until I get the key logger quarantined, I can't use the computer for anything."

He stopped pacing and went to his deck, where he stared at his computer for a long time, his hands on his hips. Then he straightened up and disappeared into the bedroom. I heard a drawer open and shut, decisively.

"Trey?"

He reappeared in the living room wearing his shoulder holster. He headed right for the bottom desk drawer, keys in hand, and my stomach flipped.

"What are you doing?"

"I'm getting my weapon."

Oh great, I thought, he's gone vigilante. I jumped up from the sofa. "Are you sure that's necessary?"

He unlocked the drawer and then the gun case. "The security of my home and my belongings has been compromised. For your safety as well as mine…"

He stopped talking and stared into the drawer. Then he shut it. Then he looked at me.

"My gun is gone."

"What!"

"The magazines and ammo too."

Another flip of the stomach. "Trey, I swear to you, I didn't—"

"I know. You don't have the keys to the desk, and you don't know where I keep them. Only two other people do." He grabbed his jacket from the chair and was out the door in two seconds, not even looking to see if I was keeping up.

But I was. "You'd better wait for me, Trey Seaver! And you'd better be headed where I think you're headed!"

The attendant at the day spa was, like all of Gabriella's employees, gorgeous and tall and as poreless as a magazine page. This one, whose nametag read Arion, had a forehead like a black onyx cliff face and eyes like shards of obsidian. She also had no idea where her employer was.

"Check her book," Trey said.

"I did."

"Not that book."

"There's nothing in that book either."

"Show me."

Arion opened a drawer and pulled out a leather portfolio, which she then spread open on the counter. There was a note inside addressed to Trey. She looked startled to see it, but Trey seemed to have been expecting it all along.

"What does it say?" I said.

He slipped it in his jacket. "It's says that she's sorry and that she'll explain later, after tonight." He addressed Arion. "Would you please double-check my delivery order? Everything should be scheduled to arrive no later than four."

Arion looked relieved to have something to do. "Of course, Mr. Seaver."

She tapped some information into the computer. The boutique portion of the store was empty, and the soft sounds of the spa seemed very far away.

"That thing at Lake Oconee is tonight," I said. "I'd completely forgotten."

"Cocktails at six, dinner at seven-thirty."

"You think Gabriella will be there?"

"She's Charley's stylist. She's at every event the Beaumonts attend." He looked at me as if seeing me for the first time. "Would you like to come?"

I blinked in surprise. "I wasn't invited."

"You don't need an invitation, not if you're with me."

"I don't have a dress."

He ran his eyes over my body, lingering at the hips, then looked around the gallery. He went to the red dress that had caught his eye on our first visit, ran his hand along the seam. "Have this delivered too, please," he said. Then he looked at my feet. "Size eight?"

"Wide."

He nodded at Arion. "Shoes too. I'll leave the choice to you."

"Certainly." She was looking at me differently now too. "Will this be on the Phoenix account as well?"

"No, my personal account."

His expression was composed, the same old Trey Seaver I was fast becoming accustomed to. But his eyes held something flickery and sharp, right at the center. I shook my head.

"Marisa will ream you out if you bring me."

"It doesn't matter. She's going to fire me for losing my weapon and allowing a third party to access Phoenix property."

I linked my arm with his and patted his bicep. "I can't help you with your computer problem."

"I know."

"But as for the missing weapon…well, being partners with a gun shop owner has its benefits."

Chapter Forty-Three

Dexter didn't have a P7M8 in stock, but his reference list proved invaluable, especially when I mentioned that money was no object to this particular client. The piece was delivered in less than an hour, and Trey's Amex Platinum was down $1500. He insisted on breaking down and inspecting it—a decision I totally agreed with—so while he cleaned it, I fetched some ammo.

"On the house," I said.

He fed the eight rounds into the magazine and inserted it. "I have to try this before we go."

"Of course. I'd like to try mine out too."

He noticed the purse then, this snappy black leather bag.

"I'm testing it for the shop," I said, showing it to him. "Zipper opening, holster insert. Lockable. Plus a separate place for lipstick should I ever decide to start wearing it."

"You have your carry permit?"

I held up the piece of paper. "Came in the mail this morning."

I could see the gears whirring in his head. But he knew the law as well as I did, and he knew I was within my rights to bring a weapon. The Beaumont reception was a private gathering on private property, teeming with conservative Second Amendment zealots. Unless someone asked me to leave, I had every legal right to be there.

"What do you have in there?"

"A revolver, Smith and Wesson Model 40. Compact, light, hammer cover to prevent it from snagging on a fancy dress."

I saw that twitch at the corner of his mouth. I smiled. "You didn't think I'd arm you to the teeth and then carry around just a nail file for myself, did you?"

We went by the range on the way out. Trey as usual exterminated the target. I did pretty well myself. Georgia's castle doctrine required no retreat before reasonably resorting to deadly force. And considering all that had gone on, a purse full of deadly force swinging on my hip felt really good.

Traffic out to Lake Oconee was unusually heavy, and I guessed from the way the helicopters hovered in a knot above the interstate that there was an accident up ahead, or some other perversity that I couldn't possibly predict. I played with the air vents and watched the city inch by, surrounded by the sounds of a thousand other motors of a thousand other people.

"Can I ask you something? Not about the case or Gabriella, about you."

He nodded. Two small travel cases rested behind us, toiletries for me, a satchel of paperwork for him.

"When I was at your desk, I found this magazine, and I couldn't help wondering…it's hard to figure out the question I want to ask."

Trey offered no help whatsoever. I stumbled on.

"Garrity said that after the accident, you bought this car, the apartment, the suits, all of it very different from how you were before. And then I noticed that the *GQ* magazine dated from when you got out of the hospital, and it had everything in it, just like Garrity described. And I thought, this can't be a coincidence."

"It's not." He kept his eyes on the road. "But I had to do something. And having a template worked. It still works. The decisions are too hard otherwise."

"I don't understand."

"It's hard to explain. Knowing what you like comes from knowing who you are. And I don't know anymore."

I'd never considered such a thing. I liked low-slung jeans and chunky boots. Shrimp, but not scallops. The color yellow. How did I know these things?

"Are you mad?"

He frowned. "Why would I be mad?"

"Well, if I had a secret, I'd be mad if someone stumbled onto it."

"It's not a secret. It's just information that I tell very few people."

"Like Gabriella."

The mention of her name sounded like a warning bell. Of the two people closest to him in the whole world, one had apparently betrayed him. I pressed on, however.

"Why won't you admit that she's up to something?"

He thought about it. "I told you, I need evidence. Her guilt contradicts other facts about her that I already have."

"So replace the facts."

"It's not that easy. I think it used to be, before the accident. Garrity says I had good instincts. He says I was very intuitive. But I'm not anymore. I can sort fact from fiction, but I can't figure out what they mean." He looked at the glove compartment. "Like those. They used to mean something to me. I keep thinking I'll remember what, but I never do."

I remembered then, from the car chase. "The rosary beads?"

"They were my mother's. Garrity was looking for them for the funeral. He thinks they were lost in the accident."

His voice was steady and calm, with no hint of emotion, but I felt the impact nonetheless.

I fingered the glove compartment handle. "May I?"

He nodded, and I took them out. They were cool to the touch, small round stones of gray-green marble with a finely chased silver crucifix.

"Connemara marble," he said, "from Ireland. That's where my grandparents were born. County Donegal."

I held them in my hand, and they felt like faith is supposed to feel—solid, soothing, tangible. He was still looking straight ahead, his hands resting lightly on the wheel.

"I'm trying to explain something to you," he said, "and I can't. It's about those, and Gabriella, and about the accident itself, but...I'm looking for a word."

I shook my head. "There isn't one. It's too much for words."

He thought about that.

"Yes," he said finally. "Perhaps you're right."

Chapter Forty-Four

Beaumont Waterway rose out of nowhere, this colossal white-columned spread that bloomed on the edge of Lake Oconee like a crop of enormous mushrooms. Inside, the main hall was decorated with muscular grandeur—stag-horn chandeliers, gray stone floors, and a massive fireplace I could have stood in.

Phoenix had two suites reserved for its agents. Trey gave me the key to one and he took the other. I opened it to find my garment bag hung on the bathroom door and a fully stocked bar with fresh ice. Through the patio doors, the lake rippled silver in the clear diffuse light. I opened them, and the astringent scent of pine blew in.

Down at the lake edge, segregated from the main complex, I saw the Beaumonts' private cabin. Charley loitered on the wrap-around porch, talking on her cell phone. She wore a white summer sweater and Jackie O sunglasses. Beside the pool, Mark enjoyed a drink with Marisa underneath a green canvas umbrella. Landon stood at her elbow, sipping something amber and neat. And there was my brother, spic and span in his Brooks Brothers casual, pouring a red wine.

Everyone but Gabriella.

I watched for several minutes, the casual glamour of it more fascinating than I cared to admit, until I heard a soft knock on my door. I turned and saw Trey. Just as I'd suspected, he was the very man tuxedos were created for, from the pitch and hang of the sleeves to the cut and break of the jacket.

I walked over and made a pretense of straightening his tie. "Did you tell anyone I was coming?"

"No."

"Not even Eric?'

"No."

"Oh good—I like surprises."

Trey's eyes were tight. I put my hand to his forehead and found his skin smooth and cool, still unfevered. Somewhere on the lake I heard the low drone of a motorboat, a distant conversation layered with laughter.

"I'll leave you to get dressed," he said. "Find me when you get to the reception."

"Oh no, you don't. We're going together. Stay put."

I grabbed the dress and the shoe box and went into the bathroom. The dress slithered from its bag, this slinky length of red, heavy with beading, cool as water.

"Do you have a plan?" I called.

"For what?"

"Finding Gabriella, of course." I stuck my head out the door. "I'd think locating her would be your first priority."

He looked annoyed. "We don't know the specifics of the situation, therefore I can't create a response plan."

I struggled into the dress. It was like trying to shove my entire leg into a glove. "So let's pretend I have proof that she took your gun and bugged your computer, solid evidence."

"I can't—"

"Pretend it's a simulation." I undid my ponytail and ran my fingers through my hair. "Pretend you had proof that a hypothetical person with connections to the Beaumonts had stolen Landon's firearm and tapped his computer, and that said person was headed this way. What would your next move as security officer be?"

"Alert perimeter control and establish a BOLO. Double-check entry and exit procedures. Inform the head of operations."

"Okay, whoa." I stuck my head back out. "Can you skip that last part? I mean, if Landon finds out about this…"

"Not Landon. Marisa. And procedure requires—"

"This is all hypothetical, remember? As you keep pointing out, you don't know for sure that Gabriella has done anything. So let's take it a step at a time, shall we?"

I returned to the main area and shook my hair out, my purse strap slung across my chest like a bandolier. The effect was not exactly Vogue-worthy, but it would do. Better tacky than dead.

Trey examined me. There was scrutiny in the look, but appreciation too. And puzzlement. I could see him sorting and analyzing, his neural circuits trying to make a connection.

I slipped into my shoes. They were beaded three-inch pumps the same flaming scarlet as the dress. I stood up, wobbled a bit, but held steady. "What exactly does perimeter control entail?"

"Alerting Steve Simpson."

"Then let's do it. And keep the part about the missing gun to yourself, can you do that?"

He considered. "For now, yes."

I took his arm. A team, I'd told him.

Yes, indeed.

◇◇◇

We found Steve in his native habitat—the surveillance van. It was parked near the entrance and could have been mistaken for a catering van except for the periscope extending through the roof. Inside, multiple screens captured feeds from around the resort, including real-time footage of the van itself. I also spotted a microwave, a coffeemaker, and a tiny, well-appointed restroom.

Steve swiveled back and forth in a gray velour captain's chair, a can of Sprite in hand. "If it isn't James Bond," he said, then grinned at me. "Which one are you, Ursula Andress?"

I ignored him. Trey ducked his head to keep from crashing into the periscope viewfinder. "I need to review the access protocols."

"You want real time or archived?"

"Neither. I need to see the incoming and outgoing attendance rosters."

Simpson rolled the chair to a massive console. "I've got entrance but not exit, and before you start, that wasn't my idea."

"But we need the exit roster to—"

"I said, don't start. Not my decision."

"Whose then?"

"Marisa's. The guests were miffed enough at getting inspected on the way in—she didn't want them to have to go through a checkpoint on the way out. Leave them with that happy generous feeling, you know?"

Trey's jaw tightened. Suddenly the interior of the van felt a lot smaller. I bent over the console and read down the list. Bingo—Gabriella's name was near the top. "It says she hasn't arrived yet."

Trey straightened up, narrowly avoiding a swinging remote control. "Have you seen Gabriella?"

"The redhead from the spa? Not tonight." Steve double-checked the column of figures. "There's other people from her shop here, and they brought a truckload of formal wear. But not the madam herself."

Trey scratched a number on a notepad. "If she arrives, please let me know as soon as possible. Use this code."

Steve accepted the piece of paper. "Why, what's she done?"

"Earlier this afternoon, Tai discovered a key logger on my computer. We suspect Gabriella might have some information about it."

Steve's eyes widened. "Really? Whoa."

I sensed it then, the shift. Steve was suddenly nervous. I wasn't an expert in micro-emotive readings, but I knew "technically true but deliberately evasive" when I saw it.

"He knows something," I said.

"I know," Trey replied. He took a step closer to the captain's chair.

Steve panicked. "Dude, I wasn't, I mean, I didn't…" He drew himself up. To his credit, he was a lot cooler than I would have been. At that moment, Trey radiated more menace than a snake-bit pit bull.

"Landon's orders," Steve finally said.

"What was?"

"The key logger. I installed it before the computer was even assigned to you. And then Landon assigned me to your cases, so I could report back to him if you were acting weird—which you were, always."

"Why?"

"How should I know? I don't ask questions, I just follow orders. Isn't that what you do too?"

The piss and vinegar was coming back once he decided that Trey wasn't going to strangle him. To me, it wasn't a smart bet, but Steve kept talking.

"Landon doesn't like you, and he doesn't trust you. But you already know that, so why harass me? Take it up with him."

He was talking too loudly, nervous again. But Trey was done. He pushed past me, heaved open the bulkhead door and disappeared. I tried to follow, but the step-down was impossible. I took off the heels and eased down backwards, cursing to myself.

"This is why I don't wear dresses," I muttered.

Trey waited for me, looking like someone had sprung his compass. I sympathized. Not only was his mistress a thief, his employer was spying on him. If I'd gotten a one-two like that, I'd have been standing bewildered on the asphalt too.

"It makes no sense," he said. "All Landon had to do was ask me to turn over the computer. It's Phoenix property. He has full access."

"He didn't want you to know about it."

"Why not?"

Trey was honestly confused. Like Gabriella, Landon was behaving illogically, and Trey couldn't formulate a motive beyond logical progression.

"He thought you were up to something," I explained, "and this was his way of catching you unaware."

"What would I be up to?"

"I don't know, Trey. I told you, these are some snaky people."

"You never said that."

"Well, I should have."

I was annoyed at myself. I'd been blinded by the assumption that Gabriella had been guilty of both misdeeds. Just like Trey, I'd only followed the one path. He needed me to do better than that.

"We need to find Landon," I said.

"Why?"

"I want to hear what he has to say about this. And I want you to tell me if it's the truth."

This wasn't what I had planned. But thinking Trey's way did have a certain logic. Start with the evidence you have, and see where it goes next. And right now the evidence showed that Landon was even more of an unscrupulous bastard than I'd thought he was.

I slipped my shoes back on, adjusted my purse strap. "Come on, Mr. Seaver. We've got a suspect to question."

Chapter Forty-Five

Down by the lake, we moved through tables scattered like seed pearls all over the sloping lawn. The wait-staff glided around silver platters filled with itty-bitty ham biscuits while the elite mingled and laughed and ignored the food. The alcohol flowed, however, and each couple trailed a handsome black-suited man wearing shades and an earpiece—a faux bodyguard, included in the ticket price. I was surprised they hadn't hired fake paparazzi.

I scanned the crowd. No Gabriella, and no Beaumonts either. I saw my brother at the bar, however. He raised his glass at me, a puzzled look on his face. I'd been hoping to escape his attention. Luckily he was busy with extremely important people. He stayed in his circle, and I stayed in mine.

I nudged Trey's shoulder. "There's Landon."

He stood separate from the crowd, a lone figure by the star-spangled dais, wearing a dark gray tuxedo that made him look almost handsome. As we approached, he shook his head. "You brought a date to work? How unlike you."

"There's no rule against it," Trey replied.

He glanced at my purse knowingly. "Remind me to make one."

Just then the buzz of conversation cranked up a notch—the Beaumonts had arrived, walking up the path from their cabin, arm in arm. The mass of well-wishers parted for them, pressing close at times, but always separate.

"I talked to Simpson," Trey said. "He told me about the key logger."

"I heard." Landon snagged a white wine from a passing waiter. "Don't hold it against him; he was just following orders. That's what we all do, isn't it? Me, you, him. All of us."

He said this with his eyes focused on the entrance. Marisa circulated among the people now with much smiling and chatting and patting of backs. Her hair tumbled about her shoulders, and her white column dress glowed like an opal in the low lights.

"Why?" Trey insisted. "Why not just ask me for it?"

"That defeats the purpose of undercover surveillance, now doesn't it?"

"It was still wrong," I said, "and probably illegal."

"Trey's computer is Phoenix property. He signed away his privacy when he signed his contract. So if either of you want to get your feelings hurt, I suggest you do it on your own time."

He turned to leave, but I stepped into his path. "I heard Dylan Flint got shot to death and dumped in the Hooch. That was illegal, for sure."

"You say that like Phoenix had something to do with it."

"You broke into his house, destroyed his stuff, and then he's killed before he can make a statement to the police, and you wonder why I think Phoenix had something to do with his death?"

I heard the rapid-fire vibrato of violins from somewhere behind me. Landon turned his face to the music. "He was in the business of betraying people for money, and he isn't anymore. That's something we can all be grateful for, especially you, Ms. Randolph."

"Why me?"

"He broke into your shop, threatened you with those ridiculous bull's eyes. I'd think you'd be glad to be rid of him."

"He said he didn't...wait a minute, how did you know about that?"

"We found the mock-ups on his computer. Pictures of you and a bull's eye graphic."

I glared at him. "You probably put them there yourself."

Landon laughed, hearty and rich. "Contrary to what you may think, Ms. Randolph, I've got better things to do with my time than annoy you." He looked at Trey. "Because I'll make you the same promise I made Marisa when she decided to hire you—this firm is not going to turn into Psycho Central, at least not under my watch."

And then he just walked off. Trey watched him go, his expression composed. But his eyes held a scimitar gleam.

"Was he telling the truth?" I said.

"Mostly. He was hiding something, though."

"I imagine Landon's always hiding something."

"Hence the problem—he reads as lying even when he's telling the truth. But there was no equivocation on the last part—he doesn't want me at Phoenix. He thinks I'm psychotic."

I put a hand on his arm. "This is what Landon does, you know. It's not about you."

"No, I understand that. He was just following orders."

Marisa noticed us at this point. She shot me a hot glare, then covered it with a smile and a wave Trey's way.

"I have to go," he said. "Wait here."

"Don't you think we should be looking for Gabriella?"

"We've alerted Simpson and reviewed the access protocols. The next step is informing Marisa to be on the lookout, not looking for Gabriella."

I suppressed the urge to scream at him and instead took a deep breath. This is what we did, followed the rules. I was grateful his timing was flexible if not his procedure.

"Fine. I'll wait here."

He nodded and then left. As he approached Marisa's little coterie, she smiled broadly and introduced him. He was part of the show tonight, a neat professional package to impress the clientele. There came the moment, however, when he said something to her. Her mouth tightened, and she took him by the elbow as if to lead him away, but he wasn't budging. He just stared at her hand until she pulled it away. Then he walked off without saying a word to anybody, not her, not Landon, not even me.

I got out my cell phone and punched in Garrity's number. I got his voice mail. "Call me," I said, "and soon. The Ice Man runneth over."

◇◇◇

For the next half hour, the Champagne flowed freely as the Beaumonts greeted the crowd. Charley wore a terra cotta sheath, while Mark sported an old-fashioned white tuxedo jacket, the kind that came with black tie and black pants. They were the center of an enchanted circle, hazy and light-dazzled, Trey ever-present in their wake.

I stayed at the bar, desperate for a cigarette, making do with faux martinis. As the crowd thickened, I scanned the new faces for Gabriella, but unless she was a mistress of disguise, she was nowhere to be seen. I ordered Trey a drink too, as an excuse to find him.

Then I heard a familiar voice at my elbow. "Grey Goose and lime, please."

I sighed. "Whatever happened to Bacardi?"

"Whatever happened to Southern Comfort?" Eric turned to face me, gestured toward my fancy fake.

"I guess people change," I said.

"Of course they do. That's what makes us people, not rocks."

I kept my eyes on Trey. I wasn't about to take the bait, not now. Later Eric and I could argue about who'd changed the most, and how, and whose fault the whole mess was. Later he could tell me all the awful things about Trey that I already knew, and maybe some I didn't.

I moved to leave, and Eric grabbed my arm. "Look, I don't know what you're up to now, and I don't want to know—."

"Good."

"—but you'd better be careful, that's all I have to say."

He looked hard at me. With his hair edging to gray and his gold-rimmed glasses, he reminded me of Dad more and more—stern, authoritative, adult. He knew what was best. He was trying to make me see it. He didn't get why this was a betrayal.

I shook free. "Really? Is that all?"

He looked conflicted for a second. But then the bartender brought his drink, and he turned away from me. "That's all."

I left for real then, taking Trey's Pellegrino with me. By now, the Beaumonts had joined Senator Adams on the dais. Trey waited in the wings, unobtrusive and alert.

I handed him the glass. "Here."

He frowned. "What's this?"

"It's Pellegrino."

"It's in a martini glass." He held it up and examined it. "And there's an olive in it."

"Jeez, Trey, it's an olive. Just go with it, won't you?"

The music suddenly died down, and Mark Beaumont moved behind a microphone stand. His whole aspect was silvery and cool, like a black-and-white matinee idol, and like the movies, he stood larger than life. Charley waited below, at the edge of the crowd, her face glowing.

"Ladies and gentlemen," Mark said, "I am proud to give you our next governor, Senator Harrison Adams!"

And then Adams moved forward, all barrel-chested goodwill, his soft elegant wife at his side. The applause thundered, and the foot-stomping too, laced with whistles and other sounds of approval.

Charley applauded more enthusiastically than anyone else. On her left, to my astonishment, I saw Jake Whitaker. At first glance, he fit right in with his broad shoulders and dark tuxedo, but his expression was brittle and his eyes ping-ponged about the crowd. He said something to Charley, and she snapped her head around and spoke sharply back. On the other side of the crowd, Landon saw the movement and headed their way.

I put a hand on Trey's arm. "There's something—"

"I know."

He moved forward just as I glimpsed a familiar face at the edge of the crowd. I snatched Trey back.

"Gabriella!"

"Where?"

I pointed. She blew us a kiss. She wore a silver blouse and white pants and she had a big spangled purse gripped in both hands. Her smile was dazzling.

Landon reached the edge of the dais just as Jake grabbed Charley's elbow. She shook him off, but he yanked her to him and pressed his mouth against her ear.

"Stay here," Trey said.

I hiked up my skirt. "Screw that. You take Charley, I'm taking Gabriella."

He hesitated, but only for a second. And then he sprinted toward the dais. He was within ten feet of it when Charley's eyes rolled back in her head, and she collapsed onto the wet grass.

Chapter Forty-Six

The Phoenix team descended like a thunderstorm, and Trey disappeared into the chaos. I didn't have time to ponder the rescue mission, however—I was shoving my way through a sea of perplexed rich people, keeping my eyes on Gabriella. She stood beside the vanishing edge pool, her hair loose and rippling, her expression curious. She didn't attempt to flee, but by the time I reached her, my sides heaved from my sprint across the courtyard.

"Stay where you are!" I yelled.

She shrugged. "Why would I run?"

And she didn't, she just stepped behind a cabana out of sight of the other partygoers. This wasn't how I'd expected the encounter to go, but if she wanted to surrender, that was cool with me. Of course if she didn't, and I had to wrestle her to the ground and throw her thieving French self into the pool, I was okay with that too.

Once I got Trey's gun back.

"Here," she said, "it's unloaded."

She handed me her purse. It was like holding a brick. I peeked inside and saw Trey's H&K snuggled in the red velvet lining, the magazine nestled beside it.

I closed it back up. "Why?"

"Why did I take it? Or why did I bring it back?"

"Both."

She sighed. "You won't believe me."

"Try me."

"Very well. I had a vision."

I stared at her. "A what?"

"It was horrible—blood everywhere, and Trey…" She trailed off, one pale hand trembling at her temple. "All I could think about was what happened last time, when he shot that man at the convenience store. Do you know that story?"

I folded my arms. "I don't see—"

"The vision wasn't clear, but I could tell he was angry, and that he was very close to hurting someone, just like then. And I knew I had to stop it from happening."

"So you decided to steal his weapon?"

She ignored me. "Only once I got home, I realized I might have misinterpreted the vision. So I laid out the cards. And there it was—Justice. And I knew then that no matter what, he'd be all right, being of pure heart. So I brought the gun back."

She laid the story out so simply, as if this happened to everyone all the time. Visions, cards, thievery, pure hearts. I was at a loss.

"You went in his computer."

"I sent him an e-mail, to explain. Didn't he read it?"

"No, he didn't read it! There was a freaking key logger…" I rubbed my temples. Why was I explaining this to her? "Never mind. Just tell me—how did you get on the property tonight with *that* in your purse?"

She waved her hand dismissively, as if that were the dumbest question ever. "I bribed the person in the van, the curly-haired one? Two thousand dollars." She made a face. "Terribly rude young man. But he knows how to bargain, I'll give him that."

Trey sent me a message about an hour later, telling me to meet him on the deck behind the Beaumonts' cabin. I found him standing at the railing, his hands resting lightly on the white wood, one finger tap-tap-tapping a steady rhythm.

I handed him the purse. "Your girlfriend is a fucking lunatic— I'll explain why later. Other than that, I have nothing to report."

Trey looked inside the purse and his jaw clenched. "How did she get past security with this?"

"She waved two thousand dollars at Steve Simpson and he let her through. When I see him again, I am going to strangle him with his own hair."

"This is what happens when people break the rules. I try to explain this, but nobody listens."

He checked the gun—it was unloaded. The secondary magazine was full, but unengaged. Satisfied, he handed the purse back to me. "Take this to the suite, please, and secure it in the safe. I'll use the one you provided for the rest of the night."

He looked exhausted. I imagined his every sinew pulled tight, every nerve stretched thin. I put a hand on his shoulder and the muscle tensed beneath my palm.

"How's Charley?"

"She's resting. One of the guests gave her a tranquilizer."

Nothing like a classy Schedule IV opiate to make things all better, I thought. "What happened?"

"She said she got dizzy because she hadn't eaten and that Jake grabbed her to steady her."

"Bullshit! Jake said something to her, and it upset her so much that she fainted. She can't blame that on an empty stomach."

I leaned on the railing beside Trey. In the distance, the sun set in a slow melt of honey and amber. I kicked my shoes off and wiggled my toes. The wood under my stocking feet felt cool and moist.

"What happened to Jake?"

"Mark had him thrown off the premises."

"And that's it?"

The tap-tapping of Trey's finger on the wood railing intensified.

"Look," I said, "something's up and nobody's talking, not Charley, and especially not Mark."

"Mark and Landon are heading back to the reception. Charley's staying in the cabin."

"She shouldn't be left alone, not with Jake lurking about."

"Mark asked me to stay with her. Charley wants the cabin empty, however, so I'm supposed to wait here until she goes to sleep."

He looked across the lake as he spoke, the polished water a darkening void before him. And suddenly nothing made sense, nothing in the whole world, and all I wanted to do was get out of my ridiculous dress and into some jeans.

And I especially wanted to lose the heavy cargo in the spangled purse. One gun was protection, but two was a burden. Dexter was right—guns aren't easy things.

Trey buttoned his jacket. "What will you do now?"

"Wait for you in the suite. My stint as girl detective is over for the night. Find me when you're done?"

He took his eyes of the horizon for the first time. They were tired, but steady. Dark, like the coming night. "I'll find you."

I walked back to the main resort, shoes in hand. I'd left Trey at attention on the deck, his only concession to comfort a fresh bottle of Pellegrino. I could hear the party still going on by the swimming pool and could see the aura of the lights, bright and contained like a football stadium. It held no appeal anymore, none whatsoever.

I plodded on in the dark. I'd just hit the main property when I saw a figure duck behind one of the columns along the front entrance.

Jake!

I threw down my shoes and Gabriella's purse and drew my own weapon. It was more baffling in the dark than I would have predicted, but I got it in hand quickly. Was I willing to use it? Or was it just a cold metal bluff?

The figure slid from the shadows into a pool of light. And then I saw the chestnut tumble of curls.

Not Jake.

Steve Simpson.

I pointed the gun right at him. "You!"

He spun around and threw his hands in the air. "For crissakes, put that away!"

"Why aren't you in the van?"

"I'm getting a cup of coffee."

"Bullshit! You've got a coffeemaker in there, I saw it!"

He put his hands down. "Fine. You caught me. I'm running away. Happy now?"

I kept the gun on him. "Running from what?"

"In case you haven't noticed, fucked-up shit is happening, and I'm not talking about Trey's usual weirdness or Charley passing out or that crazy French chick."

"You're the one who let the crazy French chick in!"

"So what? I quit. A little wire tapping is one thing, but people are getting killed, and I don't want to be next."

"Why do you think you might be?"

"Because I know stuff." He folded his arms. "And so do you. Which means I'd keep that gun ready to go if I were you. But not aimed at me, okay?"

I watched him in the light at the edge of the darkness, the groomed safety of the hedges behind him. He held the key to the whole mess, I knew he did, and if I didn't think of a way to get it out of him, he'd vanish into the night, and the Parade of Almost Truth and Sorta Justice would keep marching on.

"You know," I said, "if you know something and don't tell anyone, that makes you accessory after the fact. All I have to do is get out my cell phone and bam—you're a fugitive from justice."

"Get real. The cops don't care about the truth."

"I know one who does."

He hesitated. I waited, ready to fire if he made one wrong move. Then I noticed the bulge in his shirt pocket.

"You smoke?"

"Yeah?"

I lowered the gun, took my finger off the trigger. "Come on, I know someplace out of the way. You tell me what you know, I'll tell you what I know. Maybe we can work something out."

I took him down to the lake edge, far enough away from the party that we could have some privacy, but close enough that I could scream and be heard easily. Excellent girl detective behavior.

"We'd had Eliza under surveillance for about six months," he began, "ever since she showed up in Atlanta. I didn't ask why. That's part of the job, you know—do what you're told and don't ask questions—and frankly, I didn't give a shit."

We were in the boathouse, which was deserted except for a few party yachts bobbing in the water. Aside from the distant drone of the party and the slap slap of waves against wood, it was silent.

"Anyway, Landon made sure that the camera outside her apartment was functional from the get-go, and that we had our own copies of the footage. He had me reviewing those—when she left, who came over, how long they stayed. Nothing exciting. And then he asked me to put in the phone tap."

"Those are illegal."

"Yeah. But Landon said he had APD authorization."

"And you believed that?"

He blew out a stream of smoke. "Nope. But I didn't argue. I figured if it blew up, I had deniability and could throw the shit back uphill. We didn't get anything interesting, though. Eliza was loose, but she wasn't creepy. Jake Whitaker, now, that's a different story."

"Let me guess—he liked to watch."

"Yeah, peeping in people's windows, messing with the sur-veillance cameras. He had the one outside Eliza's either pointed at the pool or the piece of lawn where people sunbathed, not at the apartments. And he used his passkey to get into women's apartments when they weren't home."

"Did you tell Landon?"

"Yes. But he didn't care."

"Not even about the misuse of the security cameras?"

"Not enough to fix the problem."

"Did you?"

"Not my job to care."

My first drag on the cigarette sent a shot of nicotine right into my brain, like getting splashed with cold water. But it calmed me too. It made me forget I was sitting in a boathouse with a stranger, and with a killer on the loose. Of course I still had two guns in my lap, so there was that.

"How did Dylan Flint fit into the picture?"

"The papparazzi wannabe? Eliza e-mailed him, IM'd and texted too. They traded pictures a lot."

"Did you help ransack his place?"

Steve shrugged. "Landon's orders. Dylan had a lot of shots of the Beaumonts that we didn't think he needed to have."

I tapped the ash into the water. Something was trying to connect in my brain. "Jake said something to Charley that freaked her out so badly she fainted. He said it because he knew he was getting fired, and he was thinking he could coerce her into intervening. He found out something, probably by snooping on Eliza, and whatever it was, he'd been saving it for a while. Any idea what that might be?"

Steve licked his lips. "Eliza was seriously into Charley—she had hundreds of pictures of her. She sent e-mails too, lots of them."

I didn't know whether I wanted to kiss him or smack him. "Did Charley ever send anything back?"

"Just the usual form reply."

"Nothing? No cease and desist warnings?"

"Why? Eliza was a dumb kid, annoying but harmless."

Dumb, perhaps, but smart enough to call Eric and ask about confidentiality. By that time, she was out of her league and scared to death. So many clashing motivations and backstories—Jake, Dylan, Eliza, the Beaumonts, Phoenix, my brother. I knew there was a thread somewhere in there, a thread that connected everything. Pull the wrong thread, though, and everything unraveled. I knew that too.

"So why didn't the cops find the Phoenix surveillance equipment when they searched her apartment?"

"Beats me. All I know is, the cops show up Friday night and that place is as clean as a whistle. I just assumed Landon pulled some strings."

It was coming together, like an astrological convergence. I could feel planets sliding into place, meteors colliding, stars imploding.

"I need a flow chart."

"A what?"

I handed Steve the rest of my cigarette. "Here. I've got to go find a legal pad."

He took it. I grabbed my guns and my shoes and started up the stairs.

"Where are you going?"

"I've got to talk to Trey."

"You can't just leave me here! What if—"

I gave him my revolver. "Here. It's small and simple, loaded too. Point and shoot."

He stared at it in bewilderment. I threw Gabriella's spangled purse, now empty, into his lap and kept Trey's Phoenix-issue H&K for myself. I loaded it with a full magazine of eight. And then I squeezed the grip, watching with satisfaction as the firing pin pulled back with an oily snick. I disengaged the squeeze cock and tucked it in my leather purse.

"And Steve? You'd best be cutting yourself a deal, and soon. Call Dan Garrity, he's a good guy. And tell him all hell's about to break loose."

◇◇◇

I tried calling Trey on my way back to the Beaumont cabin, but got no answer. It didn't matter—I was already on the porch. I tapped on the door, lightly, so I wouldn't wake Charley. Still no answer. I tried the door and it opened easily, revealing the dark interior. No lights, no noise.

"Trey?"

I saw him then, on the floor, and my stomach clenched. But before I could make a move, Charley Beaumont stepped out of the shadows.

With a gun. Which she had pointed right at me.

"Close the door," she said. "And don't even think about screaming."

Chapter Forty-Seven

I did as she said.

"Now put your hands up."

I did that too. Trey hadn't moved, and it was too dark to tell if he was even breathing. "What did you do to him?"

"Dumped a couple of those tranquilizers in his drink." She moved to stand over him, nudged him with her toe. "Took a water pitcher to the head to take him down, though."

"So he's alive."

"Yeah, but I probably fucked up his last normal brain cell." She kicked at him. "Of course there's always the chance he might not wake up this time."

Anger bloodied my vision at the edges, and I suddenly understood why people describe rage as red. I felt the weight of the purse on my hip—Trey's old gun, fully loaded, heavy with possibility.

"I swear to God, if you hurt him—"

"Shut up. Get on your knees."

I sank. From that angle, I could see Trey better, and I didn't like what I saw. He was on his stomach, his face toward me, eyes closed, and there was blood right at his temple. I was suddenly mad at him—God, he was SWAT-trained, how could he let a creature like Charley Beaumont get the better of him?—but then the anger burned clean.

I suddenly had this wild hope that he was just pretending, that any minute he would jump up and wrench that gun from her hand and crack her upside the head with it.

He didn't move. I still couldn't tell if he was breathing.

Charley lowered the gun and stepped forward. I saw that it was Trey's, the new P7M8 I'd found for him. She probably had his wallet too, maybe his car keys. And she was agitated. Whatever she was trying to do, she hadn't planned it very well. I lowered my hands a millimeter.

She raised the gun. "Don't try it. I've got no problem blowing a hole in your head. His either."

"Just like Eliza."

"Shut up! You don't know anything!"

"I know you cared about her. Very much."

Charley stared at me. The gun wobbled.

"And I know that you didn't want to kill her."

She tightened her grip. "If she'd just taken the money and kept her damn mouth shut, none of this would have happened. I told him to put a stop to it, but he beat her instead. It's how he solves everything."

The bruises where someone had banged Eliza up three days before she died. Everyone blamed Bulldog, but that scenario was fast dissolving. No way Charley would have had anything to do with that pathetic loser, especially not sending him to take care of a problem like blackmail.

"Who beat her up?"

Charley was still talking, more to herself than to me. "He said it would teach her a lesson."

"It did—it scared her into trying to tell my brother what was going on."

Charley didn't reply. The gun shook harder, and her eyes skittered from me to Trey to the door. She was ready to bolt, but I knew I had to keep her in place until one of the damn rent-a-cops noticed something hinky was going on.

I dropped my voice, as if we were in it together. "You used Gabriella's as the drop off point, didn't you? You'd tuck the money somewhere inside and then leave, and Eliza would pick it up later—that way the two of you were never seen together. But Gabriella noticed. She told you Eliza was stalking you, which meant you had to find a different way of paying her off. She got restless in the meantime, didn't she? Called up Dylan Flint, got some pictures taken so that you couldn't deny knowing her."

Charley breathed harder. The gun wavered.

"I know some other things too, like Phoenix had Eliza's place bugged. I know somebody heard her call Eric and say she was on her way over, and I know that somebody killed her right after that and cleaned all the surveillance equipment out of her apartment."

"It wasn't supposed to be that way. He said—"

"Who said?"

She let out a sob, cut it short with another sharp inhale.

"Who, Charley? Who did it? Who killed Eliza?"

She looked at me as if I'd lost my mind. And then she swung the gun in Trey's direction. "He did, you stupid bitch!"

I froze. "No, Trey would never—"

"Of course he did, you idiot! That's why he's here now, to kill me too!"

My eyes were now accustomed to the dark and I could see her better. Trey too. I shook my head. "I don't believe you."

"Of course you don't, you think he's some kind of hero." She laughed, but it was caustic. "He beat her up, but that didn't stop her, so he killed her instead, and Landon had to cover it up. Stupid little dyke, it's all her fault, if she'd have just shut the fuck up…"

Charley continued to rant. I wasn't quite sure what I was hearing anymore—he this, Trey that, Landon this. She kept using the word "dyke" and other slurs, which didn't make any sense for the scenario I'd constructed, the one I was sure Jake Whitaker had constructed too.

The one where Charley and Eliza were having an affair.

And then suddenly I got it—South Carolina and Tennessee, so close, and Eliza's fascination with Charley, with Charley's history, and though it all, Janie's refrain. Flesh and blood, flesh and blood.

"You're her mother," I said.

Charley breathed in rapid shallow shudders. I thought for a second she was going to shoot me. But she didn't move to pull the trigger. She just stared.

"You're the girl from out of town," I said. "You abandoned Eliza with Janie's brother, and he abandoned her with Janie's family. Jake knew Eliza was obsessed with you. He snooped in her apartment, probably in her e-mail, and thought you were having an affair with her. That's what he told you at the reception, isn't it? But he had it all wrong."

She was shaking harder now. "Eliza found me in Miami. She was barely sixteen, looking for money."

"How did she know where to look?"

"Her idiot father. She tracked him down first in some half-way house and he spilled the beans, the bastard, right before he died. She just typed my name into some directory, she said, and there I was—my address, my phone number, everything. But once she saw I was as broke as she was, she didn't want anything to do with me. Which was fine by me—I didn't need a kid, especially not some teenage brat. But then I became somebody, and suddenly she wanted plenty."

The mystery of the cash-stuffed shoebox and the bank account. "She got greedy."

"She started coming to my parties, bringing her stupid friends. Then she came crying to me, said this photographer had pictures he was threatening to sell to the tabloids along with the whole story. I told her if that happened, she'd go to jail for blackmail."

Which explained all those questions Eliza had asked my brother about confidentiality. Eliza wasn't as dumb as everyone assumed.

"But I didn't care if she told or not—I'd had it with her—but he said it couldn't get out, that it would ruin us."

There was the word "he" again. Not Bulldog, and not Trey, no matter what she said. She'd wanted the secret to come out, and "he" had said no. And I had a pretty good guess who "he" was.

Mark Beaumont. I wondered where he was, if he had any idea that Charley was fleeing and leaving the whole mess in his lap. I hoped he didn't, because I was in double trouble then.

"Why didn't you talk to the cops?"

"Because they wouldn't understand."

"But you have no money, no way to—"

She let loose a high acidic laugh, and I realized my mistake. Of course she had money. She'd probably been socking it away for years. Unfortunately, there was one problem, or two rather. And she had them both at gunpoint.

She waved the gun at Trey. "Where's Landon?"

"I don't know."

"Liar." She swung the gun up. "You tell me where he is and how many men he's got and where they are, or I swear to God, I'll blow your head off!"

Something snapped inside me. "You will not. You don't even know what you're doing with that thing."

She aimed dead center at my chest. "We'll see."

We were only fifteen feet apart—even she could hit me at that distance. But I saw her hands shaking, her tiny weak hands, and I knew she couldn't do it. Hell, it had taken me almost an hour to get the hang of the H&K squeeze cocker, and it took strength and know-how to pull it off.

She couldn't do it.

Probably not anyway.

I edged my hands a few inches downward. Then I heard a rasp of breath, and Trey moved his head. Charley heard it too, and swung the gun in his direction. I saw her elbows tense, saw her close her eyes and brace herself for the blast, and I screamed just as Trey looked up.

The shots came from behind and caught her in the chest— one and then two—and she snapped like she'd caught on a tripwire. And then she went down, eyes wide. And then she fell forward. All I'd heard was the pneumatic pop pop of a silencer.

I whipped around to see Landon stepping out of the shadows. He had the gun still trained on Charley. It didn't wobble at all.

"Are you okay?"

I tried to nod, but the nausea swelled and crested. "I think I'm going to be sick."

And then I was on all fours, retching, but nothing was coming up. I heard Trey stir, saw Landon swing the gun his way, smoothly, with no hesitation.

"Stay where you are, Trey."

Trey stood, but he obeyed. He had blood on his forehead and moved slowly, unsteady on his feet. I started to stand up too, but Landon put a hand on my shoulder. "Do it easy."

Trey watched from across the room as Landon helped me up. I started to move toward him, but Landon caught me by the elbow.

"Stay here with me, Ms. Randolph. Do you understand?"

I shook free. "I need to—"

"You need to stay still. No sudden moves."

There was something in the way he said it, like Garrity had. *Lay off brandishing that weapon, you do not want to trigger that Special-Ops training.* My heart pounded, my head emptied, but I was calm, so calm.

Trey wasn't the killer. He couldn't be.

Landon lowered his gun. He seemed calm too, as did Trey, who waited at the other end of the room, head cocked, the dead woman sprawled at his feet. He didn't seem to notice. He was watching us intently, steady now.

Landon exhaled slowly. "I want you to check her pulse."

Trey knelt at Charley's side and laid two fingers on her neck. He examined her chest, watching for the rise and fall. There wasn't one. He shook his head. "No pulse, no respiration. We should—"

"First, get the gun."

Trey frowned. "That's not—"

"Get back your gun, Trey. Now."

"Why?"

"You don't get to ask why, you just follow orders!" Landon's voice rose. "I don't know how she got your weapon, and I don't want to know, but we're taking care of this mess right now! I want you to wipe that gun clean and put it back in your holster, and if anybody asks, I want you to deny it was ever anywhere else, do you understand?"

Trey stood. "I do now."

And then suddenly, in a rush of understanding, I knew too. I took one tentative step away from Landon. He caught the movement. "Don't."

But I stayed where I was. "No, he'll play it as it lies. I'll vouch for him. And you, I'll vouch for you. That Charley was going to kill Trey, that you had no choice."

"Except that he did," Trey said.

And I was thinking, shut up Trey, just shut up. But it was too late. Landon's expression switched into something predatory. But still calm, very very calm. "I don't know what you're talking about."

"She had my gun," Trey replied. "You knew that. You have the same gun. So you knew that she'd have no idea how to work the squeeze cocker."

Landon listened with interest. Then he sighed, loudly, dramatically. "All you had to do was keep Charley from doing something stupid until I could figure this mess out, and you couldn't even manage that."

And before I could scream, he had one arm around my neck, snatching me off balance. He yanked the purse from around my neck and dropped it to the floor, then kicked it aside. Trey took a step forward, and I felt the gun against my temple, so hot it burned.

"Don't even think about it," Landon said.

All I could see was Trey, not twenty feet away, but he wasn't looking at me. He had his eyes locked on Landon. He took another step forward. Landon pressed the gun harder against my skin, and Trey stopped.

"Kick the gun over here," Landon said.

Trey hesitated. My knees went weak, and the shaking started, violent and uncontrollable. Landon dropped his voice. He sounded friendly, conspiratorial.

"Listen to me, Trey—I don't want to kill you, or Tai."

"No, you don't want to. But you have no choice."

Landon considered the remark. "You know what? You're right. No point in lying about it, is there?"

"There never was. You have to kill us. It's the logical end to every scenario. You wanted my prints on a weapon. You wanted me holding that weapon when you shot me."

I imagined what Landon would say, how he'd spin it now that Trey had refused to play along. Would he plant his own weapon on me, say I'd killed Charley, that Trey and I had been working together, that he'd had to take us both down? Landon the hero, saving the day from the psycho ex-cop and the crazy girl detective.

Landon gripped my throat tighter, and I pried at his fingers, but it was no use. I wasn't getting out of his clutches, and even if I did, it was a sure bullet to the brain. I had to get him off guard.

Off balance.

Trey cocked his head. "Why Eliza?"

"Charley came to me. It was just business, just like this. This isn't personal. You understand that, Trey, I know you do."

Trey nodded. I imagined the wheels turning in his head, behind the flat gaze. "How?"

"You were the one who pointed out how much of a safety breach that wall was at Beau Elan. Everybody worried about who might get in. Nobody gave a damn who might get out."

I remembered then, the trees along the end of the wall, how simple it would have been to hop right over it that afternoon, hop right into Phoenix. Where Landon's car was parked. How easy it would have been to find Eliza at my brother's, kill her, then drive back to Phoenix, hop back over the wall. Thanks to Jake, Eliza's security camera was focused on the sunbathing area at that time. Nothing would have shown up on the exit gate cameras, and nothing on the cameras in the Phoenix garage, not after they got smashed anyway.

Dylan hadn't been lying—he hadn't broken those cameras. It had been Landon all along.

"Dylan," I said.

Landon made a noise. "First Eliza and then that idiot. Everybody gets in over their head. Eliza, Dylan, Charley. Now you two." He put his mouth against my ear. "I told you to go home. I told you over and over in so many ways."

"The bull's eyes," I said.

"Bull's eye," he repeated.

Trey didn't speak. Neither did I. I wanted to. I wanted to beg and plead and say I'd do anything—anything—if he'd just let me go. But I couldn't make my throat open.

"You framed Bulldog," Trey said.

"Like that was a challenge. The idiot practically framed himself."

I stared at Trey. He was watching me, not Landon. I saw something shift in his eyes and in his stance. Was he reaching for a weapon? Did he have another gun?

Landon noticed too. He moved the gun from my head and pointed it at Trey. "Don't be stupid."

I caught Trey's eyes again. Did he remember? I hoped to God he did because it was the only chance we had. I closed my eyes, squeezed them tight, muttered what I hoped was a prayer...

And then I went limp.

Landon lunged to catch me, trying to swing the gun back around, but I smashed his arm up and hit the floor rolling, kicking, flailing, screaming. Trey moved so fast he was a blur, catching Landon by the throat and throwing him up against the wall. The gun flew across the room, but Trey ignored it and slammed Landon against the plaster, again and again, while Landon clawed at his hands.

I scrambled for my purse and snatched the gun free. "Let him go, Trey, I've got the gun!"

But Trey didn't let go. He still had his hands on Landon's throat, his thumbs pressed deep into his windpipe. Landon clutched at his fingers, going blue, choking and sputtering.

I stamped my foot and screamed louder. "Stop it, Trey! Let him go!"

It wasn't happening. Trey had his face right up in Landon's, and he was watching him suffocate. Watching him die.

I gripped the gun tightly, took aim, and fired. The recoil jerked my hands, but I hit my target—the crystal lamp across the room shattered in a cacophony. Trey whipped his head around to see what had happened.

"Let him go!" I screamed.

Trey shook his head, like a man waking up after a long sleep. He released his hold, and Landon collapsed to the ground, gasping and wheezing in leaky gurgles. He curled into the fetal position at Trey's feet, his face ashen.

Trey looked at the glassy shards on the floor, then at Landon, then at me. "Call 911. Tell them we have a victim with a possible crushed windpipe. Tell them to hurry." And then he held out his hand. "Give me the gun."

I did. The room smelled like blood and cordite, like the car when I'd found Eliza. I was sick again, violently so. Trey kept the gun on Landon, his eyes on me. The shaking returned, my teeth chattering with each wave.

"This is where you tell me it's going to be all right," I said.

Trey holstered the gun. "It's going to be all right."

Chapter Forty-Eight

The next hours were a blur of interrogation as first the police and then EMTs descended. They decided I was okay and tucked me in the backseat of a patrol car where I told my story over and over again. Trey told his story too, but he did it in an ambulance—where nobody would let me near him.

Steve had taken me seriously about calling Garrity, who arrived on the scene not long after Trey and I were separated. To his surprise, I threw my arms around his neck. "How's Trey?"

"He'll be okay. But I tell you what, if you ever need to slip somebody a mickey, go with Pellegrino. Bitter, fizzy, dark green bottle. Impossible to detect."

"What was it?"

"Chloral hydrate. He's shaking it off now, but it hit him harder than it would have normally—empty stomach, dehydrated from being sick. He knew something was wrong, but before he could get a call through to anyone, Charley cracked him from behind."

He also told me that they'd rushed Landon to the hospital, and that he was going to be okay. This news actually cheered me. It meant he would face a judge and jury. And it meant that Trey wouldn't.

"I knew that man was bad news the minute he stepped into my kitchen," I said.

"Of course you did. In the end, it's never a surprise. That only happens in the movies."

And then he started explaining things, like what the procedure would be when I gave my official statement, what I would need to turn over to the cops—the gun, my clothes, etc. I only half-listened. My attention kept drifting to the ambulance. Garrity noticed.

"He's gonna be fine. And so are you."

"I know."

And then I heard a familiar voice, argumentative and strong. "She's my sister, damn it, let me see her!"

Garrity smiled wanly. "Oh yeah. Eric's here."

I made an exasperated face, but it was just pretend. Eric slid into the car, right beside me. He took my chin in his hand, turned my face left, turned it right. "Are you okay?"

"I'm fine, stop yanking me around."

"I just found out, but I'm here. And I'm sorry I haven't been, I really am, but—"

"Eric?"

"Yes?"

"Shut up."

I hugged him then, pressed my face into his warm crisp shirt. He felt like home, like all things familiar and easy, and he hugged me back, abrupt and fierce. I felt tears prickling, so I let him go. "Will somebody please let me see Trey?"

Eric looked at Garrity, who nodded. Then he put both hands on my shoulders. "We'll get you there in a second. But first I want you to listen to me and listen good. You're still in shock—"

"No, I'm not."

"Yes, you are. You won't feel it for a while, not while everything's crazy, but once your life calms down again—"

I squeezed his hand. "I'll deal with it. I promise."

He seemed mollified. And I knew he was right. I knew enough about post-traumatic stress to know that it crept up in nightmares and flashbacks. And I hoped that it would, I really did, that the enormity of what had happened would crash down on me at some point.

Because at that moment, I felt nothing.

◇◇◇

I endured yet another check-up at the ER while two deputies waited in the lobby. I could see the backs of their heads through the window.

"Like I'm gonna make a run for it," I complained.

Marisa wasn't happy. In the florescent lighting, her hair looked dishwater blonde instead of platinum, and she was pissed as hell. I didn't want to be alone with her, but Eric was filling out paperwork, and Garrity was running interference with the cops, and Trey was in a different room.

She spoke without preamble. "What happened?"

I told her the whole story, and her pissed-off intensified into something volcanic. She tamped it down, though, pushed her hair behind her ears.

"Why?"

"Because if Eliza had revealed Charley's secret, that would have been the end of the Beaumonts' partnership with Senator Adams. That camp would have never tolerated an illegitimate lesbian drug-dealing—"

"Point taken."

"And they would never have tolerated Phoenix either, not after that."

"But how did Landon know she was going to tell?"

"He had her phones tapped, her computer too. He beat her good after she showed up at the Mardi Gras ball with Dylan, but that just made her decide to spill it once and for all. So she told Dylan their arrangement was over and called my brother. That's when Bulldog got in the way. She tried to meet Eric one more time, and Landon found out. That's when he killed her. Then he erased all evidence that Phoenix had her under surveillance. Then he planted that gun on Bulldog and tried to kill him. And then when Dylan decided to talk to the police—"

"I can fill in the blanks. But why did Charley still keep Landon around if she knew he'd killed her daughter?"

"She didn't—he told her Trey had done it, that he was the one who roughed her up at Mardi Gras. She believed him. He also convinced her to be an alibi for everybody who was at Beau Elan on Friday. He told her it was the only way."

Marisa had other concerns. "Phoenix is fucked. We'll never get out from under this."

I didn't argue with her.

"Trey won't even see me," she said. "He's up to his elbows in this mess, and he won't explain, not even to save himself."

"Can you blame him? You got Landon to get Simpson to spy on him."

"Trey's a pragmatist. That kind of thing doesn't bother him."

Right, I thought. Trey seemed invulnerable, the Ice Man with the bulletproof heart. But I knew what a façade that was.

"Landon screwed the pooch," I said. "I can't argue that. But depending on how you slant things, you could have a genuine hero in the next room. If he can be convinced to help your ass out of this, that is."

Marisa considered. "What do you think it will take?"

"Let me see him."

She pushed the call button without a second's hesitation.

I found him sitting on an examining table, holding a cold compress to his head. He still wore his tuxedo shirt and pants, but the tie was gone and his shirt was wrinkled and untucked.

"Your hair is a mess," I said.

He put a hand to it. "I know."

I moved to stand in front of him. "How are you?"

"Concussed."

"Which means?"

"Dizzy. Weak. A bigger headache than before."

I put my hand to his forehead. "Is that from the conk or the tranquilizers?"

"Both. The EMTs also think I was overdosed with Topamax the night before."

"What? That stuff you take for migraines? That's what had you so sick?"

"I had all the symptoms—disorientation, agitation, nausea and vomiting but no fever."

"So that wasn't food poisoning, it was deliberate poisoning?"

He nodded. And he and I both knew who'd done it—Landon. Trey kept a bottle of the stuff in his desk drawer at Phoenix, unlocked, where anyone with access to his office had access to his prescriptions. And as we'd discovered, Pellegrino was the perfect disguise for all manner of drugs.

"He did it the night Dylan died, at the meeting I wasn't allowed to come to."

Trey nodded.

"Why would Landon mess you up like that?"

"One of the detectives said it would give him an excuse to come to my apartment. He needed to retrieve the files Marisa had sent home with me and see what other information I had."

"Or perhaps set you up in some way." And then I remembered. "You were supposed to be alone that night."

"I was, yes."

"But you weren't alone."

"No. You were there."

I smiled at him, suddenly relieved. His expression was open, almost vulnerable, despite the wrinkle furrowed deep between his eyes.

"Are the police finished with you?" he said.

"For the time being. But you know what? I don't want to talk about that right now."

He nodded, wincing. "Okay."

I moved my hand to his face. He closed his eyes.

"You still trust me?" I said.

He nodded.

"In that case, I have a proposition for you." And then I put my mouth next to his ear and told him about it.

His eyes widened. "Now?"

"No, Trey, not now. Later."

"Tonight?"

"No, not tonight."

"Why not tonight?"

"Because you're concussed. And poisoned."

"Overdosed."

"Twice. Two times."

"But that doesn't impair my sexual ability," he protested. "Does it?"

This last question was directed to the doctor who'd moved to stand beside me. He was young and scrappy-looking, like a rock musician or a street fighter. But he had a white coat and stethoscope, so I was willing to give him the benefit of the doubt.

He got out a penlight. "That's an odd question. Look straight ahead."

Trey complied. "I ask odd questions."

"Is it a trick question, like that old joke?"

"What old joke?"

"Look left." He shined the light in his eyes. "You know, the one where the man asks the doctor if he'll be able to play the piano after surgery, and the doctor says sure, and the man says, good, I always wanted to play the piano. Now look right."

Trey obeyed. "I don't know that one."

"It's an old standard." He looked intently into Trey's eyes. "Any double vision, blurring?"

"No."

"Nausea? Vomiting?"

"No."

"Dizziness?"

"Some."

The doctor stepped back, folded his arms. "You're going to have a major headache for a while, and all I can give you is acetaminophen. And we want to admit you overnight so we can watch your vitals. But after that, I'll tell you what I tell everybody else with a mild concussion—no caffeine, no painkillers, lots of rest. No strenuous activity for a while."

Trey cocked his head. "Strenuous?"

"Your call." He looked my way. "This the lucky woman?"
Trey just nodded.

"Is she gentle?"

Trey considered. "She can be."

I covered my face with my hand. "Oh, good Lord."

The doctor clapped him on the shoulder and turned to leave.
"Lie down for now, and then we'll get you in a room."

And then we were alone, face to face. He lowered the compress onto the table. There was so much to talk about. But it would wait.

I moved closer, right up against him, and took his hand. He didn't flinch or stiffen like I was expecting, just kind of froze. Then he put his other hand on my back, resting it between my shoulder blades. He patted softly, tentatively, like he wasn't sure it was the right thing to do.

But it was.

That night I slept in a very uncomfortable chair in the lobby, right between Garrity and Eric. The next morning, Rico showed up with a box of hot Krispy Kremes for everyone and an espresso shot cappuccino for me. He had one for Eric too, who shook his hand gravely.

They released Trey right before noon. He immediately wanted to retrieve his Ferrari, but Garrity insisted he and Eric would take care of that. I volunteered to drive Trey home in Eric's Jaguar, and to my surprise, both Trey and Eric agreed to let me do it.

As Eric went to bring the car around, I saw the story on the TV in the lobby. All the reporters wore black or gray and mused intensely about the notoriety of celebrity. Trey didn't stay to watch—he went on to the pick-up area. Garrity touched my elbow.

"I meant to tell you," he said. "They found Nikki."

"Oh no! Was she—"

"Dead? Not on your life. She was hiding out with relatives in California. Once she talked to the cops, she bolted."

"Smart girl."

"Too bad she was the only one."

I couldn't argue. But I hadn't been thinking as much about Eliza as I'd expected, probably because it was too painful. I'd wanted an innocent victim that I could somehow avenge, but she wasn't that. No glory for the victors, no garlands, no laurel crowns. But it was over. I was grateful for that at least.

"One more thing," Garrity said. "You might be getting a call from a friend of mine, a cop."

"Crap. What have I done this time?"

"It's nothing official. It's just that he got engaged recently and his fiancée is skittish about the weapon thing. I told him you might could help, but then, that was before all this went down."

I noticed then that Eric had the car waiting, that he and Trey were standing beside it, deep in conversation. Trey had his arms folded, but then Eric clapped him on the shoulder, and they shook hands like men sealing a land deal.

Garrity was still talking. "It's not like he wants her to be Annie Oakley or anything, but—"

"What does the fiancée want?"

Garrity smiled. "That's a good question. Tell you what, I'll have *her* give you a call on Monday. If you're feeling up to it."

Would I be? I tried to access the memories—the dead girl across the street, Charley being shot right in front of my eyes, the feel of the hot metal against my temple and the cold metal in my hands—and all I got was blank numbness. I knew that would change. But at the moment I was grateful for it.

"I don't know what I'll be up for," I admitted. "But tell her to call me at the shop. I'll be putting some flower boxes out front, marigolds maybe. My mother loved marigolds."

I drove Trey home. He stared out the window the whole way. Once I saw him put his hand to the glass, count to five.

"We're going to have to talk about Gabriella," I said.

He nodded. "And the cigarettes."

This caught me off guard, but I rolled with it, a skill I was going to have to practice. I pulled up in front of his building. "Are you sure you don't want me to come up?"

"I'm sure. I have a lot to think about."

He didn't move to get out, however. He just sat there, looking out the window. On the sidewalk, a construction crew passed. They were talking loudly, laughing, still wearing their orange hardhats. In the distance I saw the gleam of an I-beam, swinging in the clear sharp sunlight. Always going up, Atlanta was. Always something higher and better.

"I didn't see any of it," he said. "I can tell when people are lying, but I can't see real deception. I would have been able to figure it out before the accident. But I can't see anything except what's right in front of me now."

"You couldn't have seen this. Landon was too good."

"I know Marisa wants to talk to me. But I don't know if I want to talk to her." He didn't look at me. "Phoenix was all I had."

"No, it wasn't. And it never will be."

He turned to face me. There was something achy and tender and afraid in his expression. But strength too, and goodness, and bravery.

"This is where you kiss me," I said.

He leaned forward, touched his lips to mine. It was all I could do not to fall against him and bury my face in his shoulder.

But I let him go. And he did go, without saying another word. As I pulled away from the curb, he stopped at the entrance and looked back. I watched him in the rearview mirror, still standing under the awning as I turned the corner.

I hadn't even reached the stoplight when my phone rang.

"Did you mean it?" he said.

I took a deep breath. "Give me three minutes."

A soft click, then empty air. I swung into the left lane and made a U-turn.

To receive a free catalog of Poisoned Pen Press titles, please contact us in one of the following ways:

Phone: 1-800-421-3976
Facsimile: 1-480-949-1707
Email: info@poisonedpenpress.com
Website: www.poisonedpenpress.com

Poisoned Pen Press
6962 E. First Ave. Ste. 103
Scottsdale, AZ 85251